D0593184

THE NEW WINDMILL SERIES

General Editors: Anne and Ian Serraillier

174

D. H. LAWRENCE

SELECTED TALES

This collection contains some of Lawrence's best
short stories. Full of vitality and insight, these are
masterpieces in their own right, besides making a
fine introduction to his longer and more difficult
novels.

D. H. LAWRENCE

Selected Tales

INTRODUCED BY
IAN SERRAILLIER

HEINEMANN EDUCATIONAL BOOKS
LONDON

Heinemann Educational Books Ltd
22 Bedford Square, London WC1B 3HH

LONDON EDINBURGH MELBOURNE AUCKLAND
HONG KONG SINGAPORE KUALA LUMPUR NEW DELHI
IBADAN NAIROBI JOHANNESBURG
EXETER (NH) KINGSTON PORT OF SPAIN

ISBN 0 435 12174 1

Printed and bound in Great Britain by
Morrison & Gibb Ltd, London and Edinburgh

Contents

Introduction   vii

The Rocking-Horse Winner   1

Odour of Chrysanthemums   19

Strike-Pay   43

The Christening   54

Tickets, Please   65

Monkey Nuts   80

Fanny and Annie   96

You Touched Me   114

The Man who loved Islands   134

Things   164

Daughters of the Vicar   176

Acknowledgements

I should like to acknowledge the help of my wife
with the editorial work and selection of stories,
and also the authors of the following books on
which I have drawn for my introduction: *D. H.
Lawrence* by Anthony Beal (Oliver and Boyd 1961);
D. H. Lawrence: Novelist by F. R. Leavis (Chatto
and Windus 1955); *The Intelligent Heart* by Harry
T. Moore (Heinemann 1955); and the pamphlet
published by the BBC to accompany the Autumn
Term 1961 Broadcasts for Schools in the series
Books, Plays, Poems.

The stories included in this volume are used by
kind permission of Laurence Pollinger Ltd. The
Complete Short Stories are published in three
volumes by William Heinemann Ltd.

IAN SERRAILLIER

Introduction

D. H. LAWRENCE was born in 1885 in the ugly mining village of Eastwood, near Nottingham. In the street where he was born the miners' houses were crowded together on the hillside, not far from the ash pits. When he was six the family moved to Walker Street, where the house looked out on to woods and open country. His father, a black-bearded giant of a man, worked in one of the six pits, the colliery at Brinsley. His mother had come from quite a different environment. She had been a school teacher and had written verses, and before her marriage had little idea of what a miner's life was like. The first evening that her husband returned from the pit, his face was so grimy with coal that she did not recognize him; she thought he was a negro. The marriage turned out none too happily. There was constant tension between the parents and endless quarrels, in which the five children generally sided with their mother. She was proud of them, enjoyed their companionship, and wanted to do the best she could for them. She was determined that the girls, Ada and Emily, should not become servants, and that the sons should not go into the mines.

There was no question of David Herbert, the youngest of the three sons, going into the mines – he was not strong enough. In a brief account of his life up to his first literary success he writes:

> I was a delicate pale brat with a snuffy nose, whom most people treated quite gently as just an ordinary delicate lad. When I was twelve I got a county council scholarship, twelve pounds a year, and went to Nottingham High School.

After leaving school I was a clerk for three months, then had a very serious pneumonia illness, in my seventeenth year, that damaged my health for life.

A year later I became a school teacher, and after three years' savage teaching of collier lads I went to take the 'normal' course in Nottingham University.

As I was glad to leave school, I was glad to leave college. It had meant mere disillusion, instead of the living contact of men. From college I went down to Croydon, near London, to teach in a new elementary school at a hundred pounds a year.

It was while I was at Croydon, when I was twenty-three, that the girl who had been the chief friend of my youth, and who was herself a school teacher in a mining village at home, copied out some of my poems, and without telling me, sent them to the *English Review*, which had just had a glorious rebirth under Ford Madox Hueffer.

Hueffer was most kind. He printed the poems, and asked me to come and see him. The girl had launched me, so easily, on my literary career, like a princess cutting a thread, launching a ship.

The girl was Jessie Chambers, his first sweetheart, who lived at Hagg's Farm, a two-mile walk out into the country from Eastwood. He was a schoolboy when he first met her, and their friendship lasted for a dozen years. That he did not marry her was probably due in part to the dominating influence that his mother had over him; he was more devoted to her than to Jessie. The woman he eventually married was a very different type of person – Frieda von Richthofen, the German wife of a Nottingham University professor. She left her husband and two children and went abroad with him, and they were married in 1914 after her divorce. Though they returned to England, Lawrence seldom visited Nottingham and the scenes of his childhood again.

The years of the First World War were an unpleasant and embittering time for both of them, for they had to contend with much anti-German feeling as well as hostility to his writings. In 1919, in despair of ever getting a sympathetic hearing, he left England and became a wanderer for the rest of his life. He visited Italy, Sicily, Germany, Mexico, Australia, and the United States, but never settled anywhere for long. He died of tuberculosis in the south of France in 1930, when he was only forty-four.

Lawrence was poet, novelist, essayist, and travel-writer. His greatest achievement was in his novels, but not all of them make easy reading. The best approach to his work is through the short stories, and we have made this selection from the forty-seven that he completed. Of these all but a very few are of the highest quality. They are not written to formula, with surprise endings and other tricks borrowed from hack story writers, but are the product of a great creative artist working within a limited compass. They have the vitality and insight of his finest writing, but greater concentration and economy. Like the novels they can also be enjoyed for what they reveal of Lawrence's own life and personality. Few great writers have put more of themselves and their background into their writing.

In *Odour of Chrysanthemums* and *The Christening* Lawrence portrays the life that he knew as a boy, that of the miner's home. The wife in the former story, which was written before 1911, is modelled on his own Aunt Polly, who lost her first husband in a mining disaster. The whole atmosphere – the burning pit-banks, the locomotive engine clanking with its full wagons through the raw afternoon, the lighting of the candle in the cold damp room of the miner's home – is distilled from his earliest memories. *Strike-Pay* shows what it means to a family when the wage-earner loses his strike-money and the wife has only a few shillings to manage on. *Monkey Nuts* and *Tickets, Please* re-create war-time experiences on the home front; the first, about a reluctant courtship between a soldier and a land girl, and the second about the girl-conductors on the Ripley to Nottingham tramway, a tough lot of 'fearless young hussies' who knock down an inspector who annoys them and try to rip off his clothes. As a young man Lawrence had a similar experience when he was attacked by a gang of factory girls. Anyone that he met was liable to figure in his stories, not always

in a flattering light. In *Things*, one of his later stories, there is
a touch of meanness and cruelty in the way he satirizes two
idealistic American friends whom he met on Capri. He laughs
at them for their naïve interest in painting and Buddhism, for
their habit of collecting 'things' wherever they go – things
which, in their eventual disillusionment, they grow to hate. He
even wrote to tell them about the story – 'a most amusing story
of mine in the American *Bookman* . . . – you'll think it's you,
but it isn't'. But they were not deceived. It is to their credit that
they did not allow it to sour their regard for him, and they
remained his firm friends till his death. Other friends were less
forgiving. The best-selling novelist who had rented an island
to retire to and whom Lawrence satirizes in *The Man who
Loved Islands* tried to prevent the story being republished.

Lawrence's work reveals him as a man of unconventional
views and habits, at odds with the materialistic outlook of his
day, serious-minded and deeply sincere. He could not bear pre-
tence of any kind. He believed that industrialism and machinery
degraded people, and he bitterly blamed 'the moneyed classes
and promoters of industry' for the ugliness to which it con-
demned the workers – the sort of ugliness in which he had himself grown up. In one of his last essays he wrote, 'The human
soul needs actual beauty more than bread,' and to beauty in its
many forms he was acutely sensitive. The whole universe was
for him a living thing, and he saw nature with a poet's eye:

> There was a field of hay, the foxgloves stood looking
> down. In a little cove, the sun was on the pale granite
> where you bathed, and the shadow was in the rocks.

The same freshness and radiant simplicity informs all the nature
passages in *The Man who Loved Islands*. Here is a description
of a gull in the same story:

> He was big, and pearl-grey, and his roundnesses were
> as smooth and lovely as a pearl . . . And as the gull
> walked back and forth, back and forth in front of the
> cabin, strutting on pale-dusky gold feet, holding up his

pale yellow beak, that was curved at the tip, with curious alien importance, the man wondered over him. He was portentous, he had a meaning.

The bird appears for only a brief moment before flying away, but Lawrence has penetrated into its very being. His sympathy for people irrespective of class and his ability to reach down to their inmost feelings is profound, as any of the stories will show. He believed that life should be lived and enjoyed to the full. In *Daughters of the Vicar*, the longest and in many ways the finest of the stories, the atmosphere of repression in the narrow life of the vicarage is shown as a destructive force, isolating the family from the parish and causing nothing but misery. The children grew up 'unwarmed' and 'rigid', while gradually their parents 'lost all hold on life, and spent their hours, weeks and years merely haggling to make ends meet, and bitterly repressing and pruning their children into gentility'. Yet in Louisa's 'fixed will to love, to have the man she loves', the forces of life triumph.

Since his death Lawrence's reputation has continued to grow and several of his novels have become very widely known. His short stories do not seem to have achieved the full recognition they deserve, although F. R. Leavis in *D. H. Lawrence: Novelist* devotes more than half his book to a discussion of them. Praising them for their first-hand experience of life and their profound interest in human experience, he claims that they represent one of the major creative achievements of literature. Furthermore, they have great relevance to the needs of today. 'Any creative writer who has not had his due is a power for life wasted,' he says. 'But the insight, the wisdom, the revived and re-educated feeling for health, that Lawrence brings are what, as our civilization goes, we desperately need.' These words would have pleased Lawrence, for, though he was largely indifferent to material success for himself, he always wanted to be understood, and he knew that he had something of value to give to mankind.

IAN SERRAILLIER

The Rocking-Horse Winner

THERE was a woman who was beautiful, who started with all the advantages, yet she had no luck. She married for love, and the love turned to dust. She had bonny children, yet she felt they had been thrust upon her, and she could not love them. They looked at her coldly, as if they were finding fault with her. And hurriedly she felt she must cover up some fault in herself. Yet what it was that she must cover up she never knew. Nevertheless, when her children were present, she always felt the centre of her heart go hard. This troubled her, and in her manner she was all the more gentle and anxious for her children, as if she loved them very much. Only she herself knew that at the centre of her heart was a hard little place that could not feel love, no, not for anybody. Everybody else said of her: 'She is such a good mother. She adores her children.' Only she herself, and her children themselves, knew it was not so. They read it in each other's eyes.

There were a boy and two little girls. They lived in a pleasant house, with a garden, and they had discreet servants, and felt themselves superior to anyone in the neighbourhood.

Although they lived in style, they felt always an anxiety in the house. There was never enough money. The mother had a small income, and the father had a small income, but not nearly enough for the social position which they had to keep up. The father went into town to some office. But though he had good prospects, these prospects never materialized. There was always the grinding sense of the shortage of money, though the style was always kept up.

At last the mother said: 'I will see if *I* can't make something.' But she did not know where to begin. She racked her brains, and tried this thing and the other, but could not find anything successful. The failure made deep lines come into her face. Her children were growing up, they would have to go to school. There must be more money, there must be more money. The father, who was always very handsome and expensive in his tastes, seemed as if he never *would* be able to do anything worth doing. And the mother, who had a great belief in herself, did not succeed any better, and her tastes were just as expensive.

And so the house came to be haunted by the unspoken phrase: *There must be more money! There must be more money!* The children could hear it all the time, though nobody said it aloud. They heard it at Christmas, when the expensive and splendid toys filled the nursery. Behind the shining modern rocking-horse, behind the smart doll's house, a voice would start whispering: 'There *must* be more money! There *must* be more money!' And the children would stop playing, to listen for a moment. They would look into each other's eyes, to see if they had all heard. And each one saw in the eyes of the other two that they too had heard. 'There *must* be more money! There *must* be more money!'

It came whispering from the springs of the still-swaying rocking-horse, and even the horse, bending his wooden, champing head, heard it. The big doll, sitting so pink and smirking in her new pram, could hear it quite plainly, and seemed to be smirking all the more self-consciously because of it. The foolish puppy, too, that took the place of the teddy-bear, he was looking so extraordinarily foolish for no other reason but that he heard the secret whisper all over the house: 'There *must* be more money!'

Yet nobody ever said it aloud. The whisper was everywhere, and therefore no one spoke it. Just as no one ever says: 'We are breathing!' in spite of the fact that breath is coming and going all the time.

'Mother,' said the boy Paul one day, 'why don't we keep a car of our own? Why do we always use uncle's, or else a taxi?'

'Because we're the poor members of the family,' said the mother.

'But why *are* we, mother?'

'Well – I suppose,' she said slowly and bitterly, 'it's because your father has no luck.'

The boy was silent for some time.

'Is luck money, mother?' he asked, rather timidly.

'No, Paul. Not quite. It's what causes you to have money.'

'Oh!' said Paul vaguely. 'I thought when Uncle Oscar said *filthy lucker*, it meant money.'

'*Filthy lucre* does mean money,' said the mother. 'But it's lucre, not luck.'

'Oh!' said the boy. 'Then what *is* luck, mother?'

'It's what causes you to have money. If you're lucky you have money. That's why it's better to be born lucky than rich. If you're rich, you may lose your money. But if you're lucky, you will always get more money.'

'Oh! Will you? And is father not lucky?'

'Very unlucky, I should say,' she said bitterly.

The boy watched her with unsure eyes.

'Why?' he asked.

'I don't know. Nobody ever knows why one person is lucky and another unlucky.'

'Don't they? Nobody at all? Does *nobody* know?'

'Perhaps God. But He never tells.'

'He ought to then. And aren't you lucky either, mother?'

'I can't be, if I married an unlucky husband.'

'But by yourself, aren't you?'

'I used to think I was, before I married. Now I think I am very unlucky indeed.'

'Why?'

'Well – never mind! Perhaps I'm not really,' she said.

The child looked at her to see if she meant it. But he saw, by the lines of her mouth, that she was only trying to hide something from him.

'Well, anyhow,' he said stoutly, 'I'm a lucky person.'

'Why?' said his mother, with a sudden laugh.

He stared at her. He didn't even know why he had said it.

'God told me,' he asserted, brazening it out.

'I hope He did, dear!' she said, again with a laugh, but rather bitter.

'He did, mother!'

'Excellent!' said the mother, using one of her husband's exclamations.

The boy saw she did not believe him; or rather, that she paid no attention to his assertion. This angered him somewhere, and made him want to compel her attention.

He went off by himself, vaguely, in a childish way, seeking for the clue to 'luck'. Absorbed, taking no heed of other people, he went about with a sort of stealth, seeking inwardly for luck. He wanted luck, he wanted it, he wanted it. When the two girls were playing dolls in the nursery, he would sit on his big rocking-horse, charging madly into space, with a frenzy that made the little girls peer at him uneasily. Wildly the horse careered, the waving dark hair of the boy tossed, his eyes had a strange glare in them. The little girls dared not speak to him.

When he had ridden to the end of his mad little journey, he climbed down and stood in front of his rocking-horse, staring fixedly into its lowered face. Its red face was slightly open, its big eye was wide and glassy-bright.

'Now!' he would silently command the snorting steed. 'Now, take me to where there is luck! Now take me!'

And he would slash the horse on the neck with the little whip he had asked Uncle Oscar for. He *knew* the horse could take him to where there was luck, if only he forced it. So he would mount again and start on his furious ride, hoping at last to get there. He knew he could get there.

'You'll break your horse, Paul!' said the nurse.

'He's always riding like that! I wish he'd leave off!' said his elder sister Joan.

But he only glared down on them in silence. Nurse gave him up. She could make nothing of him. Anyhow, he was growing beyond her.

One day his mother and his Uncle Oscar came in when he was on one of his furious rides. He did not speak to them.

'Hallo, you young jockey! Riding a winner?' said his uncle.

'Aren't you growing too big for a rocking-horse? You're not a very little boy any longer, you know,' said his mother.

But Paul only gave a blue glare from his big, rather close-set eyes. He would speak to nobody when he was in full tilt. His mother watched him with an anxious expression on her face.

At last he suddenly stopped forcing his horse into the mechanical gallop and slid down.

'Well, I got there!' he announced fiercely, his blue eyes still flaring, and his sturdy long legs straddling apart.

'Where did you get to?' asked his mother.

'Where I wanted to go,' he flared back at her.

'That's right, son!' said Uncle Oscar. 'Don't you stop till you get there. What's the horse's name?'

'He doesn't have a name,' said the boy.

'Gets on without all right?' asked the uncle.

'Well, he has different names. He was called Sansovino last week.'

'Sansovino, eh? Won the Ascot. How did you know his name?'

'He always talks about horse-races with Bassett,' said Joan.

The uncle was delighted to find that his small nephew was posted with the racing news. Bassett, the young gardener, who had been wounded in the left foot in the war and had got his present job through Oscar Cresswell, whose batman he had been, was a perfect blade of the 'turf'. He lived in the racing events, and the small boy lived with him.

Oscar Cresswell got it all from Bassett.

'Master Paul comes and asks me, so I can't do more than tell him, sir,' said Bassett, his face terribly serious, as if he were speaking of religious matters.

'And does he ever put anything on a horse he fancies?'

'Well – I don't want to give him away – he's a young sport, a fine sport, sir. Would you mind asking him himself? He sort of takes a pleasure in it, and perhaps he'd feel I was giving him away, sir, if you don't mind.'

Bassett was serious as a church.

The uncle went back to his nephew and took him off for a ride in the car.

'Say, Paul, old man, do you ever put anything on a horse?' the uncle asked.

The boy watched the handsome man closely.

'Why, do you think I oughtn't to?' he parried.

'Not a bit of it! I thought perhaps you might give me a tip for the Lincoln.'

The car sped on into the country, going down to Uncle Oscar's place in Hampshire.

'Honour bright?' said the nephew.

'Honour bright, son!' said the uncle.

'Well, then, Daffodil.'

'Daffodil! I doubt it, sonny. What about Mirza?'

'I only know the winner,' said the boy. 'That's Daffodil.'

'Daffodil, eh?'

There was a pause. Daffodil was an obscure horse comparatively.

'Uncle!'

'Yes, son?'

'You won't let it go any further, will you? I promised Bassett.'

'Bassett be damned, old man! What's he got to do with it?'

'We're partners. We've been partners from the first. Uncle, he lent me my first five shillings, which I lost. I promised him, honour bright, it was only between me and him; only you gave me that ten-shilling note I started winning with, so I thought you were lucky. You won't let it go any further, will you?'

The boy gazed at his uncle from those big, hot, blue eyes, set rather close together. The uncle stirred and laughed uneasily.

'Right you are, son! I'll keep your tip private. Daffodil, eh? How much are you putting on him?'

'All except twenty pounds,' said the boy. 'I keep that in reserve.'

The uncle thought it a good joke.

'You keep twenty pounds in reserve, do you, you young romancer? What are you betting, then?'

'I'm betting three hundred,' said the boy gravely. 'But it's between you and me, Uncle Oscar! Honour bright?'

The uncle burst into a roar of laughter.

'It's between you and me all right, you young Nat Gould,' he said, laughing. 'But where's your three hundred?'

'Bassett keeps it for me. We're partners.'

'You are, are you! And what is Bassett putting on Daffodil?'

'He won't go quite as high as I do, I expect. Perhaps he'll go a hundred and fifty.'

'What, pennies?' laughed the uncle.

'Pounds,' said the child, with a surprised look at his uncle. 'Bassett keeps a bigger reserve than I do.'

Between wonder and amusement Uncle Oscar was silent. He pursued the matter no further, but he determined to take his nephew with him to the Lincoln races.

'Now, son,' he said, 'I'm putting twenty on Mirza, and I'll

put five on for you on any horse you fancy. What's your pick?'

'Daffodil, uncle.'

'No, not the fiver on Daffodil!'

'I should if it was my own fiver,' said the child.

'Good! Good! Right you are! A fiver for me and a fiver for you on Daffodil.'

The child had never been to a race-meeting before, and his eyes were blue fire. He pursed his mouth tight and watched. A Frenchman just in front had put his money on Lancelot. Wild with excitement, he flayed his arms up and down, yelling 'Lancelot! Lancelot!' in his French accent.

Daffodil came in first, Lancelot second, Mirza third. The child, flushed and with eyes blazing, was curiously serene. His uncle brought him four five-pound notes, four to one.

'What am I to do with these?' he cried, waving them before the boy's eyes.

'I suppose we'll talk to Bassett,' said the boy. 'I expect I have fifteen hundred now; and twenty in reserve; and this twenty.'

His uncle studied him for some moments.

'Look here, son!' he said. 'You're not serious about Bassett and that fifteen hundred, are you?'

'Yes, I am. But it's between you and me, uncle. Honour bright?'

'Honour bright all right, son! But I must talk to Bassett.'

'If you'd like to be a partner, uncle, with Bassett and me, we could all be partners. Only, you'd have to promise, honour bright, uncle, not to let it go beyond us three. Bassett and I are lucky, and you must be lucky, because it was your ten shillings I started winning with. . . .'

Uncle Oscar took both Bassett and Paul into Richmond Park for an afternoon, and there they talked.

'It's like this, you see, sir,' Bassett said. 'Master Paul would get me talking about racing events, spinning yarns, you know, sir. And he was always keen on knowing if I'd made or if I'd lost. It's about a year since, now, that I put five shillings on Blush of Dawn for him: and we lost. Then the luck turned, with that ten shillings he had from you: that we put on Singhalese. And since that time, it's been pretty steady, all things considering. What do you say, Master Paul?'

'We're all right when we're sure,' said Paul. 'It's when we're not quite sure that we go down.'

'Oh, but we're careful then,' said Bassett.

'But when are you *sure*?' smiled Uncle Oscar.

'It's Master Paul, sir,' said Bassett in a secret, religious voice. 'It's as if he had it from heaven. Like Daffodil, now, for the Lincoln. That was as sure as eggs.'

'Did you put anything on Daffodil?' asked Oscar Cresswell.

'Yes, sir. I made my bit.'

'And my nephew?'

Bassett was obstinately silent, looking at Paul.

'I made twelve hundred, didn't I, Bassett? I told uncle I was putting three hundred on Daffodil.'

'That's right,' said Bassett, nodding.

'But where's the money?' asked the uncle.

'I keep it safe locked up, sir. Master Paul he can have it any minute he likes to ask for it.'

'What, fifteen hundred pounds?'

'And twenty! And *forty*, that is, with the twenty he made on the course.'

'It's amazing!' said the uncle.

'If Master Paul offers you to be partners, sir, I would, if I were you: if you'll excuse me,' said Bassett.

Oscar Cresswell thought about it.

'I'll see the money,' he said.

They drove home again, and, sure enough, Bassett came round to the garden-house with fifteen hundred pounds in notes. The twenty pounds reserve was left with Joe Glee, in the Turf Commission deposit.

'You see, it's all right, uncle, when I'm *sure*! Then we go strong, for all we're worth. Don't we, Bassett?'

'We do that, Master Paul.'

'And when are you sure?' said the uncle, laughing.

'Oh, well, sometimes I'm *absolutely* sure, like about Daffodil,' said the boy; 'and sometimes I have an idea; and sometimes I haven't even an idea, have I, Bassett? Then we're careful, because we mostly go down.'

'You do, do you! And when you're sure, like about Daffodil, what makes you sure, sonny?'

'Oh, well, I don't know,' said the boy uneasily. 'I'm sure, you know, uncle; that's all.'

'It's as if he had it from heaven, sir,' Bassett reiterated.

'I should say so!' said the uncle.

But he became a partner. And when the Leger was coming on Paul was 'sure' about Lively Spark, which was a quite inconsiderable horse. The boy insisted on putting a thousand on the horse, Bassett went for five hundred, and Oscar Cresswell two hundred. Lively Spark came in first, and the betting had been ten to one against him. Paul had made ten thousand.

'You see,' he said, 'I was absolutely sure of him.'

Even Oscar Cresswell had cleared two thousand.

'Look here, son,' he said, 'this sort of thing makes me nervous.'

'It needn't, uncle! Perhaps I shan't be sure again for a long time.'

'But what are you going to do with your money?' asked the uncle.

'Of course,' said the boy, 'I started it for mother. She said she had no luck, because father is unlucky, so I thought if *I* was lucky, it might stop whispering.'

'What might stop whispering?'

'Our house. I *hate* our house for whispering.'

'What does it whisper?'

'Why – why' – the boy fidgeted – 'why, I don't know. But it's always short of money, you know, uncle.'

'I know it, son, I know it.'

'You know people send mother writs, don't you, uncle?'

'I'm afraid I do,' said the uncle.

'And then the house whispers, like people laughing at you behind your back. It's awful, that is! I thought if I was lucky--'

'You might stop it,' added the uncle.

The boy watched him with big blue eyes, that had an uncanny cold fire in them, and he said never a word.

'Well, then!' said the uncle. 'What are we doing?'

'I shouldn't like mother to know I was lucky,' said the boy.

'Why not, son?'

'She'd stop me.'

'I don't think she would.'

'Oh!' – and the boy writhed in an odd way – 'I *don't* want her to know, uncle.'

'All right, son! We'll manage it without her knowing.'

They managed it very easily. Paul, at the other's suggestion, handed over five thousand pounds to his uncle, who deposited it with the family lawyer, who was then to inform Paul's mother that a relative had put five thousand pounds into his hands, which sum was to be paid out a thousand pounds at a time, on the mother's birthday, for the next five years.

'So she'll have a birthday present of a thousand pounds for five successive years,' said Uncle Oscar. 'I hope it won't make it all the harder for her later.'

Paul's mother had her birthday in November. The house had been 'whispering' worse than ever lately, and, even in spite of his luck, Paul could not bear up against it. He was very anxious to see the effect of the birthday letter, telling his mother about the thousand pounds.

When there were no visitors, Paul now took his meals with his parents, as he was beyond the nursery control. His mother went into town nearly every day. She had discovered that she had an odd knack of sketching furs and dress materials, so she worked secretly in the studio of a friend who was the chief 'artist' for the leading drapers. She drew the figures of ladies in furs and ladies in silk and sequins for the newspaper advertisements. This young woman artist earned several thousand pounds a year, but Paul's mother only made several hundreds, and she was again dissatisfied. She so wanted to be first in something, and she did not succeed, even in making sketches for drapery advertisements.

She was down to breakfast on the morning of her birthday. Paul watched her face as she read her letters. He knew the lawyer's letter. As his mother read it, her face hardened and became more expressionless. Then a cold, determined look came on her mouth. She hid the letter under the pile of others, and said not a word about it.

'Didn't you have anything nice in the post for your birthday, mother?' said Paul.

'Quite moderately nice,' she said, her voice cold and absent.

She went away to town without saying more.

But in the afternoon Uncle Oscar appeared. He said Paul's mother had had a long interview with the lawyer, asking if the whole five thousand could not be advanced at once, as she was in debt.

'What do you think, uncle?' said the boy.

'I leave it to you, son.'

'Oh, let her have it, then! We can get some more with the other,' said the boy.

'A bird in the hand is worth two in the bush, laddie!' said Uncle Oscar.

'But I'm sure to *know* for the Grand National; or the Lincolnshire, or else the Derby. I'm sure to know for *one* of them,' said Paul.

So Uncle Oscar signed the agreement, and Paul's mother

touched the whole five thousand. Then something very curious happened. The voices in the house suddenly went mad, like a chorus of frogs on a spring evening. There were certain new furnishings, and Paul had a tutor. He was *really* going to Eton, his father's school, in the following autumn. There were flowers in the winter, and a blossoming of the luxury Paul's mother had been used to. And yet the voices in the house, behind the sprays of mimosa and almond-blossom, and from under the piles of iridescent cushions, simply trilled and screamed in a sort of ecstasy: 'There *must* be more money! Oh-h-h; there *must* be more money. Oh, now, now-w! Now-w-w – there *must* be more money! – more than ever! More than ever!'

It frightened Paul terribly. He studied away at his Latin and Greek with his tutor. But his intense hours were spent with Bassett. The Grand National had gone by: he had not 'known', and had lost a hundred pounds. Summer was at hand. He was in agony for the Lincoln. But even for the Lincoln he didn't 'know', and he lost fifty pounds. He became wild-eyed and strange, as if something were going to explode in him.

'Let it alone, son! Don't you bother about it!' urged Uncle Oscar. But it was as if the boy couldn't really hear what his uncle was saying.

'I've got to know for the Derby! I've got to know for the Derby!' the child reiterated, his big blue eyes blazing with a sort of madness.

His mother noticed how overwrought he was.

'You'd better go to the seaside. Wouldn't you like to go now to the seaside, instead of waiting? I think you'd better,' she said, looking down at him anxiously, her heart curiously heavy because of him.

But the child lifted his uncanny blue eyes.

'I couldn't possibly go before the Derby, mother!' he said. 'I couldn't possibly!'

'Why not?' she said, her voice becoming heavy when she

was opposed. 'Why not? You can still go from the seaside to see the Derby with your Uncle Oscar, if that's what you wish. No need for you to wait here. Besides, I think you care too much about these races. It's a bad sign. My family has been a gambling family, and you won't know till you grow up how much damage it has done. But it has done damage. I shall have to send Bassett away, and ask Uncle Oscar not to talk racing to you, unless you promise to be reasonable about it: go away to the seaside and forget it. You're all nerves!'

'I'll do what you like, mother, so long as you don't send me away till after the Derby,' the boy said.

'Send you away from where? Just from this house?'

'Yes,' he said, gazing at her.

'Why, you curious child, what makes you care about this house so much, suddenly? I never knew you loved it.'

He gazed at her without speaking. He had a secret within a secret, something he had not divulged, even to Bassett or to his Uncle Oscar.

But his mother, after standing undecided and a little bit sullen for some moments, said:

'Very well, then! Don't go to the seaside till after the Derby, if you don't wish it. But promise me you won't let your nerves go to pieces. Promise you won't think so much about horse-racing and *events*, as you call them!'

'Oh no,' said the boy casually. 'I won't think much about them, mother. You needn't worry. I wouldn't worry, mother, if I were you.'

'If you were me and I were you,' said his mother, 'I wonder what we *should* do.'

'But you know you needn't worry, mother, don't you?' the boy repeated.

'I should be awfully glad to know it,' she said wearily.

'Oh, well, you *can*, you know. I mean, you *ought* to know you needn't worry,' he insisted.

'Ought I? Then I'll see about it,' she said.

Paul's secret of secrets was his wooden horse, that which had no name. Since he was emancipated from a nurse and a nursery-governess, he had had his rocking-horse removed to his own bedroom at the top of the house.

'Surely you're too big for a rocking-horse!' his mother had remonstrated.

'Well, you see, mother, till I can have a *real* horse, I like to have *some* sort of animal about,' had been his quaint answer.

'Do you feel he keeps you company?' she laughed.

'Oh yes! He's very good, he always keeps me company, when I'm there,' said Paul.

So the horse, rather shabby, stood in an arrested prance in the boy's bedroom.

The Derby was drawing near, and the boy grew more and more tense. He hardly heard what was spoken to him, he was very frail, and his eyes were really uncanny. His mother had sudden strange seizures of uneasiness about him. Sometimes, for half an hour, she would feel a sudden anxiety about him that was almost anguish. She wanted to rush to him at once, and know he was safe.

Two nights before the Derby, she was at a big party in town, when one of her rushes of anxiety about her boy, her first-born, gripped her heart till she could hardly speak. She fought with the feeling, might and main, for she believed in common sense. But it was too strong. She had to leave the dance and go downstairs to telephone to the country. The children's nursery-governess was terribly surprised and startled at being rung up in the night.

'Are the children all right, Miss Wilmot?'

'Oh yes, they are quite all right.'

'Master Paul? Is he all right?'

'He went to bed as right as a trivet. Shall I run up and look at him?'

'No,' said Paul's mother reluctantly. 'No! Don't trouble. It's all right. Don't sit up. We shall be home fairly soon.' She did not want her son's privacy intruded upon.

'Very good,' said the governess.

It was about one o'clock when Paul's mother and father drove up to their house. All was still. Paul's mother went to her room and slipped off her white fur cloak. She had told her maid not to wait up for her. She heard her husband downstairs, mixing a whisky and soda.

And then, because of the strange anxiety at her heart, she stole upstairs to her son's room. Noiselessly she went along the upper corridor. Was there a faint noise? What was it?

She stood, with arrested muscles, outside his door, listening. There was a strange, heavy, and yet not loud noise. Her heart stood still. It was a soundless noise, yet rushing and powerful. Something huge, in violent, hushed motion. What was it? What in God's name was it? She ought to know. She felt that she knew the noise. She knew what it was.

Yet she could not place it. She couldn't say what it was. And on and on it went, like a madness.

Softly, frozen with anxiety and fear, she turned the door-handle.

The room was dark. Yet in the space near the window, she heard and saw something plunging to and fro. She gazed in fear and amazement.

Then suddenly she switched on the light, and saw her son, in his green pyjamas, madly surging on the rocking-horse. The blaze of light suddenly lit him up, as he urged the wooden horse, and lit her up, as she stood, blonde, in her dress of pale green and crystal, in the doorway.

'Paul!' she cried. 'Whatever are you doing?'

'It's Malabar!' he screamed in a powerful, strange voice. 'It's Malabar!'

His eyes blazed at her for one strange and senseless second, as he ceased urging his wooden horse. Then he fell with a crash to the ground, and she, all her tormented motherhood flooding upon her, rushed to gather him up.

But he was unconscious, and unconscious he remained, with some brain-fever. He talked and tossed, and his mother sat stonily by his side.

'Malabar! It's Malabar! Bassett, Bassett, I *know*! It's Malabar!'

So the child cried, trying to get up and urge the rocking-horse that gave him his inspiration.

'What does he mean by Malabar?' asked the heart-frozen mother.

'I don't know,' said the father stonily.

'What does he mean by Malabar?' she asked her brother Oscar.

'It's one of the horses running for the Derby,' was the answer.

And, in spite of himself, Oscar Cresswell spoke to Bassett, and himself put a thousand on Malabar: at fourteen to one.

The third day of the illness was critical: they were waiting for a change. The boy, with his rather long, curly hair, was tossing ceaselessly on the pillow. He neither slept nor regained consciousness, and his eyes were like blue stones. His mother sat, feeling her heart had gone, turned actually into a stone.

In the evening, Oscar Cresswell did not come, but Bassett sent a message, saying could he come up for one moment, just one moment? Paul's mother was very angry at the intrusion, but on second thoughts she agreed. The boy was the same. Perhaps Bassett might bring him to consciousness.

The gardener, a shortish fellow with a little brown moustache and sharp little brown eyes, tiptoed into the room, touched his imaginary cap to Paul's mother, and stole to the bedside, staring with glittering, smallish eyes at the tossing, dying child.

'Master Paul!' he whispered. 'Master Paul! Malabar came in first all right, a clean win. I did as you told me. You've made over seventy thousand pounds, you have; you've got over eighty thousand. Malabar came in all right, Master Paul.'

'Malabar! Malabar! Did I say Malabar, mother? Did I say Malabar? Do you think I'm lucky, mother? I knew Malabar, didn't I? Over eighty thousand pounds! I call that lucky, don't you, mother? Over eighty thousand pounds! I knew, didn't I know I knew? Malabar came in all right. If I ride my horse till I'm sure, then I tell you, Bassett, you can go as high as you like. Did you go for all you were worth, Bassett?'

'I went a thousand on it, Master Paul.'

'I never told you, mother, that if I can ride my horse, and *get there*, then I'm absolutely sure – oh, absolutely! Mother, did I ever tell you? I *am* lucky!'

'No, you never did,' said his mother.

But the boy died in the night.

And even as he lay dead, his mother heard her brother's voice saying to her: 'My God, Hester, you're eighty-odd thousand to the good, and a poor devil of a son to the bad. But, poor devil, poor devil, he's best gone out of a life where he rides his rocking-horse to find a winner.'

Odour of Chrysanthemums

I

THE small locomotive engine, Number 4, came clanking, stumbling down from Selston with seven full wagons. It appeared round the corner with loud threats of speed, but the colt that it startled from among the gorse, which still flickered indistinctly in the raw afternoon, out-distanced it at a canter. A woman, walking up the railway line to Underwood, drew back into the hedge, held her basket aside, and watched the footplate of the engine advancing. The trucks thumped heavily past, one by one, with slow inevitable movement, as she stood insignificantly trapped between the jolting black wagons and the hedge; then they curved away towards the coppice where the withered oak leaves dropped noiselessly, while the birds, pulling at the scarlet hips beside the track, made off into the dusk that had already crept into the spinney. In the open, the smoke from the engine sank and cleaved to the rough grass. The fields were dreary and forsaken, and in the marshy strip that led to the whimsey, a reedy pit-pond, the fowls had already abandoned their run among the alders, to roost in the tarred fowl-house. The pit-bank loomed up beyond the pond, flames like red sores licking its ashy sides, in the afternoon's stagnant light. Just beyond rose the tapering chimneys and the clumsy black headstocks of Brinsley Colliery. The two wheels were spinning fast up against the sky, and the winding engine rapped out its little spasms. The miners were being turned up.

The engine whistled as it came into the wide bay of railway lines beside the colliery, where rows of trucks stood in harbour.

Miners, single, trailing and in groups, passed like shadows diverging home. At the edge of the ribbed level of sidings squat a low cottage, three steps down from the cinder track. A large bony vine clutched at the house, as if to claw down the tiled roof. Round the bricked yard grew a few wintry primroses. Beyond, the long garden sloped down to a bush-covered brook course. There were some twiggy apple trees, winter-crack trees, and ragged cabbages. Beside the path hung dishevelled pink chrysanthemums, like pink cloths hung on bushes. A woman came stooping out of the felt-covered fowl-house, half-way down the garden. She closed and padlocked the door, then drew herself erect, having brushed some bits from her white apron.

She was a tall woman of imperious mien, handsome, with definite black eyebrows. Her smooth black hair was parted exactly. For a few moments she stood steadily watching the miners as they passed along the railway: then she turned towards the brook course. Her face was calm and set, her mouth was closed with disillusionment. After a moment she called:

'John!' There was no answer. She waited, and then said distinctly:

'Where are you?'

'Here!' replied a child's sulky voice from among the bushes. The woman looked piercingly through the dusk.

'Are you at that brook?' she asked sternly.

For answer the child showed himself before the raspberry-canes that rose like whips. He was a small, sturdy boy of five. He stood quite still, defiantly.

'Oh!' said the mother, conciliated. 'I thought you were down at that wet brook – and you remember what I told you—'

The boy did not move or answer.

'Come, come on in,' she said more gently, 'it's getting dark. There's your grandfather's engine coming down the line!'

The lad advanced slowly, with resentful, taciturn movement. He was dressed in trousers and waistcoat of cloth that was too thick and hard for the size of the garments. They were evidently cut down from a man's clothes.

As they went slowly towards the house he tore at the ragged wisps of chrysanthemums and dropped the petals in handfuls among the path.

'Don't do that – it does look nasty,' said his mother. He refrained, and she, suddenly pitiful, broke off a twig with three or four wan flowers and held them against her face. When mother and son reached the yard her hand hesitated, and instead of laying the flower aside, she pushed it in her apron-band. The mother and son stood at the foot of the three steps looking across the bay of lines at the passing home of the miners. The trundle of the small train was imminent. Suddenly the engine loomed past the house and came to a stop opposite the gate.

The engine-driver, a short man with round grey beard, leaned out of the cab high above the woman.

'Have you got a cup of tea?' he said in a cheery, hearty fashion.

It was her father. She went in, saying she would mash. Directly, she returned.

'I didn't come to see you on Sunday,' began the little grey-bearded man.

'I didn't expect you,' said his daughter.

The engine-driver winced; then, reassuming his cheery, airy manner, he said:

'Oh, have you heard then? Well, and what do you think—?'

'I think it is soon enough,' she replied.

At her brief censure the little man made an impatient gesture, and said coaxingly, yet with dangerous coldness:

'Well, what's a man to do? It's no sort of life for a man of my years, to sit at my own hearth like a stranger. And if I'm going to marry again it may as well be soon as late – what does it matter to anybody?'

The woman did not reply, but turned and went into the house. The man in the engine-cab stood assertive, till she returned with a cup of tea and a piece of bread and butter on a plate. She went up the steps and stood near the footplate of the hissing engine.

'You needn't 'a' brought me bread an' butter,' said her father. 'But a cup of tea' – he sipped appreciatively – 'it's very nice.' He sipped for a moment or two, then: 'I hear as Walter's got another bout on,' he said.

'When hasn't he?' said the woman bitterly.

'I heerd tell of him in the "Lord Nelson" braggin' as he was going to spend that b—— afore he went: half a sovereign that was.'

'When?' asked the woman.

'A' Sat'day night – I know that's true.'

'Very likely,' she laughed bitterly. 'He gives me twenty-three shillings.'

'Aye, it's a nice thing, when a man can do nothing with his money but make a beast of himself!' said the grey-whiskered man. The woman turned her head away. Her father swallowed the last of his tea and handed her the cup.

'Aye,' he sighed, wiping his mouth. 'It's a settler, it is—'

He put his hand on the lever. The little engine strained and groaned, and the train rumbled towards the crossing. The woman again looked across the metals. Darkness was settling over the spaces of the railway and trucks: the miners, in grey sombre groups, were still passing home. The winding engine pulsed hurriedly, with brief pauses. Elizabeth Bates looked at the dreary flow of men, then she went indoors. Her husband did not come.

The kitchen was small and full of firelight; red coals piled glowing up the chimney mouth. All the life of the room seemed in the white, warm hearth and the steel fender reflecting the red fire. The cloth was laid for tea; cups glinted in the shadows. At the back, where the lowest stairs protruded into the room, the boy sat struggling with a knife and a piece of whitewood. He was almost hidden in the shadow. It was half-past four. They had but to await the father's coming to begin tea. As the mother watched her son's sullen little struggle with the wood, she saw herself in his silence and pertinacity; she saw the father in her child's indifference to all but himself. She seemed to be occupied by her husband. He had probably gone past his home, slung past his own door, to drink before he came in, while his dinner spoiled and wasted in waiting. She glanced at the clock, then took the potatoes to strain them in the yard. The garden and fields beyond the brook were closed in uncertain darkness. When she rose with the saucepan, leaving the drain steaming into the night behind her, she saw the yellow lamps were lit along the high road that went up the hill away beyond the space of the railway lines and the field.

Then again she watched the men trooping home, fewer now and fewer.

Indoors the fire was sinking and the room was dark red. The woman put her saucepan on the hob, and set a batter-pudding near the mouth of the oven. Then she stood unmoving. Directly, gratefully, came quick young steps to the door. Someone hung on the latch a moment, then a little girl entered and began pulling off her outdoor things, dragging a mass of curls, just ripening from gold to brown, over her eyes with her hat.

Her mother chid her for coming late from school, and said she would have to keep her at home the dark winter days.

'Why, mother, it's hardly a bit dark yet. The lamp's not lighted, and my father's not home.'

'No, he isn't. But it's a quarter to five! Did you see anything of him?'

The child became serious. She looked at her mother with large, wistful blue eyes.

'No, mother, I've never seen him. Why? Has he come up an' gone past, to Old Brinsley? He hasn't, mother, 'cos I never saw him.'

'He'd watch that,' said the mother bitterly, 'he'd take care as you didn't see him. But you may depend upon it, he's seated in the "Prince o' Wales". He wouldn't be this late.'

The girl looked at her mother piteously.

'Let's have our teas, mother, should we?' said she.

The mother called John to table. She opened the door once more and looked out across the darkness of the lines. All was deserted: she could not hear the winding-engines.

'Perhaps,' she said to herself, 'he's stopped to get some ripping done.'

They sat down to tea. John, at the end of the table near the door, was almost lost in the darkness. Their faces were hidden from each other. The girl crouched against the fender slowly moving a thick piece of bread before the fire. The lad, his face a dusky mark on the shadow, sat watching her who was transfigured in the red glow.

'I do think it's beautiful to look in the fire,' said the child.

'Do you?' said her mother. 'Why?'

'It's so red, and full of little caves – and it feels so nice, and you can fair smell it.'

'It'll want mending directly,' replied her mother, 'and then if your father comes he'll carry on and say there never is a fire when a man comes home sweating from the pit. A public-house is always warm enough.'

There was silence till the boy said complainingly: 'Make haste, our Annie.'

'Well, I am doing! I can't make the fire do it no faster, can I?'

'She keeps wafflin' it about so's to make 'er slow,' grumbled the boy.

'Don't have such an evil imagination, child,' replied the mother.

Soon the room was busy in the darkness with the crisp sound of crunching. The mother ate very little. She drank her tea determinedly, and sat thinking. When she rose her anger was evident in the stern unbending of her head. She looked at the pudding in the fender, and broke out:

'It is a scandalous thing as a man can't even come home to his dinner! If it's crozzled up to a cinder I don't see why I should care. Past his very door he goes to get to a public-house, and here I sit with his dinner waiting for him—'

She went out. As she dropped piece after piece of coal on the red fire, the shadows fell on the walls, till the room was almost in total darkness.

'I canna see,' grumbled the invisible John. In spite of herself, the mother laughed.

'You know the way to your mouth,' she said. She set the dust-pan outside the door. When she came again like a shadow on the hearth, the lad repeated, complaining sulkily:

'I canna see.'

'Good gracious!' cried the mother irritably, 'you're as bad as your father if it's a bit dusk!'

Nevertheless, she took a paper spill from a sheaf on the mantelpiece and proceeded to light the lamp that hung from the ceiling in the middle of the room. As she reached up, her figure displayed itself just rounding with maternity.

'Oh, mother—!' exclaimed the girl.

'What?' said the woman, suspended in the act of putting the lamp-glass over the flame. The copper reflector shone hand-somely on her, as she stood with uplifted arm, turning to face her daughter.

'You've got a flower in your apron!' said the child, in a little rapture at this unusual event.

'Goodness me!' exclaimed the woman, relieved. 'One would think the house was afire.' She replaced the glass and waited a moment before turning up the wick. A pale shadow was seen floating vaguely on the floor.

'Let me smell!' said the child, still rapturously, coming forward and putting her face to her mother's waist.

'Go along, silly!' said the mother, turning up the lamp. The light revealed their suspense so that the woman felt it almost unbearable. Annie was still bending at her waist. Irritably, the mother took the flowers out from her apron-band.

'Oh, mother – don't take them out!' Annie cried, catching her hand and trying to replace the sprig.

'Such nonsense!' said the mother, turning away. The child put the pale chrysanthemums to her lips, murmuring:

'Don't they smell beautiful!'

Her mother gave a short laugh.

'No,' she said, 'not to me. It was chrysanthemums when I married him, and chrysanthemums when you were born, and the first time they ever brought him home drunk, he'd got brown chrysanthemums in his button-hole.'

She looked at the children. Their eyes and their parted lips were wondering. The mother sat rocking in silence for some time. Then she looked at the clock.

'Twenty minutes to six!' In a tone of fine bitter carelessness she continued: 'Eh, he'll not come now till they bring him. There he'll stick! But he needn't come rolling in here in his pit-dirt, for *I* won't wash him. He can lie on the floor— Eh, what a fool I've been, what a fool! And this is what I came here for, to this dirty hole, rats and all, for him to slink past his very door. Twice last week – he's begun now—'

She silenced herself, and rose to clear the table.

While for an hour or more the children played, subduedly

intent, fertile of imagination, united in fear of the mother's wrath, and in dread of their father's home-coming, Mrs Bates sat in her rocking-chair making a 'singlet' of thick cream-coloured flannel, which gave a dull wounded sound as she tore off the grey edge. She worked at her sewing with energy, listening to the children, and her anger wearied itself, lay down to rest, opening its eyes from time to time and steadily watching, its ears raised to listen. Sometimes even her anger quailed and shrank, and the mother suspended her sewing, tracing the footsteps that thudded along the sleepers outside; she would lift her head sharply to bid the children 'hush', but she recovered herself in time, and the footsteps went past the gate, and the children were not flung out of their play-world.

But at last Annie sighed, and gave in. She glanced at her wagon of slippers, and loathed the game. She turned plaintively to her mother.

'Mother!' – but she was inarticulate.

John crept out like a frog from under the sofa. His mother glanced up.

'Yes,' she said, 'just look at those shirt-sleeves!'

The boy held them out to survey them, saying nothing. Then somebody called in a hoarse voice away down the line, and suspense bristled in the room. till two people had gone by outside, talking.

'It is time for bed,' said the mother.

'My father hasn't come,' wailed Annie plaintively. But her mother was primed with courage.

'Never mind. They'll bring him when he does come – like a log.' She meant there would be no scene. 'And he may sleep on the floor till he wakes himself. I know he'll not go to work tomorrow after this!'

The children had their hands and faces wiped with a flannel. They were very quiet. When they had put on their night-dresses, they said their prayers, the boy mumbling. The mother looked down at them, at the brown silken bush of intertwining curls in the nape of the girl's neck, at the little black head of the lad, and her heart burst with anger at their father, who caused all three such distress. The children hid their faces in her skirts for comfort.

When Mrs Bates came down, the room was strangely empty, with a tension of expectancy. She took up her sewing and stitched for some time without raising her head. Meantime her anger was tinged with fear.

II

The clock struck eight and she rose suddenly, dropping her sewing on her chair. She went to the stairfoot door, opened it, listening. Then she went out, locking the door behind her.

Something scuffled in the yard, and she started, though she knew it was only the rats with which the place was over-run. The night was very dark. In the great bay of railway lines, bulked with trucks, there was no trace of light, only away back she could see a few yellow lamps at the pit-top, and the red smear of the burning pit-bank on the night. She hurried along the edge of the track, then, crossing the converging lines, came to the stile by the white gates, whence she emerged on the road. Then the fear which had led her shrank. People were walking up to New Brinsley; she saw the lights in the houses; twenty yards farther on were the broad windows of the 'Prince of Wales', very warm and bright, and the loud voices of men could be heard distinctly. What a fool she had been to imagine that anything had happened to him! He was merely drinking over there at the 'Prince of Wales'. She faltered. She had never yet been to fetch him, and she never would go. So she continued her walk towards the long straggling line of houses, standing back on the highway. She entered a passage between the dwellings.

'Mr Rigley? – Yes! Did you want him? No, he's not in at this minute.'

The raw-boned woman leaned forward from her dark scullery and peered at the other, upon whom fell a dim light through the blind of the kitchen window.

'Is it Mrs Bates?' she asked in a tone tinged with respect.

'Yes. I wondered if your Master was at home. Mine hasn't come yet.'

' 'Asn't 'e! Oh, Jack's been 'ome an' 'ad 'is dinner an' gone out. 'E's just gone for 'alf an hour afore bed-time. Did you call at the "Prince of Wales"?'

'No—'

'No, you didn't like—! It's not very nice.' The other woman was indulgent. There was an awkward pause. 'Jack never said nothink about – about your Mester,' she said.

'No! – I expect he's stuck in there!'

Elizabeth Bates said this bitterly, and with recklessness. She knew that the woman across the yard was standing at her door listening, but she did not care. As she turned:

'Stop a minute! I'll just go and ask Jack if 'e knows anythink,' said Mrs Rigley.

'Oh no – I wouldn't like to put—!'

'Yes, I will, if you'll just step inside an' see as th' childer doesn't come downstairs and set theirselves afire.'

Elizabeth Bates, murmuring a remonstrance, stepped inside. The other woman apologized for the state of the room.

The kitchen needed apology. There were little frocks and trousers and childish undergarments on the squab and on the floor, and a litter of playthings everywhere. On the black American cloth of the table were pieces of bread and cake, crusts, slops, and a teapot with cold tea.

'Eh, ours is just as bad,' said Elizabeth Bates, looking at the woman, not at the house. Mrs Rigley put a shawl over her head and hurried out, saying:

'I shanna be a minute.'

The other sat, noting with faint disapproval the general untidiness of the room. Then she fell to counting the shoes of various sizes scattered over the floor. There were twelve. She sighed and said to herself: 'No wonder!' – glancing at the litter. There came the scratching of two pairs of feet on the yard, and the Rigleys entered. Elizabeth Bates rose. Rigley was a big man, with very large bones. His head looked particularly bony. Across his temple was a blue scar, caused by a wound got in the pit, a wound in which the coal-dust remained blue like tattooing.

''Asna 'e come whoam yit?' asked the man, without any form of greeting, but with deference and sympathy. 'I couldna say wheer he is – 'e's non ower theer!' – he jerked his head to signify the 'Prince of Wales'.

' 'E's 'appen gone up to th' "Yew",' said Mrs Rigley.

There was another pause. Rigley had evidently something to get off his mind:

'Ah left 'im finishin' a stint,' he began. 'Loose-all 'ad bin gone about ten minutes when we com'n away, an' I shouted: "Are ter comin', Walt?" an' 'e said: "Go on, Ah shanna be but a'ef a minnit," so we com'n ter th' bottom, me an' Bowers, thinkin' as 'e wor just behint, an' 'ud come up i' th' next bantle—'

He stood perplexed, as if answering a charge of deserting his mate. Elizabeth Bates, now again certain of disaster, hastened to reassure him:

'I expect 'e's gone up to th' "Yew Tree", as you say. It's not the first time. I've fretted myself into a fever before now. He'll come home when they carry him.'

'Ay, isn't it too bad!' deplored the other woman.

'I'll just step up to Dick's an' see if 'e is theer,' offered the man, afraid of appearing alarmed, afraid of taking liberties.

'Oh, I wouldn't think of bothering you that far,' said Elizabeth

Bates, with emphasis, but he knew she was glad of his offer.

As they stumbled up the entry, Elizabeth Bates heard Rigley's wife run across the yard and open her neighbour's door. At this, suddenly all the blood in her body seemed to switch away from her heart.

'Mind!' warned Rigley. 'Ah've said many a time as Ah'd fill up them ruts in this entry, sumb'dy 'll be breakin' their legs yit.'

She recovered herself and walked quickly along with the miner.

'I don't like leaving the children in bed, and nobody in the house,' she said.

'No, you dunna!' he replied courteously. They were soon at the gate of the cottage.

'Well, I shanna be many minnits. Dunna you be frettin' now, 'e'll be all right,' said the butty.

'Thank you very much, Mr Rigley,' she replied.

'You're welcome!' he stammered, moving away. 'I shanna be many minnits.'

The house was quiet. Elizabeth Bates took off her hat and shawl, and rolled back the rug. When she had finished, she sat down. It was a few minutes past nine. She was startled by the rapid chuff of the winding-engine at the pit, and the sharp whirr of the brakes on the rope as it descended. Again she felt the painful sweep of her blood, and she put her hand to her side, saying aloud: 'Good gracious! – it's only the nine o'clock deputy going down,' rebuking herself.

She sat still, listening. Half an hour of this, and she was wearied out.

'What am I working myself up like this for?' she said piti-ably to herself. 'I s'll only be doing myself some damage.'

She took out her sewing again.

At a quarter to ten there were footsteps. One person! She watched for the door to open. It was an elderly woman, in a black bonnet and a black woollen shawl – his mother. She was about sixty years old, pale, with blue eyes, and her face all wrinkled and lamentable. She shut the door and turned to her daughter-in-law peevishly.

'Eh, Lizzie, whatever shall we do, whatever shall we do!' she cried.

Elizabeth drew back a little, sharply.

'What is it, mother?' she said.

The elder woman seated herself on the sofa.

'I don't know, child, I can't tell you!' – she shook her head slowly. Elizabeth sat watching her, anxious and vexed.

'I don't know,' replied the grandmother, sighing very deeply. 'There's no end to my troubles, there isn't. The things I've gone through, 'm sure it's enough—!' She wept without wiping her eyes, the tears running.

'But, mother,' interrupted Elizabeth, 'what do you mean? What is it?'

The grandmother slowly wiped her eyes. The fountains of her tears were stopped by Elizabeth's directness. She wiped her eyes slowly.

'Poor child! Eh, you poor thing!' she moaned. 'I don't know what we're going to do, I don't – and you as you are – it's a thing, it is indeed!'

Elizabeth waited.

'Is he dead?' she asked, and at the words her heart swung violently, though she felt a slight flush of shame at the ultimate extravagance of the question. Her words sufficiently frightened the old lady, almost brought her to herself.

'Don't say so, Elizabeth! We'll hope it's not as bad as that; no, may the Lord spare us that, Elizabeth. Jack Rigley came just as I was sittin' down to a glass afore going to bed, an' 'e said: " 'Appen you'll go down th' line, Mrs Bates. Walt's had an accident. 'Appen you'll go an' sit wi' 'er till we can get him home." I hadn't time to ask him a word afore he was gone. An' I put my bonnet on an' come straight down, Lizzie. I thought to myself: "Eh, that poor blessed child, if anybody should come an' tell her of a sudden, there's no knowin' what'll 'appen to 'er.' You mustn't let it upset you, Lizzie – or you know what to expect. How long is it, six months – or is it five, Lizzie? Ay!' – the old woman shook her head – 'time slips on, it slips on! Ay!'

Elizabeth's thoughts were busy elsewhere. If he was killed – would she be able to manage on the little pension and what she could earn? – she counted up rapidly. If he was hurt – they wouldn't take him to the hospital – how tiresome he would be to nurse! – but perhaps she'd be able to get him away from the drink and his hateful ways. She would – while he was ill. The tears offered to come to her eyes at the picture. But what sentimental luxury was this she was beginning? She turned to consider the children. At any rate she was absolutely necessary for them. They were her business.

'Ay!' repeated the old woman, 'it seems but a week or two since he brought me his first wages. Ay – he was a good lad, Elizabeth, he was, in his way. I don't know why he got to be such a trouble, I don't. He was a happy lad at home, only full of spirits. But there's no mistake he's been a handful of trouble, he has! I hope the Lord'll spare him to mend his ways. I hope so, I hope so. You've had a sight o' trouble with him, Elizabeth, you have indeed. But he was a jolly enough lad wi' me, he was, I can assure you. I don't know how it is. . . .'

The old woman continued to muse aloud, a monotonous irritating sound, while Elizabeth thought concentratedly, startled once, when she heard the winding-engine chuff quickly, and the brakes skirr with a shriek. Then she heard the engine more slowly, and the brakes made no sound. The old woman did not notice. Elizabeth waited in suspense. The mother-in-law talked, with lapses into silence.

'But he wasn't your son, Lizzie, an' it makes a difference. Whatever he was, I remember him when he was little, an' I learned to understand him and to make allowances. You've got to make allowances for them—'

It was half-past ten, and the old woman was saying: 'But it's trouble from beginning to end; you're never too old for trouble, never too old for that—' when the gate banged back, and there were heavy feet on the steps.

'I'll go, Lizzie, let me go,' cried the old woman, rising. But Elizabeth was at the door. It was a man in pit-clothes.

'They're bringin' 'im, Missis,' he said. Elizabeth's heart halted a moment. Then it surged on again, almost suffocating her.

'Is he – is it bad?' she asked.

The man turned away, looking at the darkness:

'The doctor says 'e'd been dead hours. 'E saw 'im i' th' lamp-cabin.'

The old woman, who stood just behind Elizabeth, dropped into a chair, and folded her hands, crying: 'Oh, my boy, my boy!'

'Hush!' said Elizabeth, with a sharp twitch of a frown. 'Be still, mother, don't waken th' children: I wouldn't have them down for anything!'

The old woman moaned softly, rocking herself. The man was drawing away. Elizabeth took a step forward.

'How was it?' she asked.

'Well, I couldn't say for sure,' the man replied, very ill at ease. ''E wor finishin' a stint an' th' butties 'ad gone, an' a lot o' stuff come down atop 'n 'im.'

'And crushed him?' cried the widow, with a shudder.

'No,' said the man, 'it fell at th' back of 'im. 'E wor under th' face, an' it niver touched 'im. It shut 'im in. It seems 'e wor smothered.'

Elizabeth shrank back. She heard the old woman behind her cry:

'What? – what did 'e say it was?'

The man replied, more loudly: ''E wor smothered!'

Then the old woman wailed aloud, and this relieved Elizabeth.

'Oh, mother,' she said, putting her hand on the old woman, don't waken th' children, don't waken th' children.'

She wept a little, unknowing, while the old mother rocked herself and moaned. Elizabeth remembered that they were bringing him home, and she must be ready. 'They'll lay him in the parlour,' she said to herself, standing a moment pale and perplexed.

Then she lighted a candle and went into the tiny room. The air was cold and damp, but she could not make a fire, there was no fireplace. She set down the candle and looked round. The candlelight glittered on the lustre-glasses, on the two vases that held some of the pink chrysanthemums, and on the dark mahogany. There was a cold, deathly smell of chrysanthemums in the room. Elizabeth stood looking at the flowers. She turned away, and calculated whether there would be room to lay him on the floor, between the couch and the chiffonier. She pushed the chairs aside. There would be room to lay him down and to step around him. Then she fetched the old red tablecloth, and another old cloth, spreading them down to save her bit of carpet. She shivered on leaving the parlour; so, from the dresser drawer she took a clean shirt and put it at the fire to air. All the time her mother-in-law was rocking herself in the chair and moaning.

'You'll have to move from there, mother,' said Elizabeth. 'They'll be bringing him in. Come in the rocker.'

The old mother rose mechanically, and seated herself by the fire, continuing to lament. Elizabeth went into the pantry for another candle, and there, in the little pent-house under the naked tiles, she heard them coming. She stood still in the pantry doorway, listening. She heard them pass the end of the house, and come awkwardly down the three steps, a jumble of shuffling footsteps and muttering voices. The old woman was silent. The men were in the yard.

Then Elizabeth heard Matthews, the manager of the pit, say: 'You go in first, Jim. Mind!'

The door came open, and the two women saw a collier backing into the room, holding one end of a stretcher, on which they could see the nailed pit-boots of the dead man. The two carriers halted, the man at the head stooping to the lintel of the door.

'Wheer will you have him?' asked the manager, a short, white-bearded man.

Elizabeth roused herself and came from the pantry carrying the unlighted candle.

'In the parlour,' she said.

'In there, Jim!' pointed the manager, and the carriers backed round the tiny room. The coat with which they had covered the body fell off as they awkwardly turned through the two doorways, and the women saw their man, naked to the waist, lying stripped for work. The old woman began to moan in a low voice of horror.

'Lay th' stretcher at th' side,' snapped the manager, 'an' put 'im on th' cloths. Mind now, mind! Look you now—!'

One of the men had knocked off a vase of chrysanthemums. He stared awkwardly, then they set down the stretcher. Elizabeth did not look at her husband. As soon as she could get in the room, she went and picked up the broken vase and the flowers.

'Wait a minute!' she said.

The three men waited in silence while she mopped up the water with a duster.

'Eh, what a job, what a job, to be sure!' the manager was saying, rubbing his brow with trouble and perplexity. 'Never knew such a thing in my life, never! He'd no business to ha' been left. I never knew such a thing in my life! Fell over him clean as a whistle, an' shut him in. Not four foot of space, there wasn't – yet it scarce bruised him.'

He looked down at the dead man, lying prone, half naked, all grimed with coal-dust.

' " 'Sphyxiated", the doctor said. It is the most terrible job I've ever known. Seems as if it was done o' purpose. Clean over him, an' shut 'im in, like a mouse-trap' – he made a sharp, descending gesture with his hand.

The colliers standing by jerked aside their heads in hopeless comment.

The horror of the thing bristled upon them all.

Then they heard the girl's voice upstairs calling shrilly: 'Mother, mother – who is it? Mother, who is it?'

Elizabeth hurried to the foot of the stairs and opened the door:

'Go to sleep!' she commanded sharply. 'What are you shouting about? Go to sleep at once – there's nothing—'

Then she began to mount the stairs. They could hear her on the boards, and on the plaster floor of the little bedroom. They could hear her distinctly:

'What's the matter now? – what's the matter with you, silly thing?' – her voice was much agitated, with an unreal gentleness.

'I thought it was some men come,' said the plaintive voice of the child. 'Has he come?'

'Yes, they've brought him. There's nothing to make a fuss about. Go to sleep now, like a good child.'

They could hear her voice in the bedroom, they waited whilst she covered the children under the bedclothes.

'Is he drunk?' asked the girl, timidly, faintly.

'No! No – he's not! He – he's asleep.'

'Is he asleep downstairs?'

'Yes – and don't make a noise.'

There was silence for a moment, then the men heard the frightened child again:

'What's that noise?'

'It's nothing, I tell you, what are you bothering for?'

The noise was the grandmother moaning. She was oblivious of everything, sitting on her chair rocking and moaning. The manager put his hand on her arm and bade her 'Sh – sh! !'

The old woman opened her eyes and looked at him. She was shocked by this interruption, and seemed to wonder.

'What time is it?' the plaintive thin voice of the child, sinking back unhappily into sleep, asked this last question.

'Ten o'clock,' answered the mother more softly. Then she must have bent down and kissed the children.

Matthews beckoned to the men to come away. They put on their caps and took up the stretcher. Stepping over the body, they tiptoed out of the house. None of them spoke till they were far away from the wakeful children.

When Elizabeth came down she found her mother alone on the parlour floor, leaning over the dead man, the tears dropping on him.

'We must lay him out,' the wife said. She put on the kettle, then returning knelt at the feet, and began to unfasten the knotted leather laces. The room was clammy and dim with only one candle, so that she had to bend her face almost to the floor. At last she got off the heavy boots and put them away.

'You must help me now,' she whispered to the old woman. Together they stripped the man.

When they arose, saw him lying in the naïve dignity of death, the women stood arrested in fear and respect. For a few moments they remained still, looking down, the old mother whimpering. Elizabeth felt countermanded. She saw him, how utterly inviolable he lay in himself. She had nothing to do with him. She could not accept it. Stooping, she laid her hand on him, in claim. He was still warm, for the mine was hot where he had died. His mother had his face between her hands, and was murmuring incoherently. The old tears fell in succession as drops from wet leaves; the mother was not weeping, merely her tears flowed. Elizabeth embraced the body of her husband, with cheek and lips. She seemed to be listening, inquiring, trying to get some connection. But she could not. She was driven away. He was impregnable.

She rose, went into the kitchen, where she poured warm water into a bowl, brought soap and flannel and a soft towel.

'I must wash him,' she said.

Then the old mother rose stiffly, and watched Elizabeth as she carefully washed his face, carefully brushing the big blond moustache from his mouth with the flannel. She was afraid with a bottomless fear, so she ministered to him. The old woman, jealous, said:

'Let me wipe him!' – and she kneeled on the other side drying slowly as Elizabeth washed, her big black bonnet sometimes brushing the dark head of her daughter-in-law. They worked thus in silence for a long time. They never forgot it was death, and the touch of the man's dead body gave them strange emotions, different in each of the women; a great dread possessed them both, the mother felt the lie was given to her womb, she was denied; the wife felt the utter isolation of the human soul, the child within her was a weight apart from her.

At last it was finished. He was a man of handsome body, and his face showed no traces of drink. He was blond, full-fleshed, with fine limbs. But he was dead.

'Bless him,' whispered his mother, looking always at his face, and speaking out of sheer terror. 'Dear lad – bless him!' She spoke in a faint, sibilant ecstasy of fear and mother love.

Elizabeth sank down again to the floor, and put her face against his neck, and trembled and shuddered. But she had to draw away again. He was dead, and her living flesh had no place against his. A great dread and weariness held her: she was so unavailing. Her life was gone like this.

'White as milk he is, clear as a twelve-month baby, bless him, the darling!' the old mother murmured to herself. 'Not a mark on him, clear and clean and white, beautiful as ever a child was made,' she murmured with pride. Elizabeth kept her face hidden.

'He went peaceful, Lizzie – peaceful as sleep. Isn't he beautiful, the lamb? Ay – he must ha' made his peace, Lizzie. 'Appen he made it all right, Lizzie, shut in there. He'd have time. He wouldn't look like this if he hadn't made his peace. The lamb, the dear lamb. Eh, but he had a hearty laugh. I loved to hear it. He had the heartiest laugh, Lizzie, as a lad—'

Elizabeth looked up. The man's mouth was fallen back, slightly open under the cover of the moustache. The eyes, half shut, did not show glazed in the obscurity. Life with its smoky burning gone from him, had left him apart and utterly alien to her. And she knew what a stranger he was to her. In her womb was ice of fear, because of this separate stranger with whom she had been living as one flesh. Was this what it all meant – utter, intact separateness, obscured by heat of living? In dread she turned her face away. The fact was too deadly. There had been nothing between them, and yet they had come together, exchanging their nakedness repeatedly. Each time he had taken her, they had been two isolated beings, far apart as now. He was no more responsible than she. The child was like ice in her womb. For as she looked at the dead man, her mind, cold and detached, said clearly: 'Who am I? What have I been doing? I have been fighting a husband who did not exist. *He* existed all the time. What wrong have I done? What was that I have been living with? There lies the reality, this man.' And her soul died in her for fear: she knew she had never seen him, he had never seen her, they had met in the dark and had fought in the dark, not knowing whom they met nor whom they fought. And now she saw, and turned silent in seeing. For she had been wrong. She had said he was something he was not; she had felt familiar with him. Whereas he was apart all the while, living as she never lived, feeling as she never felt.

In fear and shame she looked at his naked body, that she had
known falsely. And he was the father of her children. Her soul
was torn from her body and stood apart. She looked at his
naked body and was ashamed, as if she had denied it. After all,
it was itself. It seemed awful to her. She looked at his face,
and she turned her own face to the wall. For his look was
other than hers, his way was not her way. She had denied him
what he was – she saw it now. She had refused him as himself.
And this had been her life, and his life. She was grateful to
death, which restored the truth. And she knew she was not
dead.

And all the while her heart was bursting with grief and pity
for him. What had he suffered? What stretch of horror for
this helpless man! She was rigid with agony. She had not been
able to help him. He had been cruelly injured, this naked man,
this other being, and she could make no reparation. There were
the children – but the children belonged to life. This dead man
had nothing to do with them. He and she were only channels
through which life had flowed to issue in the children. She was
a mother – but how awful she knew it now to have been a
wife. And he, dead now, how awful he must have felt it to
be a husband. She felt that in the next world he would be a
stranger to her. If they met there, in the beyond, they would
only be ashamed of what had been before. The children had
come, for some mysterious reason, out of both of them. But
the children did not unite them. Now he was dead, she knew
how eternally he was apart from her, how eternally he had
nothing more to do with her. She saw this episode of her life
closed. They had denied each other in life. Now he had with-
drawn. An anguish came over her. It was finished then: it had
become hopeless between them long before he died. Yet he
had been her husband. But how little!

'Have you got his shirt, 'Lizabeth?'

Elizabeth turned without answering, though she strove to

weep and behave as her mother-in-law expected. But she could not, she was silenced. She went into the kitchen and returned with the garment.

'It is aired,' she said, grasping the cotton shirt here and there to try. She was almost ashamed to handle him; what right had she or anyone to lay hands on him: but her touch was humble on his body. It was hard work to clothe him. He was so heavy and inert. A terrible dread gripped her all the while: that he could be so heavy and utterly inert, unresponsive, apart. The horror of the distance between them was almost too much for her – it was so infinite a gap she must look across.

At last it was finished. They covered him with a sheet and left him lying, with his face bound. And she fastened the door of the little parlour, lest the children should see what was lying there. Then, with peace sunk heavy on her heart, she went about making tidy the kitchen. She knew she submitted to life, which was her immediate master. But from death, her ultimate master, she winced with fear and shame.

Strike-Pay

S TRIKE-MONEY is paid in the Primitive Methodist
Chapel. The crier was round quite early on Wednesday
morning to say that paying would begin at ten o'clock.

The Primitive Methodist Chapel is a big barn of a place, built,
designed, and paid for by the colliers themselves. But it
threatened to fall down from its first form, so that a professional
architect had to be hired at last to pull the place together.

It stands in the Square. Forty years ago, when Bryan and
Wentworth opened their pits, they put up the 'squares' of
miners' dwellings. They are two great quadrangles of houses,
enclosing a barren stretch of ground, littered with broken pots
and rubbish, which forms a square, a great, sloping, lumpy
playground for the children, a drying-ground for many women's
washing.

Wednesday is still wash-day with some women. As the men
clustered round the Chapel, they heard the thud-thud-thud of
many pouches, women pounding away at the wash-tub with
a wooden pestle. In the Square the white clothes were waving
in the wind from a maze of clothes-lines, and here and there
women were pegging out, calling to the miners, or to the
children who dodged under the flapping sheets.

Ben Townsend, the Union agent, has a bad way of paying.
He takes the men in order of his round, and calls them by
name. A big, oratorical man with a grey beard, he sat at the
table in the Primitive school-room, calling name after name.

43

The room was crowded with colliers, and a great group pushed up outside. There was much confusion. Ben dodged from the Scargill Street list to the Queen Street. For this Queen Street men were not prepared. They were not to the fore.

'Joseph Grooby – Joseph Grooby! Now, Joe, where are you?'

'Hold on a bit, Sorry!' cried Joe from outside. 'I'm shovin' up.' There was a great noise from the men.

'I'm takin' Queen Street. All you Queen Street men should be ready. Here you are, Joe,' said the Union agent loudly.

'Five children!' said Joe, counting the money suspiciously.

'That's right, I think,' came the mouthing voice. 'Fifteen shillings, is it not?'

'A bob a kid,' said the collier.

'Thomas Sedgwick— How are you, Tom? Missis better?'

'Ay, 'er's shapin' nicely. Tha'rt hard at work to-day, Ben. This was sarcasm on the idleness of a man who had given up the pit to become a Union agent.

'Yes. I rose at four to fetch the money.'

'Dunna hurt thysen,' was the retort, and the men laughed.

'No – John Merfin!'

But the colliers, tired with waiting, excited by the strike spirit, began to rag. Merfin was young and dandiacal. He was choir-master at the Wesleyan Chapel.

'Does your collar cut, John?' asked a sarcastic voice out of the crowd.

'Hymn Number Nine.

> "Diddle-diddle dumpling, my son John
> Went to bed with his best suit on," '

came the solemn announcement.

Mr Merfin, his white cuffs down to his knuckles, picked up his half-sovereign, and walked away loftily.

'Sam Coutts!' cried the paymaster.

'Now, lad, reckon it up,' shouted the voice of the crowd, delighted.

Mr Coutts was a straight-backed ne'er-do-well. He looked at his twelve shillings sheepishly.

'Another two bob – he had twins a-Monday night – get thy money, Sam, tha's earned it – tha's addled it, Sam; dunna go be-out it. Let him ha' the two bob for 'is twins, mister,' came the clamour from the men around.

Sam Coutts stood grinning awkwardly.

'You should ha' given us notice, Sam,' said the paymaster suavely. 'We can make it all right for you next week—'

'Nay, nay, nay,' shouted a voice. 'Pay on dèlivery – the goods is there right enough.'

'Get thy money, Sam, tha's addled it,' became the universal cry, and the Union agent had to hand over another florin, to prevent a disturbance. Sam Coutts grinned with satisfaction.

'Good shot, Sam,' the men exclaimed.

'Ephraim Wharmby,' shouted the pay-man.

A lad came forward.

'Gi' him sixpence for what's on t'road,' said a sly voice.

'Nay, nay,' replied Ben Townsend; 'pay on delivery.'

There was a roar of laughter. The miners were in high spirits.

In the town they stood about in gangs, talking and laughing. Many sat on their heels in the market-place. In and out of the public-houses they went, and on every bar the half-sovereigns clicked.

'Comin' ter Nottingham wi' us, Ephraim?' said Sam Coutts to the slender, pale young fellow of about twenty-two.

'I'm non walkin' that far of a gleamy day like this.'

'He has na got the strength,' said somebody, and a laugh went up.

'How's that?' asked another pertinent voice.

'He's a married man, mind yer,' said Chris Smitheringale, 'an' it ta'es a bit o' keepin' up.'

The youth was teased in this manner for some time.

'Come on ter Nottingham wi's; tha'll be safe for a bit,' said Coutts.

A gang set off, although it was only eleven o'clock. It was a nine-mile walk. The road was crowded with colliers travelling on foot to see the match between Notts and Aston Villa. In Ephraim's gang were Sam Coutts, with his fine shoulders and his extra florin, Chris Smitheringale, fat and smiling, and John Wharmby, a remarkable man, tall, erect as a soldier, black-haired and proud; he could play any music instrument, he declared.

'I can play owt from a comb up'ards. If there's music to be got outer a thing, I back I'll get it. No matter what shape or form of instrument you set before me, it doesn't signify if I nivir clapped eyes on it before, I's warrant I'll have a tune out of it in five minutes.'

He beguiled the first two miles so. It was true, he had caused a sensation by introducing the mandoline into the townlet, filling the hearts of his fellow-colliers with pride as he sat on the platform in evening dress, a fine soldierly man, bowing his black head, and scratching the mewing mandoline with hands that had only to grasp the 'instrument' to crush it entirely.

Chris stood a can round at the 'White Bull' at Gilt Brook. John Wharmby took his turn at Kimberley top.

'We wunna drink again,' they decided, 'till we're at Cinder Hill. We'll non stop i' Nuttall.'

They swung along the high-road under the budding trees. In Nuttall churchyard the crocuses blazed with yellow at the brim of the balanced, black yews. White and purple crocuses clipt up over the graves, as if the churchyard were bursting out in tiny tongues of flame.

'Sithee,' said Ephraim, who was an ostler down pit, 'sithee, here comes the Colonel. Sithee at his 'osses how they pick their toes up, the beauties!'

The Colonel drove past the men, who took no notice of him.

'Hast heard, Sorry,' said Sam, 'as they're com'n out i' Germany, by the thousand, an' begun riotin'?'

'An' comin' out i' France simbitar,' cried Chris.

The men all gave a chuckle.

'Sorry,' shouted John Wharmby, much elated, 'we oughtna ter go back under a twenty per cent rise.'

'We should get it,' said Chris.

'An' easy! They can do nowt bi-out us, we'n on'y ter stop out long enough.'

'I'm willin',' said Sam, and there was a laugh. The colliers looked at one another. A thrill went through them as if an electric current passed.

'We'n on'y ter stick out, an' we s'll see who's gaffer.'

'Us!' cried Sam. 'Why, what can they do again' us, if we come out all over th' world?'

'Nowt!' said John Wharmby. 'Th' mesters is bobbin' about like corks on a cassivoy a'ready.' There was a large natural reservoir, like a lake, near Bestwood, and this supplied the simile.

Again there passed through the men that wave of elation, quickening their pulses. They chuckled in their throats. Beyond all consciousness was this sense of battle and triumph in the hearts of the working-men at this juncture.

It was suddenly suggested at Nuttall that they should go over the fields to Bulwell, and into Nottingham that way. They went single file across the fallow, past the wood, and over the railway, where now no trains were running. Two fields away was a troop of pit ponies. Of all colours, but chiefly of red or brown, they clustered thick in the field, scarcely moving, and the two lines of trodden earth patches showed where fodder was placed down the field.

'Theer's the pit 'osses,' said Sam. 'Let's run 'em.'

'It's like a circus turned out. See them skewbawd 'uns – seven skewbawd,' said Ephraim.

The ponies were inert, unused to freedom. Occasionally one walked round. But there they stood, two thick lines of ruddy brown and piebald and white, across the trampled field. It was a beautiful day, mild, pale blue, a 'growing day', as the men said, when there was the silence of swelling sap everywhere.

'Let's ha'e a ride,' said Ephraim.

The younger men went up to the horses.

'Come on – co-oop, Taffy – co-oop, Ginger.'

The horses tossed away. But having got over the excitement of being above-ground, the animals were feeling dazed and rather dreary. They missed the warmth and the life of the pit. They looked as if life were a blank to them.

Ephraim and Sam caught a couple of steeds, on whose backs they went careering round, driving the rest of the sluggish herd from end to end of the field. The horses were good specimens, on the whole, and in fine condition. But they were out of their element.

Performing too clever a feat, Ephraim went rolling from his mount. He was soon up again, chasing his horse. Again he was thrown. Then the men proceeded on their way.

They were drawing near to miserable Bulwell, when Ephraim, remembering his turn was coming to stand drinks, felt in his pocket for his beloved half-sovereign, his strike-pay. It was not there. Through all his pockets he went, his heart sinking like lead.

'Sam,' he said, 'I believe I'n lost that ha'ef a sovereign.'

'Tha's got it somewheer about thee,' said Chris.

They made him take off his coat and waistcoat. Chris examined the coat, Sam the waistcoat, whilst Ephraim searched his trousers.

'Well,' said Chris, 'I'n foraged this coat, an' it's non theer.'

'An I'll back my life as th' on'y bit a metal on this wa'scoat is the buttons,' said Sam.

'An't it's non in my breeches,' said Ephraim. He took off his boots and his stockings. The half-sovereign was not there. He had not another coin in his possession.

'Well,' said Chris, 'we mun go back an' look for it.'

Back they went, four serious-hearted colliers, and searched the field, but in vain.

'Well,' said Chris, 'we s'll ha'e ter share wi' thee, that's a'.'

'I'm willin',' said John Wharmby.

'An' me,' said Sam.

'Two bob each,' said Chris.

Ephraim, who was in the depths of despair, shamefully accepted their six shillings.

In Bulwell they called in a small public-house, which had one long room with a brick floor, scrubbed benches and scrubbed tables. The central space was open. The place was full of colliers, who were drinking. There was a great deal of drinking during the strike, but not a vast amount drunk. Two men were playing skittles, and the rest were betting. The seconds sat on either side the skittle-board, holding caps of money, sixpences and coppers, the wagers of the 'backers'.

Sam, Chris and John Wharmby immediately put money on the man who had their favour. In the end Sam declared himself willing to play against the victor. He was the Bestwood champion. Chris and John Wharmby backed him heavily, and even Ephraim the Unhappy ventured sixpence.

In the end, Sam had won half a crown, with which he promptly stood drinks and bread and cheese for his comrades. At half-past one they set off again.

It was a good match between Notts and Villa – no goals at half-time, two-none for Notts at the finish. The colliers were hugely delighted, especially as Flint, the forward for Notts, who was an Underwood man well known to the four comrades, did some handsome work, putting the two goals through.

Ephraim determined to go home as soon as the match was over. He knew John Wharmby would be playing the piano at the 'Punch Bowl', and Sam, who had a good tenor voice, singing, while Chris cut in with witticisms, until evening. So he bade them farewell, as he must get home. They, finding him somewhat of a damper on their spirits, let him go.

He was the sadder for having witnessed an accident near the football-ground. A navvy, working at some drainage, carting an iron tip-tub of mud and emptying it, had got with his horse on to the deep deposit of ooze which was crusted over. The crust had broken, the man had gone under the horse, and it was some time before the people had realized he had vanished. When they found his feet sticking out, and hauled him forth, he was dead, stifled dead in the mud. The horse was at length hauled out, after having its neck nearly pulled from the socket.

Ephraim went home vaguely impressed with a sense of death, and loss, and strife. Death was loss greater than his own, the strike was a battle greater than that he would presently have to fight.

He arrived home at seven o'clock, just when it had fallen dark. He lived in Queen Street with his young wife, to whom he had been married two months, and with his mother-in-law, a widow of sixty-four. Maud was the last child remaining unmarried, the last of eleven.

Ephraim went up the entry. The light was burning in the kitchen. His mother-in-law was a big, erect woman, with wrinkled, loose face, and cold blue eyes. His wife was also large, with very vigorous fair hair, frizzy like unravelled rope. She had a quiet way of stepping, a certain cat-like stealth, in spite of her large build. She was five months pregnant.

'Might we ask wheer you've been to?' inquired Mrs Marriott,

very erect, very dangerous. She was only polite when she was very angry.

'I'n bin ter th' match.'

'Oh indeed!' said the mother-in-law. 'And why couldn't we be told as you thought of jaunting off?'

'I didna know mysen,' he answered, sticking to his broad Derbyshire.

'I suppose it popped into your mind, an' so you darted off,' said the mother-in-law dangerously.

'I didna. It wor Chris Smitheringale who exed me.'

'An' did you take much invitin'?'

'I didna want ter goo.'

'But wasn't there enough man beside your jacket to say no?'

He did not answer. Down at the bottom he hated her. But he was, to use his own words, all messed up with having lost his strike-pay and with knowing the man was dead. So he was more helpless before his mother-in-law, whom he feared. His wife neither looked at him nor spoke, but kept her head bowed. He knew she was with her mother.

'Our Maud's been waitin' for some money, to get a few things,' said the mother-in-law.

In silence, he put five-and-sixpence on the table.

'Take that up, Maud,' said the mother.

Maud did so.

'You'll want it for usboard, shan't you?' she asked, furtively, of her mother.

'Might I ask if there's nothing you want to buy yourself, first?'

'No, there's nothink I want,' answered the daughter.

Mrs Marriott took the silver and counted it.

'And do you,' said the mother-in-law, towering upon the shrinking son, but speaking slowly and statelily, 'do you think I'm going to keep you and your wife for five-and-sixpence a week?'

'It's a' I've got,' he answered, sulkily.

'You've had a good jaunt, my sirs, if it's cost four-and-six-pence. You've started your game early, haven't you?'

He did not answer.

'It's a nice thing! Here's our Maud an' me been sitting since eleven o'clock this morning! Dinner waiting and cleared away, tea waiting and washed up; then in he comes crawling with five-and-sixpence. Five-and-sixpence for a man an' wife's board for a week, if you please!'

Still he did not say anything.

'You must think something of yourself, Ephraim Wharmby!' said his mother-in-law. 'You must think something of yourself. You suppose, do you, I'm going to keep you an' your wife, while you make a holiday, off on the nines to Nottingham, drink an' women.'

'I've neither had drink nor women, as you know right well,' he said.

'I'm glad we know summat about you. For you're that close, anybody'd think we was foreigners to you. You're a pretty little jockey, aren't you? Oh, it's a gala time for you, the strike is. That's all men strike for, indeed. They enjoy themselves, they do that. Ripping and racing and drinking, from morn till night, my sirs!'

'Is there ony tea for me?' he asked, in a temper.

'Hark at him! Hark-ye! Should I ask you whose house you think you're in? Kindly order me about, do. Oh, it makes him big, the strike does. See him land home after being out on the spree for hours, and give his orders, my sirs! Oh, strike sets the men up, it does. Nothing have they to do but guzzle and galli-vant to Nottingham. Their wives'll keep them, oh yes. So long as they get something to eat at home, what more do they want! What more should they want, prithee? Nothing! Let the women and children starve and scrape, but fill the man's belly, and let him have his fling. My sirs, indeed, I think so! Let tradesmen go – what do they matter! Let rent go. Let children get what they can catch. Only the man will see *he's* all right. But not here, though!'

'Are you goin' ter gi'e me ony bloody tea?'

His mother-in-law started up.

'If tha dares ter swear at me, I'll lay thee flat.'

'Are yer – goin' ter – gi'e me – any blasted, ròtten, còssed. blòody tèa?' he bawled, in a fury, accenting every other word deliberately.

'Maud!' said the mother-in-law, cold and stately, 'if you gi'e him any tea after that, you're a trollops.' Whereupon she sailed out to her other daughter's.

Maud quietly got the tea ready.

'Shall y'ave your dinner warmed up?' she asked.

'Ay.'

She attended to him. Not that she was really meek. But – he was *her* man, not her mother's.

The Christening

T H E mistress of the British School stepped down from her school gate, and instead of turning to the left as usual. she turned to the right. Two women who were hastening home to scramble their husbands' dinners together – it was five minutes to four – stopped to look at her. They stood gazing after her for a moment; then they glanced at each other with a woman's little grimace.

To be sure, the retreating figure was ridiculous: small and thin, with a black straw hat, and a rusty cashmere dress hanging full all round the skirt. For so small and frail and rusty a creature to sail with slow, deliberate stride was also absurd. Hilda Rowbotham was less than thirty, so it was not years that set the measure of her pace; she had heart disease. Keeping her face, that was small with sickness, but not uncomely, firmly lifted and fronting ahead, the young woman sailed on past the market-place, like a black swan of mournful disreputable plumage.

She turned into Berryman's, the bakers. The shop displayed bread and cakes, sacks of flour and oatmeal, flitches of bacon, hams, lard and sausages. The combination of scents was not unpleasing. Hilda Rowbotham stood for some minutes nervously tapping and pushing a large knife that lay on the counter, and looking at the tall, glittering brass scales. At last a morose man with sandy whiskers came down the step from the house-place.

'What is it?' he asked, not apologizing for his delay.

54

'Will you give me sixpennyworth of assorted cakes and pastries – and put in some macaroons, please?' she asked, in remarkably rapid and nervous speech. Her lips fluttered like two leaves in a wind, and her words crowded and rushed like a flock of sheep at a gate.

'We've got no macaroons,' said the man churlishly.

He had evidently caught that word. He stood waiting.

'Then I can't have any, Mr Berryman. Now I do feel disappointed. I like those macaroons, you know, and it's not often I treat myself. One gets so tired of trying to spoil oneself, don't you think? It's less profitable even than trying to spoil somebody else.' She laughed a quick little nervous laugh, putting her hand to her face.

'Then what'll you have?' asked the man, without the ghost of an answering smile. He evidently had not followed, so he looked more glum than ever.

'Oh, anything you've got,' replied the schoolmistress, flushing slightly. The man moved slowly about, dropping the cakes from various dishes one by one into a paper bag.

'How's that sister o' yours getting on?' he asked, as if he were talking to the flour-scoop.

'Whom do you mean?' snapped the schoolmistress.

'The youngest,' answered the stooping, pale-faced man, with a note of sarcasm.

'Emma! Oh, she's very well, thank you!' The schoolmistress was very red, but she spoke with sharp, ironical defiance. The man grunted. Then he handed her the bag, and watched her out of the shop without bidding her 'Good afternoon'.

She had the whole length of the main street to traverse, a half-mile of slow-stepping torture, with shame flushing over her neck. But she carried her white bag with an appearance of steadfast unconcern. When she turned into the field she seemed to droop a little. The wide valley opened out from her, with the far woods withdrawing into twilight, and away in the centre the great pit steaming its white smoke and chuffing as the men were being turned up. A full rose-coloured moon, like a flamingo flying low under the far, dusky east, drew out of the mist. It was beautiful, and it made her irritable sadness soften, diffuse.

Across the field, and she was at home. It was a new, substantial cottage, built with unstinted hand, such a house as an old miner could build himself out of his savings. In the rather small kitchen a woman of dark, saturnine complexion sat nursing a baby in a long white gown; a young woman of heavy, brutal cast stood at the table, cutting bread and butter. She had a downcast, humble mien that sat unnaturally on her, and was strangely irritating. She did not look round when her sister entered. Hilda put down the bag of cakes and left the room, not having spoken to Emma, nor to the baby, nor to Mrs Carlin, who had come in to help for the afternoon.

Almost immediately the father entered from the yard with a dust-pan full of coals. He was a large man, but he was going to pieces. As he passed through, he gripped the door with his free hand to steady himself, but turning, he lurched and swayed. He began putting the coals on the fire, piece by piece. One lump fell from his hands and smashed on the white hearth. Emma Rowbotham looked round, and began in a rough, loud voice of anger: 'Look at you!' Then she consciously moderated her tones. 'I'll sweep it up in a minute – don't you bother; you'll only be going head-first into the fire.'

Her father bent down nevertheless to clear up the mess he had made, saying, articulating his words loosely and slavering in his speech:

'The lousy bit of a thing, it slipped between my fingers like a fish.'

As he spoke he went tilting towards the fire. The dark-browed woman cried out; he put his hand on the hot stove to save himself; Emma swung round and dragged him off.

'Didn't I tell you!' she cried roughly. 'Now, have you burnt yourself?'

She held tight hold of the big man, and pushed him into his chair.

'What's the matter?' cried a sharp voice from the other room. The speaker appeared, a hard well-favoured woman of twenty-eight. 'Emma, don't speak like that to father.' Then, in a tone not so cold, but just as sharp: 'Now, father, what have you been doing?'

Emma withdrew to her table sullenly.

'It's nöwt,' said the old man, vainly protesting. 'It's nöwt at a'. Get on wi' what you're doin'.'

'I'm afraid 'e's burnt 'is 'and,' said the black-browed woman, speaking of him with a kind of hard pity, as if he were a cumbersome child. Bertha took the old man's hand and looked at it, making a quick tut-tutting noise of impatience.

'Emma, get that zinc ointment – and some white rag,' she commanded sharply. The younger sister put down her loaf with the knife in it, and went. To a sensitive observer, this obedience was more intolerable than the most hateful discord. The dark woman bent over the baby and made silent, gentle movements of motherliness to it. The little one smiled and moved on her lap. It continued to move and twist.

'I believe this child's hungry,' she said. 'How long is it since he had anything?'

'Just afore dinner,' said Emma dully.

'Good gracious!' exclaimed Bertha. 'You needn't starve the child now you've got it. Once every two hours it ought to be fed, as I've told you; and now it's three. Take him, poor little mite – I'll cut the bread.' She bent and looked at the bonny baby. She could not help herself: she smiled, and pressed its cheek with her finger, and nodded to it, making little noises. Then she turned and took the loaf from her sister. The woman rose and gave the child to its mother. Emma bent over the little sucking mite. She hated it when she looked at it, and saw it as a symbol, but when she felt it, her love was like fire in her blood.

'I should think 'e canna be comin',' said the father uneasily, looking up at the clock.

'Nonsense, father – the clock's fast! It's but half-past four! Don't fidget!' Bertha continued to cut the bread and butter.

'Open a tin of pears,' she said to the woman, in a much milder tone. Then she went into the next room. As soon as she was gone, the old man said again: 'I should ha'e thought he'd 'a' been 'ere by now, if he means comin'.'

Emma, engrossed, did not answer. The father had ceased to consider her, since she had become humbled.

' 'E'll come – 'e'll come!' assured the stranger.

A few minutes later Bertha hurried into the kitchen, taking off her apron. The dog barked furiously. She opened the door, commanded the dog to silence, and said: 'He will be quiet now, Mr Kendal.'

'Thank you,' said a sonorous voice, and there was the sound of a bicycle being propped against a wall. A clergyman entered, a big-boned, thin, ugly man of nervous manner. He went straight to the father.

'Ah – how are you?' he asked musically, peering down on the great frame of the miner, ruined by locomotor ataxy.

His voice was full of gentleness, but he seemed as if he could not see distinctly, could not get things clear.

'Have you hurt your hand?' he said comfortingly, seeing the white rag.

'It wor nöwt but a pestered bit o' coal as dropped, an' I put my hand on th' hub. I thought tha worna commin'.'

The familiar 'tha', and the reproach, were unconscious retaliation on the old man's part. The minister smiled, half wistfully, half indulgently. He was full of vague tenderness. Then he turned to the young mother, who flushed sullenly because her dishonoured breast was uncovered.

'How are *you*?' he asked, very softly and gently, as if she were ill and he were mindful of her.

'I'm all right,' she replied, awkwardly taking his hand without rising, hiding her face and the anger that rose in her.

'Yes – yes—' he peered down at the baby, which sucked with distended mouth upon the firm breast. 'Yes, yes.' He seemed lost in a dim musing.

Coming to, he shook hands unseeingly with the woman.

Presently they all went into the next room, the minister hesitating to help his crippled old deacon.

'I can go by myself, thank yer,' testily replied the father.

Soon all were seated. Everybody was separated in feeling and isolated at table. High tea was spread in the middle kitchen, a large, ugly room kept for special occasions.

Hilda appeared last, and the clumsy, raw-boned clergyman rose to meet her. He was afraid of this family, the well-to-do old collier, and the brutal, self-willed children. But Hilda was queen among them. She was the clever one, and had been to college. She felt responsible for the keeping up of a high standard of conduct in all the members of the family. There *was* a difference between the Rowbothams and the common collier folk. Woodbine Cottage was a superior house to most – and was built in pride by the old man. She, Hilda, was a college-trained schoolmistress; she meant to keep up the prestige of her house in spite of blows.

She had put on a dress of green voile for this special occasion. But she was very thin; her neck protruded painfully. The clergyman, however, greeted her almost with reverence, and, with some assumption of dignity, she sat down before the tray. At the far end of the table sat the broken, massive frame of her father. Next to him was the youngest daughter, nursing the restless boy. The minister sat between Hilda and Bertha, hulking his bony frame uncomfortably.

There was a great spread on the table of tinned fruits and tinned salmon, ham and cakes. Miss Rowbotham kept a keen eye on everything: she felt the importance of the occasion. The young mother who had given rise to all this solemnity ate in sulky discomfort, snatching sullen little smiles at her child, smiles which came, in spite of her, when she felt its little limbs stirring vigorously on her lap. Bertha, sharp and abrupt, was chiefly concerned with the baby. She scorned her sister, and treated her like dirt. But the infant was a streak of light to her. Miss Rowbotham concerned herself with the function and the conversation. Her hands fluttered; she talked in little volleys, exceedingly nervous. Towards the end of the meal, there came a pause. The old man wiped his mouth with his red handkerchief, then, his blue eyes going fixed and staring, he began to speak, in a loose, slobbering fashion, charging his words at the clergyman.

'Well, mester – we'n axed you to come here ter christen this childt, an' you'n come, an' I'm sure we're very thankful. I can't see lettin' the poor blessed childt miss baptizing, an' they aren't for goin' to church wi't—' He seemed to lapse into a muse. 'So,' he resumed, 'we'n axed you to come here to do the job. I'm not sayin' as it's not 'ard on us, it is. I'm breakin' up, an' mother's gone. I don't like leavin' a girl o' mine in a situation like 'ers is, but what the Lord's done, He's done, an' it's no matter murmuring. . . . There's one thing to be thankful for, an' we *are* thankful for it: they never need know the want of bread.'

Miss Rowbotham, the lady of the family, sat very stiff and pained during this discourse. She was sensitive to so many things that she was bewildered. She felt her young sister's shame, then a kind of swift protecting love for the baby, a feeling that included the mother; she was at a loss before her father's religious sentiment, and she felt and resented bitterly the mark upon the family, against which the common folk could lift their fingers. Still she winced from the sound of her father's words. It was a painful ordeal.

'It is hard for you,' began the clergyman in his soft, lingering, unworldly voice. 'It is hard for you today, but the Lord gives comfort in His time. A man child is born unto us, therefore let us rejoice and be glad. If sin has entered in among us, let us purify our hearts before the Lord. . . .'

He went on with his discourse. The young mother lifted the whimpering infant, till its face was hid in her loose hair. She was hurt, and a little glowering anger shone in her face. But nevertheless her fingers clasped the body of the child beautifully. She was stupefied with anger against this emotion let loose on her account.

Miss Bertha rose and went to the little kitchen, returning with water in a china bowl. She placed it there among the teathings.

'Well, we're all ready,' said the old man, and the clergyman began to read the service. Miss Bertha was godmother, the two men godfathers. The old man sat with bent head. The scene became impressive. At last Miss Bertha took the child and put it in the arms of the clergyman. He, big and ugly, shone with a kind of unreal love. He had never mixed with life, and women were all unliving, Biblical things to him. When he asked for the name, the old man lifted his head fiercely. 'Joseph William, after me,' he said, almost out of breath.

'Joseph William, I baptize thee . . .' resounded the strange, full, chanting voice of the clergyman. The baby was quite still.

'Let us pray!' It came with relief to them all. They knelt before their chairs, all but the young mother, who bent and hid herself over her baby. The clergyman began his hesitating, struggling prayer.

Just then heavy footsteps were heard coming up the path, ceasing at the window. The young mother, glancing up, saw her brother, black in his pit dirt, grinning in through the panes. His red mouth curved in a sneer; his fair hair shone above his blackened skin. He caught the eye of his sister and grinned. Then his black face disappeared. He had gone on into the kitchen. The girl with the child sat still and anger filled her heart. She hated now the praying clergyman and the whole emotional business; she hated her brother bitterly. In anger and bondage she sat and listened.

Suddenly her father began to pray. His familiar, loud, rambling voice made her shut herself up and become even insentient. Folks said his mind was weakening. She believed it to be true, and kept herself always disconnected from him.

'We ask Thee, Lord,' the old man cried, 'to look after this childt. Fatherless he is. But what does the earthly father matter before Thee? The childt is Thine, he is Thy childt. Lord, what father has a man but Thee? Lord, when a man says he is a father, he is wrong from the first word. For Thou art the Father, Lord. Lord, take away from us the conceit that our children are ours. Lord, Thou art Father of this childt as is fatherless here. O God, Thou bring him up. For I have stood between Thee and my children; I've had my way with them, Lord; I've stood between Thee and my children; I've cut 'em off from Thee because they were mine. And they've grown twisted, because of me. Who is their father, Lord, but Thee? But I put myself in the way, they've been plants under a stone, because of me. Lord, if it hadn't been for me, they might ha' been trees in the sunshine. Let me own it, Lord, I've done 'em mischief. It would ha' been better if they'd never known no father. No man is a father, Lord: only Thou art. They can never grow beyond Thee, but I hampered them. Lift 'em up again, and undo what I've done to my children. And let this young childt be like a willow tree beside the waters, with no father but Thee, O God.

Aye, an' I wish it had been so with my children, that they'd had no father but Thee. For I've been like a stone upon them, and they rise up and curse me in their wickedness. But let me go, an' lift Thou them up, Lord . . .'

The minister, unaware of the feelings of a father, knelt in trouble, hearing without understanding the special language of fatherhood. Miss Rowbotham alone felt and understood a little. Her heart began to flutter; she was in pain. The two younger daughters kneeled unhearing, stiffened and impervious. Bertha was thinking of the baby; and the young mother thought of the father of her child, whom she hated. There was a clatter outside in the scullery. There the youngest son made as much noise as he could, pouring out the water for his wash, muttering in deep anger:

'Blortin', slaverin' old fool!'

And while the praying of his father continued, his heart was burning with rage. On the table was a paper bag. He picked it up and read: 'John Berryman – Bread, Pastries, etc.' Then he grinned with a grimace. The father of the baby was baker's man at Berryman's. The prayer went on in the middle kitchen. Laurie Rowbotham gathered together the mouth of the bag, inflated it, and burst it with his fist. There was a loud report. He grinned to himself. But he writhed at the same time with shame and fear of his father.

The father broke off from his prayer; the party shuffled to their feet. The young mother went into the scullery.

'What art doin', fool?' she said.

The collier youth tipped the baby under the chin, singing:

> 'Pat-a-cake, pat-a-cake, baker's man,
> Bake me a cake as fast as you can. . . .'

The mother snatched the child away. 'Shut thy mouth,' she said, the colour coming into her cheek.

'Prick it and stick it and mark it with P,
And put it i' th' oven for baby an' me. . . .'

He grinned, showing a grimy, and jeering and unpleasant red mouth and white teeth.

'I s'll gi'e thee a dab ower th' mouth,' said the mother of the baby grimly. He began to sing again, and she struck out at him.

'Now what's to do?' said the father, staggering in.

The youth began to sing again. His sister stood sullen and furious.

'Why does *that* upset you?' asked the eldest Miss Rowbotham, sharply, of Emma the mother. 'Good gracious, it hasn't improved your temper.'

Miss Bertha came in, and took the bonny baby.

The father sat big and unheeding in his chair, his eyes vacant, his physique wrecked. He let them do as they would, he fell to pieces. And yet some power, involuntary, like a curse, remained in him. The very ruin of him was like a lodestone that held them in its control. The wreck of him still dominated the house, in his dissolution even he compelled their being. They had never lived; his life, his will had always been upon them and contained them. They were only half-individuals.

The day after the christening he staggered in at the doorway declaring, in a loud voice, with joy in life still: 'The daisies light up the earth, they clap their hands in multitudes, in praise of the morning.' And his daughters shrank, sullen.

Tickets, Please

THERE is in the Midlands a single-line tramway system which boldly leaves the county town and plunges off into the black, industrial countryside, up hill and down dale, through the long ugly villages of workmen's houses, over canals and railways, past churches perched high and nobly over the smoke and shadows, through stark, grimy cold little market-places, tilting away in a rush past cinemas and shops down to the hollow where the colleries are, then up again, past a little rural church, under the ash trees, on in a rush to the terminus, the last little ugly place of industry, the cold little town that shivers on the edge of the wild, gloomy country beyond. There the green and creamy coloured tram-cars seem to pause and purr with curious satisfaction. But in a few minutes – the clock on the turret of the Co-operative Wholesale Society's shops gives the time – away it starts once more on the adventure. Again there are the reckless swoops downhill, bouncing the loops: again the chilly wait in the hill-top market-place: again the breathless slithering round the precipitous drop under the church: again the patient halts at the loops, waiting for the out-coming car: so on and on, for two long hours, till at last the city looms beyond the fat gas-works, the narrow factories draw near, we are in the sordid streets of the great town, once more we sidle to a standstill at our terminus, abashed by the great crimson and cream-coloured city cars, but still perky, jaunty, somewhat dare-devil, green as a jaunty sprig of parsley out of a black colliery garden.

To ride on these cars is always an adventure. Since we are in war-time, the drivers are men unfit for active service: cripples and hunchbacks. So they have the spirit of the devil in them. The ride becomes a steeplechase. Hurray! we have leapt in a clear jump over the canal bridge – now for the four-lane corner. With a shriek and a trail of sparks we are clear again. To be sure, a tram often leaps the rails – but what matter! It sits in a ditch till other trams come to haul it out. It is quite common for a car, parked with one solid mass of living people, to come to a dead halt in the midst of unbroken blackness, the heart of nowhere on a dark night, and for the driver and the girl conductor to call: 'All get off – car's on fire!' Instead, however, of rushing out in a panic, the passengers stolidly reply: 'Get on – get on! We're not coming out. We're stopping where we are. Push on, George.' So till flames actually appear.

The reason for this reluctance to dismount is that the nights are howling cold, black, and windswept, and a car is a haven of refuge. From village to village the miners travel, for a change of cinema, of girl, of pub. The trams are desperately packed. Who is going to risk himself in the black gulf outside, to wait perhaps an hour for another tram, then to see the forlorn notice 'Depot Only', because there is something wrong! Or to greet a unit of three bright cars all so tight with people that they sail past with a howl of derision. Trams that pass in the night.

This, the most dangerous tram-service in England, as the authorities themselves declare, with pride, is entirely conducted by girls, and driven by rash young men, a little crippled, or by delicate young men, who creep forward in terror. The girls are fearless young hussies. In their ugly blue uniform, skirts up to their knees, shapeless old peaked caps on their heads, they have all the *sang-froid* of an old non-commissioned officer. With a tram packed with howling colliers, roaring hymns downstairs and a sort of antiphony of obscenities upstairs, the lasses are perfectly at their ease. They pounce on the youths who try to evade their ticket-machine. They push off the men at the end of their distance. They are not going to be done in the eye – not they. They fear nobody – and everybody fears them.

'Hello, Annie!'

'Hello, Ted!'

'Oh, mind my corn, Miss Stone. It's my belief you've got a heart of stone, for you've trod on it again.'

'You should keep it in your pocket,' replies Miss Stone, and she goes sturdily upstairs in her high boots.

'Tickets, please.'

She is peremptory, suspicious, and ready to hit first. She can hold her own in ten thousand. The step of that tram-car is her Thermopylae.

Therefore, there is a certain wild romance aboard these cars – and in the sturdy bosom of Annie herself. The time for soft romance is in the morning, between ten o'clock and one, when things are rather slack: that is, except market-day and Saturday. Thus Annie has time to look about her. Then she often hops off her car and into a shop where she has spied something, while the driver chats in the main road. There is very good feeling between the girls and the drivers. Are they not companions in peril, shipments aboard this careering vessel of a tram-car, for ever rocking on the waves of a stormy land.

Then, also, during the easy hours, the inspectors are most in evidence. For some reason, everybody employed in this tram-service is young: there are no grey heads. It would not do. Therefore the inspectors are of the right age, and one, the chief, is also good-looking. See him stand on a wet, gloomy morning, in his long oilskin, his peaked cap well down over his eyes, waiting to board a car. His face ruddy, his small brown moustache is weathered. he has a faint impudent smile. Fairly tall and agile, even in his waterproof, he springs aboard a car and greets Annie.

'Hello, Annie! Keeping the wet out?'

'Trying to.'

There are only two people in the car. Inspecting is soon over. Then for a long and impudent chat on the foot-board, a good, easy, twelve-mile chat.

The inspector's name is John Thomas Raynor – always called John Thomas, except sometimes, in malice, Coddy. His face sets in fury when he is addressed, from a distance, with this abbreviation. There is considerable scandal about John Thomas in half a dozen villages. He flirts with the girl conductors in the morning, and walks out with them in the dark night, when they leave their tram-car at the depôt. Of course, the girls quit the service frequently. Then he flirts and walks out with the newcomer: always providing she is sufficiently attractive, and that she will consent to walk. It is remarkable, however, that most of the girls are quite comely, they are all young, and this roving life aboard the car gives them a sailor's dash and recklessness. What matter how they behave when the ship is in port? Tomorrow they will be aboard again.

Annie, however, was something of a Tartar, and her sharp tongue had kept John Thomas at arm's length for many months. Perhaps, therefore, she liked him all the more: for he always came up smiling, with impudence. She watched him vanquish one girl, then another. She could tell by the movement of his mouth and eyes, when he flirted with her in the morning, that he had been walking out with this lass, or the other, the night before. A fine cock-of-the-walk he was. She could sum him up pretty well.

In this subtle antagonism they knew each other like old friends, they were as shrewd with one another almost as man and wife. But Annie had always kept him sufficiently at arm's length. Besides, she had a boy of her own.

The Statutes fair, however, came in November, at Bestwood. It happened that Annie had the Monday night off. It was a drizzling ugly night, yet she dressed herself up and went to the fair-ground. She was alone, but she expected soon to find a pal of some sort.

The roundabouts were veering round and grinding out their music, the side-shows were making as much commotion as possible. In the coconut shies there were no coconuts, but artificial war-time substitutes, which the lads declared were fastened into the irons. There was a sad decline in brilliance and luxury. None the less, the ground was muddy as ever, there was the same crush, the press of faces lighted up by the flares and the electric lights, the same smell of naphtha and a few potatoes, and of electricity.

Who should be the first to greet Miss Annie on the show-ground but John Thomas. He had a black overcoat buttoned up to his chin, and a tweed cap pulled down over his brows, his face between was ruddy and smiling and handy as ever. She knew so well the way his mouth moved.

She was very glad to have a 'boy'. To be at the Statutes without a fellow was no fun. Instantly, like the gallant he was, he took her on the dragons, grim-toothed roundabout switch-backs. It was not nearly so exciting as a tram-car actually. But, then, to be seated in a shaking, green dragon, uplifted above the sea of bubble faces, careering in a rickety fashion in the lower heavens, whilst John Thomas leaned over her, his cigarette in his mouth, was after all the right style. She was a plump, quick, alive little creature. So she was quite excited and happy.

John Thomas made her stay on for the next round. And therefore she could hardly for shame repulse him when he put his arm round her and drew her a little nearer to him, in a very warm and cuddly manner. Besides, he was fairly discreet, he kept his movement as hidden as possible. She looked down, and saw that his red, clean hand was out of sight of the crowd.

And they knew each other so well. So they warmed up to the fair.

After the dragons they went on the horses. John Thomas paid each time, so she could but be complaisant. He, of course, sat astride on the outer horse – named 'Black Bess' – and she sat sideways, towards him, on the inner horse – named 'Wildfire'. But of course John Thomas was not going to sit discreetly on 'Black Bess', holding the brass bar. Round they spun and heaved, in the light. And round he swung on his wooden steed, flinging one leg across her mount, and perilously tipping up and down, across the space, half lying back, laughing at her. He was perfectly happy; she was afraid her hat was on one side, but she was excited.

He threw quoits on a table, and won for her two large, pale blue hat-pins. And then, hearing the noise of the cinemas, announcing another performance, they climbed the boards and went in.

Of course, during these performances pitch darkness falls from time to time, when the machine goes wrong. Then there is a wild whooping, and a loud smacking of simulated kisses. In these moments John Thomas drew Annie towards him. After all, he had a wonderfully warm, cosy way of holding a girl with his arm, he seemed to make such a nice fit. And, after all, it was pleasant to be so held: so very comforting and cosy and nice. He leaned over her and she felt his breath on her hair; she knew he wanted to kiss her on the lips. And, after all, he was so warm and she fitted in to him so softly. After all, she wanted him to touch her lips.

But the light sprang up; she also started electrically, and put her hat straight. He left his arm lying nonchalantly behind her. Well, it was fun, it was exciting to be at the Statutes with John Thomas.

When the cinema was over they went for a walk across the dark, damp fields. He had all the arts of love-making. He was especially good at holding a girl, when he sat with her on a stile in the black, drizzling darkness. He seemed to be holding her in space, against his own warmth and gratification. And his kisses were soft and slow and searching.

So Annie walked out with John Thomas, though she kept her own boy dangling in the distance. Some of the tram-girls chose to be huffy. But there, you must take things as you find them, in his life.

There was no mistake about it, Annie liked John Thomas a good deal. She felt so rich and warm in herself whenever he was near. And John Thomas really liked Annie, more than usual. The soft, melting way in which she could flow into a fellow, as if she melted into his very bones, was something rare and good. He fully appreciated this.

But with a developing acquaintance there began a developing intimacy. Annie wanted to consider him a person, a man: she wanted to take an intelligent interest in him, and to have an intelligent response. She did not want a mere nocturnal presence, which was what he was so far. And she prided herself that he could not leave her.

Here she made a mistake. John Thomas intended to remain a nocturnal presence; he had no idea of becoming an all-round individual to her. When she started to take an intelligent interest in him and his life and his character, he sheered off. He hated intelligent interest. And he knew that the only way to stop it was to avoid it. The possessive female was aroused in Annie. So he left her.

It is no use saying she was not surprised. She was at first startled, thrown out of her count. For she had been so *very* sure of holding him. For a while she was staggered, and everything became uncertain to her. Then she wept with fury, indignation, desolation, and misery. Then she had a spasm of despair. And then, when he came, still impudently, on to her car, still familiar, but letting her see by the movement of his head that he had gone away to somebody else for the time being, and was enjoying pastures new, then she determined to have her own back.

She had a very shrewd idea what girls John Thomas had taken out. She went to Nora Purdy. Nora was a tall, rather pale, but well-built girl, with beautiful yellow hair. She was rather secretive.

'Hey!' said Annie, accosting her; then softly: 'Who's John Thomas on with now?'

'I don't know,' said Nora.

'Why, tha does,' said Annie, ironically lapsing into dialect. 'Tha knows as well as I do.'

'Well, I do, then,' said Nora. 'It isn't me, so don't bother.'

'It's Cissy Meakin, isn't it?'

'It is, for all I know.'

'Hasn't he got a face on him!' said Annie. 'I don't half like his cheek. I could knock him off the foot-board when he comes round at me.'

'He'll get dropped on one of these days,' said Nora.

'Ay, he will, when somebody makes up their mind to drop it on him. I should like to see him taken down a peg or two, shouldn't you?'

'I shouldn't mind,' said Nora.

'You've got quite as much cause to as I have,' said Annie. 'But we'll drop on him one of these days, my girl. What? Don't you want to?'

'I don't mind,' said Nora.

But as a matter of fact, Nora was much more vindictive than Annie.

One by one Annie went the round of the old flames. It so happened that Cissy Meakin left the tramway service in quite a short time. Her mother made her leave. Then John Thomas was on the *qui vive*. He cast his eyes over his old flock. And his eyes lighted on Annie He thought she would be safe now. Besides, he liked her.

She arranged to walk home with him on Sunday night. It so happened that her car would be in the depôt at half-past nine: the last car would come in at 10.15. So John Thomas was to wait for her there.

At the depôt the girls had a little waiting-room of their own. It was quite rough, but cosy, with a fire and an oven and a mirror, and table and wooden chairs. The half-dozen girls who knew John Thomas only too well had arranged to take service this Sunday afternoon. So, as the cars began to come in, early, the girls dropped into the waiting-room. And instead of hurrying off home, they sat around the fire and had a cup of tea. Outside was the darkness and lawlessness of war-time.

John Thomas came on the car after Annie, at about a quarter to ten. He poked his head easily into the girls' waiting-room.

'Prayer-meeting?' he asked.

'Ay,' said Laura Sharp. 'Ladies only.'

'That's me!' said John Thomas. It was one of his favourite exclamations.

'Shut the door, boy,' said Muriel Baggaley.

'Oh, which side of me?' said John Thomas.

'Which tha likes,' said Polly Birkin.

He had come in and closed the door behind him. The girls moved in their circle, to make a place for him near the fire. He took off his greatcoat and pushed back his hat.

'Who handles the teapot?' he said.

Nora Purdy silently poured him out a cup of tea.

'Want a bit o' my bread and drippin'?' said Muriel Baggaley to him.

'Ay, give us a bit.'

And he began to eat his piece of bread.

'There's no place like home, girls,' he said.

They all looked at him as he uttered this piece of impudence. He seemed to be sunning himself in the presence of so many damsels.

'Especially if you're not afraid to go home in the dark,' said Laura Sharp.

'Me! By myself I am.'

They sat till they heard the last tram come in. In a few minutes Emma Houselay entered.

'Come on, my old duck!' cried Polly Birkin.

'It *is* perishing,' said Emma, holding her fingers to the fire.

'But – I'm afraid to, go home in, the dark,' sang Laura Sharp, the tune having got into her mind.

'Who're you going with tonight, John Thomas?' asked Muriel Baggaley coolly.

'Tonight?' said John Thomas. 'Oh, I'm going home by myself tonight – all on my lonely-o.'

'That's me!' said Nora Purdy, using his own ejaculation

The girls laughed shrilly.

'Me as well, Nora,' said John Thomas.

'Don't know what you mean,' said Laura.

'Yes, I'm toddling,' said he, rising and reaching for his overcoat.

'Nay,' said Polly. 'We're all here waiting for you.'

'We've got to be up in good time in the morning,' he said, in the benevolent official manner.

They all laughed.

'Nay,' said Muriel. 'Don't leave us all lonely, John Thomas. Take one!'

'I'll take the lot, if you like,' he responded gallantly.

'That you won't, either,' said Muriel. 'Two's company; seven's too much of a good thing.'

'Nay – take one,' said Laura. 'Fair and square, all above board and say which.'

'Ay,' cried Annie, speaking for the first time. 'Pick, John Thomas; let's hear thee.'

'Nay,' he said. 'I'm going home quiet tonight. Feeling good, for once.'

'Whereabouts?' said Annie. 'Take a good un, then. But tha's got to take one of us!'

'Nay, how can I take one,' he said, laughing uneasily. 'I don't want to make enemies.'

'You'd only make *one*,' said Annie.

'The chosen *one*,' added Laura.

'Oh, my! Who said girls!' exclaimed John Thomas, again turning as if to escape. 'Well – good-night.'

'Nay, you've got to make your pick,' said Muriel. 'Turn your face to the wall, and say which one touches you. Go on – we shall only just touch your back – one of us. Go on – turn your face to the wall, and don't look, and say which one touches you.'

He was uneasy, mistrusting them. Yet he had not the courage to break away. They pushed him to a wall and stood him there with his face to it. Behind his back they all grimaced, tittering. He looked so comical. He looked around uneasily.

'Go on!' he cried.

'You're looking – you're looking!' they shouted.

He turned his head away. And suddenly, with a movement like a swift cat, Annie went forward and fetched him a box on the side of the head that sent his cap flying and himself staggering. He started round.

But at Annie's signal they all flew at him, slapping him, pinching him, pulling his hair, though more in fun than in spite or anger. He, however, saw red. His blue eyes flamed with strange fear as well as fury, and he butted through the girls to the door. It was locked. He wrenched at it. Roused, alert, the girls stood round and looked at him. He faced them, at bay. At that moment they were rather horrifying to him, as they stood in their short uniforms. He was distinctly afraid.

'Come on, John Thomas! Come on! Choose!' said Annie.

'What are you after? Open the door,' he said.

'We shan't – not till you've chosen!' said Muriel.

'Chosen what?' he said.

'Chosen the one you're going to marry,' she replied.

He hesitated a moment.

'Open the blasted door,' he said, 'and get back to your senses.' He spoke with official authority.

'You've got to choose!' cried the girls.

'Come on!' cried Annie, looking him in the eye. 'Come on! Come on!'

He went forward, rather vaguely. She had taken off her belt, and swinging it, she fetched him a sharp blow over the head with the buckle end. He sprang and seized her. But immediately the other girls rushed upon him, pulling and tearing and beating him. Their blood was now thoroughly up. He was their sport now. They were going to have their own back, out of him. Strange, wild creatures, they hung on him and rushed at him to bear him down. His tunic was torn right up the back. Nora had hold at the back of his collar, and was actually strangling him. Luckily the button burst. He struggled in a wild frenzy of fury and terror, almost mad terror. His tunic was simply torn off his back, his shirt-sleeves were torn away, his arms were naked. The girls rushed at him, clenched their hands on him and pulled at him: or they rushed at him and pushed him, butted him with all their might: or they struck him wild blows. He ducked and cringed and struck sideways. They became more intense.

At last he was down. They rushed on him, kneeling on him. He had neither breath nor strength to move. His face was bleeding with a long scratch, his brow was bruised.

Annie knelt on him, the other girls knelt and hung on to him. Their faces were flushed, their hair wild, their eyes were all glittering strangely. He lay at last quite still, with face averted, as an animal lies when it is defeated and at the mercy of the captor. Sometimes his eye glanced back at the wild faces of the girls. His breast rose heavily, his wrists were torn.

'Now, then, my fellow!' gasped Annie at length. 'Now then – now—'

At the sound of her terrifying, cold triumph, he suddenly started to struggle as an animal might, but the girls threw themselves upon him with unnatural strength and power, forcing him down.

'Yes – now, then!' gasped Annie at length.

And there was a dead silence, in which the thud of heart-beating was to be heard. It was a suspense of pure silence in every soul.

'Now you know where you are,' said Annie.

The sight of his white, bare arm maddened the girls. He lay in a kind of trance of fear and antagonism. They felt themselves filled with supernatural strength.

Suddenly Polly started to laugh – to giggle wildly – helplessly – and Emma and Muriel joined in. But Annie and Nora and Laura remained the same, tense, watchful, with gleaming eyes. He winced away from these eyes.

'Yes,' said Annie, in a curious low tone, secret and deadly. 'Yes! You've got it now. You know what you've done, don't you? You know what you've done.'

He made no sound nor sign, but lay with bright, averted eyes, and averted, bleeding face.

'You ought to be *killed*, that's what you ought,' said Annie, tensely. 'You ought to be *killed*.' And there was a terrifying lust in her voice.

Polly was ceasing to laugh, and giving long-drawn Oh-h-hs and sighs as she came to herself.

'He's got to choose,' she said vaguely.

'Oh, yes, he has,' said Laura, with vindictive decision.

'Do you hear – do you hear?' said Annie. And with a sharp movement, that made him wince, she turned his face to her.

'Do you hear?' she repeated, shaking him.

But he was quite dumb. She fetched him a sharp slap on the

face. He started, and his eyes widened. Then his face darkened with defiance, after all.

'Do you hear?' she repeated.

He only looked at her with hostile eyes.

'Speak!' she said, putting her face devilishly near his.

'What?' he said, almost overcome.

'You've got to *choose*!' she cried, as if it were some terrible menace, and as if it hurt her that she could not exact more.

'What?' he said, in fear.

'Choose your girl, Coddy. You've got to choose her now. And you'll get your neck broken if you play any more of your tricks, my boy. You're settled now.'

There was a pause. Again he averted his face. He was cunning in his overthrow. He did not give in to them really – no, not if they tore him to bits.

'All right, then,' he said, 'I choose Annie.' His voice was strange and full of malice. Annie let go of him as if he had been a hot coal.

'He's chosen Annie!' said the girls in chorus.

'Me!' cried Annie. She was still kneeling, but away from him. He was still lying prostrate, with averted face. The girls grouped uneasily around.

'Me!' repeated Annie, with a terrible bitter accent.

Then she got up, drawing away from him with strange disgust and bitterness.

'I wouldn't touch him,' she said.

But her face quivered with a kind of agony, she seemed as if she would fall. The other girls turned aside. He remained lying on the floor, with his torn clothes and bleeding, averted face.

'Oh, if he's chosen—' said Polly.

'I don't want him – he can choose again,' said Annie, with the same rather bitter hopelessness.

'Get up,' said Polly, lifting his shoulder. 'Get up.'

He rose slowly, a strange, ragged, dazed creature. The girls eyed him from a distance, curiously, furtively, dangerously.

'Who wants him?' cried Laura, roughly.

'Nobody,' they answered, with contempt. Yet each one of them waited for him to look at her, hoped he would look at her. All except Annie, and something was broken in her.

He, however, kept his face closed and averted from them all. There was a silence of the end. He picked up the torn pieces of his tunic, without knowing what to do with them. The girls stood about uneasily, flushed, panting, tidying their hair and their dress unconsciously, and watching him. He looked at none of them. He espied his cap in a corner, and went and picked it up. He put it on his head, and one of the girls burst into a shrill, hysteric laugh at the sight he presented. He, however, took no heed, but went straight to where his overcoat hung on a peg. The girls moved away from contact with him as if he had been an electric wire. He put on his coat and buttoned it down. Then he rolled his tunic-rags into a bundle, and stood before the locked door, dumbly.

'Open the door, somebody,' said Laura.

'Annie's got the key,' said one.

Annie silently offered the key to the girls. Nora unlocked the door.

'Tit for tat, old man,' she said. 'Show yourself a man, and don't bear a grudge.'

But without a word or a sign he had opened the door and gone, his face closed, his head dropped.

'That'll learn him,' said Laura.

'Coddy!' said Nora.

'Shut up, for God's sake!' cried Annie fiercely, as if in torture.

'Well, I'm about ready to go, Polly. Look sharp!' said Muriel.

The girls were all anxious to be off. They were tidying themselves hurriedly, with mute, stupefied faces.

Monkey Nuts

A T first Joe thought the job O.K. He was loading hay on the trucks, along with Albert, the corporal. The two men were pleasantly billeted in a cottage not far from the station: they were their own masters, for Joe never thought of Albert as a master. And the little sidings of the tiny village station was as pleasant a place as you could wish for. On one side, beyond the line, stretched the woods: on the other, the near side, across a green smooth field, red houses were dotted among flowering apple trees. The weather being sunny, work being easy, Albert, a real good pal, what life could be better! After Flanders, it was heaven itself.

Albert, the corporal, was a clean-shaven, shrewd-looking fellow of about forty. He seemed to think his one aim in life was to be full of fun and nonsense. In repose, his face looked a little withered, old. He was a very good pal to Joe, steady decent and grave under all his 'mischief'; for his mischief was only his laborious way of skirting his own ennui.

Joe was much younger than Albert – only twenty-three. He was a tallish, quiet youth, pleasant-looking. He was of a slightly better class than his corporal, more personable. Careful about his appearance, he shaved every day. 'I haven't got much of a face,' said Albert. 'If I was to shave every day like you, Joe, I should have none.'

There was plenty of life in the little goods-yard: three porter youths, a continual come and go of farm wagons bringing hay, wagons with timber from the woods, coal-carts loading at the trucks. The black coal seemed to make the place sleepier, hotter. Round the big white gate the station-master's children played and his white chickens walked, whilst the station-master himself, a young man getting too fat, helped his wife to peg out the washing on the clothes-line in the meadow.

The great boat-shaped wagons came up from Playcross with the hay. At first the farm-men wagoned it. On the third day one of the land-girls appeared with the first load, drawing to a standstill easily at the head of her two great horses. She was a buxom girl, young, in linen overalls and gaiters. Her face was ruddy, she had large blue eyes.

'Now that's the wagoner for us, boys,' said the corporal loudly.

'Whoa!' she said to her horses; and then to the corporal: 'Which boys do you mean?'

'We are the pick of the bunch. That's Joe, my pal. Don't you let on that my name's Albert,' said the corporal to his private. 'I'm the corporal.'

'And I'm Miss Stokes,' said the land-girl coolly, 'if that's all the boys you are.'

'You know you couldn't want more, Miss Stokes,' said Albert politely. Joe, who was bare-headed, whose grey flannel sleeves were rolled up to the elbow, and whose shirt was open at the breast, looked modestly aside as if he had no part in the affair.

'Are you on this job regular then?' said the corporal to Miss Stokes.

'I don't know for sure,' she said, pushing a piece of hair under her hat, and attending to her splendid horses.

'Oh, make it a certainty,' said Albert.

She did not reply. She turned and looked over the two men coolly. She was pretty, moderately blonde, with crisp hair, a good skin, and large blue eyes. She was strong, too, and the work went on leisurely and easily.

'Now!' said the corporal, stopping as usual to look round, 'pleasant company makes work a pleasure – don't hurry it, boys.' He stood on the truck surveying the world. That was one of his great and absorbing occupations: to stand and look out on things in general. Joe, also standing on the truck, also turned round to look what was to be seen. But he could not become blankly absorbed, as Albert could.

Miss Stokes watched the two men from under her broad felt hat. She had seen hundreds of Alberts, khaki soldiers standing in loose attitudes, absorbed in watching nothing in particular. She had seen also a good many Joes, quiet, good-looking young soldiers with half-averted faces. But there was something in the turn of Joe's head, and something in his quiet, tender-looking form, young and fresh -- which attracted her eye. As she watched him closely from below, he turned as if he felt her, and his dark-blue eye met her straight, light-blue gaze. He faltered and turned aside again and looked as if he were going to fall off the truck. A slight flush mounted under the girl's full, ruddy face. She liked him.

Always, after this, when she came into the sidings with her team, it was Joe she looked for. She acknowledged to herself that she was sweet on him. But Albert did all the talking. He was so full of fun and nonsense. Joe was a very shy bird, very brief and remote in his answers. Miss Stokes was driven to indulge in repartee with Albert, but she fixed her magnetic attention on the younger fellow. Joe would talk with Albert, and laugh at his jokes. But Miss Stokes could get little out of him. She had to depend on her silent forces. They were more effective than might be imagined.

Suddenly, on Saturday afternoon, at about two o'clock, Joe received a bolt from the blue – a telegram: 'Meet me Belbury Station 6.00 p.m. today. M.S.' He knew at once who M.S. was. His heart melted, he felt weak as if he had had a blow.

'What's the trouble, boy?' asked Albert anxiously.

'No – no trouble – it's to meet somebody.' Joe lifted his dark, blue eyes in confusion towards his corporal.

'Meet somebody!' repeated the corporal, watching his young pal with keen blue eyes. 'It's all right, then; nothing wrong?'

'No – nothing wrong. I'm not going,' said Joe.

Albert was old and shrewd enough to see that nothing more should be said before the housewife. He also saw that Joe did not want to take him into confidence. So he held his peace, though he was piqued.

The two soldiers went into town, smartened up. Albert knew a fair number of the boys round about; there would be plenty of gossip in the market-place, plenty of lounging in groups on the Bath Road, watching the Saturday evening shoppers. Then a modest drink or two, and the movies. They passed an agreeable, casual, nothing-in-particular evening, with which Joe was quite satisfied. He thought of Belbury Station, and of M.S. waiting there. He had not the faintest intention of meeting her. And he had not the faintest intention of telling Albert.

And yet, when the two men were in their bedroom, half undressed, Joe suddenly held out the telegram to his corporal, saying: 'What d'you think of that?'

Albert was just unbuttoning his braces. He desisted, took the telegram form, and turned towards the candle to read it.

'*Meet me Belbury Station 6.00 p.m. today. M.S.*,' he read, *sotto voce*. His face took on its fun-and-nonsense look.

'Who's M.S.?' he asked, looking shrewdly at Joe.

'You know as well as I do,' said Joe, non-committal.

'*M.S.*,' repeated Albert. 'Blamed if I know, boy. Is it a woman?'

The conversation was carried on in tiny voices, for fear of disturbing the householders.

'I don't know,' said Joe, turning. He looked full at Albert, the two men looked straight into each other's eyes. There was a lurking grin in each of them.

'Well, I'm – *blamed*!' said Albert at last, throwing the telegram down emphatically on the bed.

'Wha – at?' said Joe, grinning rather sheepishly, his eyes clouded, none the less.

Albert sat on the bed and proceeded to undress, nodding his head with mock gravity all the while. Joe watched him foolishly.

'What?' he repeated faintly.

Albert looked up at him with a knowing look.

'If that isn't coming it quick, boy!' he said. 'What the blazes! What ha' you bin doing?'

'Nothing!' said Joe.

Albert slowly shook his head as he sat on the side of the bed.

'Don't happen to me when *I've* bin doin' nothing,' he said. And he proceeded to pull off his stockings.

Joe turned away, looking at himself in the mirror as he unbuttoned his tunic.

'You didn't want to keep the appointment?' Albert asked, in a changed voice, from the bedside.

Joe did not answer for a moment. Then he said:

'I made no appointment.'

'I'm not saying you did, boy. Don't be nasty about it. I mean you didn't want to answer the – unknown person's summons – shall I put it that way?'

'No,' said Joe.

'What was the deterring motive?' asked Albert, who was now lying on his back in bed.

'Oh,' said Joe, suddenly looking round rather haughtily, 'I didn't want to.' He had a well-balanced head, and could take on a sudden distant bearing.

'Didn't want to – didn't cotton on, like. Well – *they be artful, the women*—' he mimicked his landlord. 'Come on into bed, boy. Don't loiter about as if you'd lost something.'

Albert turned over, to sleep.

On Monday Miss Stokes turned up as usual, striding beside her team. Her 'whoa!' was resonant and challenging, she looked up at the truck as her steeds came to a standstill. Joe had turned aside, and had his face averted from her. She glanced him over – save for his slender succulent tenderness she would have despised him. She sized him up in a steady look. Then she turned to Albert, who was looking down at her and smiling in his mischievous turn. She knew his aspects by now. She looked straight back at him, though her eyes were hot. He saluted her.

'Beautiful morning, Miss Stokes.'

'Very,' she replied.

'Handsome is as handsome looks,' said Albert.

Which produced no response.

'Now, Joe, come on here,' said the corporal. 'Don't keep the ladies waiting – it's the sign of a weak heart.'

Joe turned and the work began. Nothing more was said for the time being. As the week went on all parties became more comfortable. Joe remained silent, averted, neutral, a little on his dignity. Miss Stokes was off-hand and masterful. Albert was full of mischief.

The great theme was a circus, which was coming to the market town on the following Saturday.

'You'll go to the circus, Miss Stokes?' said Albert.

'I may go. Are you going?'

'Certainly. Give us the pleasure of escorting you?'

'No, thanks.'

'That's what I call a flat refusal – what, Joe? You don't mean that you have no liking for our company, Miss Stokes?'

'Oh, I don't know,' said Miss Stokes. 'How many are there of you?'

'Only me and Joe.'

'Oh, is that all?' she said satirically.

Albert was a little nonplussed.

'Isn't that enough for you?' he asked.

'Too many by half,' blurted out Joe, jeeringly, in a sudden fit of uncouth rudeness that made both the others stare.

'Oh, I'll stand out of the way, boy, if that's it,' said Albert to Joe. Then he turned mischievously to Miss Stokes. 'He wants to know what M. stands for,' he said confidentially.

'Monkeys,' she replied, turning to her horses.

'What's M.S.?' said Albert.

'Monkey nuts,' she retorted, leading off her team.

Albert looked after her a little discomfited. Joe had flushed dark, and cursed Albert in his heart.

On the Saturday afternoon the two soldiers took the train into town. They would have to walk home. They had tea at six o'clock, and lounged about till half-past seven. The circus was in a meadow near the river – a great red-and-white striped tent. Caravans stood at the side. A great crowd of people was gathered round the ticket-caravan.

Inside the tent the lamps were lighted, shining on a ring of faces, a great circular bank of faces round the green grassy centre. Along with some comrades, the two soldiers packed themselves on a thin plank seat, rather high. They were delighted with the flaring lights, the wild effect. But the circus performance did not affect them deeply. They admired the lady in black velvet with rose-purple legs who leapt so neatly on to the galloping horse; they watched the feats of strength, and laughed at the clown. But they felt a little patronizing, they missed the sensational drama of the cinema.

Half-way through the performance Joe was electrified to see the face of Miss Stokes not very far from him. There she was, in her khaki and her felt hat, as usual; he pretended not to see her. She was laughing at the clown; she also pretended not to see him. It was a blow to him, and it made him angry. He would not even mention it to Albert. Least said, soonest mended. He liked to believe she had not seen him. But he knew, fatally, that she had.

When they came out it was nearly eleven o'clock; a lovely night, with a moon and tall, dark, noble trees: a magnificent May night. Joe and Albert laughed and chaffed with the boys. Joe looked round frequently to see if he were safe from Miss Stokes. It seemed so.

But there were six miles to walk home. At last the two soldiers set off, swinging their canes. The road was white between tall hedges, other stragglers were passing out of the town towards the villages; the air was full of pleased excitement.

They were drawing near to the village when they saw a dark figure ahead. Joe's heart sank with pure fear. It was a figure wheeling a bicycle; a land-girl; Miss Stokes. Albert was ready with his nonsense. Miss Stokes had a puncture.

'Let me wheel the rattler,' said Albert.

'Thank you,' said Miss Stokes. 'You *are* kind.'

'Oh, I'd be kinder than that, if you'd show me how,' said Albert.

'Are you sure?' said Miss Stokes.

'Doubt my words?' said Albert. 'That's cruel of you, Miss Stokes.'

Miss Stokes walked between them, close to Joe.

'Have you been to the circus?' she asked him.

'Yes,' he replied mildly.

'Have *you* been?' Albert asked her.

'Yes. I didn't see you,' she replied.

'What! – you say so! Didn't see us! Didn't think us worth looking at,' began Albert. 'Aren't I as handsome as the clown, now? And you didn't as much as glance in our direction? I call it a downright oversight.'

'I never *saw* you,' reiterated Miss Stokes. 'I didn't know you saw me.'

'That makes it worse,' said Albert.

The road passed through a belt of dark pine-wood. The village, and the branch road, was very near. Miss Stokes put out her fingers and felt for Joe's hand as it swung at his side. To say he was staggered is to put it mildly. Yet he allowed her softly to clasp his fingers for a few minutes. But he was a mortified youth.

At the cross-road they stopped – Miss Stokes should turn off. She had another mile to go.

'You'll let us see you home,' said Albert.

'Do me a kindness,' she said. 'Put my bike in your shed, and take it to Baker's on Monday, will you?'

'I'll sit up all night and mend it for you, if you like.'

'No, thanks. And Joe and I'll walk on.'

'Oh – ho! Oh – ho!' sang Albert. 'Joe! Joe! What do you say to that, boy? Aren't you in luck's way? And I get the bloomin' old bike for my pal. Consider it again, Miss Stokes.'

Joe turned aside his face, and did not speak.

'Oh, well! I wheel the grid, do I? I leave you, boy—'

'I'm not keen on going any farther,' barked out Joe, in an un-couth voice. 'She bain't my choice.'

The girl stood silent, and watched the two men.

There now!' said Albert. 'Think o' that! If it was *me* now—' But he was uncomfortable. 'Well, Miss Stokes, have me,' he added.

Miss Stokes stood quite still, neither moved nor spoke. And so the three remained for some time at the lane end. At last Joe began kicking the ground – then he suddenly lifted his face. At that moment Miss Stokes was at his side. She put her arm deli-cately round his waist.

'Seems I'm the one extra, don't you think?' Albert inquired of the high bland moon.

Joe had dropped his head and did not answer. Miss Stokes stood with her arm lightly round his waist. Albert bowed, saluted, and bade good-night. He walked away, leaving the two standing.

Miss Stokes put a light pressure on Joe's waist, and drew him down the road. They walked in silence. The night was full of scent – wild cherry, the first bluebells. Still they walked in silence. A nightingale was singing. They approached nearer and nearer, till they stood close by his dark bush. The powerful notes sounded from the cover, almost like flashes of light – then the interval of silence – then the moaning notes, almost like a dog faintly howling, followed by the long, rich trill, and flashing notes. Then a short silence again.

Miss Stokes turned at last to Joe. She looked up at him, and in the moonlight he saw her faintly smiling. He felt maddened, but helpless. Her arm was round his waist, she drew him closely to her with a soft pressure that made all his bones rotten.

Meanwhile Albert was waiting at home. He put on his overcoat, for the fire was out, and he had had malarial fever. He looked fitfully at the *Daily Mirror* and the *Daily Sketch*, but he saw nothing. It seemed a long time. He began to yawn widely, even to nod. At last Joe came in.

Albert looked at him keenly. The young man's brow was black, his face sullen.

'All right, boy?' asked Albert.

Joe merely grunted for a reply. There was nothing more to be got out of him. So they went to bed.

Next day Joe was silent, sullen. Albert could make nothing of him. He proposed a walk after tea.

'I'm going somewhere,' said Joe.

'Where – Monkey nuts?' asked the corporal. But Joe's brow only became darker.

So the days went by. Almost every evening Joe went off alone, returning late. He was sullen, taciturn and had a hang-dog look, a curious way of dropping his head and looking dangerously from under his brows. And he and Albert did not get on so well any more with one another. For all his fun and nonsense, Albert was really irritable, soon made angry. And Joe's stand-offish sulkiness and complete lack of confidence riled him, got on his nerves. His fun and nonsense took a biting, sarcastic turn, at which Joe's eyes glittered occasionally, though the young man turned unheeding aside. Then again Joe would be full of odd, whimsical fun, out-shining Albert himself.

Miss Stokes still came to the station with the wain: Monkey nuts, Albert called her, though not to her face. For she was very clear and good-looking, almost she seemed to gleam. And Albert was a tiny bit afraid of her. She very rarely addressed Joe whilst the hay-loading was going on, and that young man always turned his back to her. He seemed thinner, and his limber figure looked more slouching. But still it had the tender, attractive appearance, especially from behind. His tanned face, a little thinned and darkened, took a handsome, slightly sinister look.

'Come on, Joe!' the corporal urged sharply one day. 'What're you doing, boy? Looking for beetles on the bank?'

Joe turned round swiftly, almost menacing, to work.

'He's a different fellow these days, Miss Stokes,' said Albert to the young woman. 'What's got him? Is it Monkey nuts that don't suit him, do you think?'

Choked with chaff, more like,' she retorted. 'It's as bad as feeding a threshing machine, to have to listen to some folks.'

'As bad as what?' said Albert. 'You don't mean *me*, do you, Miss Stokes?'

'No,' she cried. 'I don't mean you.'

Joe's face became dark red during these sallies, but he said nothing. He would eye the young woman curiously, as she swung so easily at the work, and he had some of the look of a dog which is going to bite.

Albert, with his nerves on edge, began to find the strain rather severe. The next Sunday evening, when Joe came in more black-browed than ever, he watched him, determined to have it out with him.

When the boy went upstairs to bed, the corporal followed him. He closed the door behind him carefully, sat on the bed and watched the younger man undressing. And for once he spoke in a natural voice, neither chaffing nor commanding.

'What's gone wrong, boy?'

Joe stopped a moment as if he had been shot. Then he went on unwinding his puttees, and did not answer or look up.

'You can hear, can't you?' said Albert, nettled.

'Yes, I can hear,' said Joe, stooping over his puttees till his face was purple.

'Then why don't you answer?'

Joe sat up. He gave a long, sideways look at the corporal. Then he lifted his eyes and stared at a crack in the ceiling.

The corporal watched these movements shrewdly.

'And *then* what?' he asked ironically.

Again Joe turned and stared him in the face. The corporal smiled very slightly, but kindly.

'There'll be murder done one of these days,' said Joe, in a quiet, unimpassioned voice.

'So long as it's by daylight—' replied Albert. Then he went over, sat down by Joe, put his hand on his shoulder affectionately, and continued: 'What is it, boy? What's gone wrong? You can trust me, can't you?'

Joe turned and looked curiously at the face so near to his.

'It's nothing, that's all,' he said laconically.

Albert frowned.

'Then who's going to be murdered? – and who's going to do the murdering? – me or you – which is it, boy?' He smiled gently at the stupid youth, looking straight at him all the while, into his eyes. Gradually the stupid, hunted, glowering look died out of Joe's eyes. He turned his head aside, gently, as one rousing from a spell.

'I don't want her,' he said, with fierce resentment.

'Then you needn't have her,' said Albert. 'What do you go for, boy?'

But it wasn't as simple as all that. Joe made no remark.

'She's a smart-looking girl. What's wrong with her, my boy? I should have thought you were a lucky chap, myself.'

'I don't want 'er,' Joe barked, with ferocity and resentment.

'Then tell her so and have done,' said Albert. He waited a while. There was no response. 'Why don't you?' he added.

'Because I don't,' confessed Joe sulkily.

Albert pondered – rubbed his head.

'You're too soft-hearted, that's where it is, boy. You want your mettle dipping in cold water, to temper it. You're too soft-hearted—'

He laid his arm affectionately across the shoulders of the younger man. Joe seemed to yield a little towards him.

'When are you going to see her again?' Albert asked. For a long time there was no answer.

'When is it, boy?' persisted the softened voice of the corporal.

'Tomorrow,' confessed Joe.

'Then let me go,' said Albert. 'Let me go, will you?'

The morrow was Sunday, a sunny day, but a cold evening. The sky was grey, the new foliage very green, but the air was chill and depressing. Albert walked briskly down the white road towards Beeley. He crossed a larch plantation, and followed a narrow by-road, where blue speedwell flowers fell from the banks into the dust. He walked swinging his cane, with mixed sensations. Then having gone a certain length, he turned and began to walk in the opposite direction.

So he saw a young woman approaching him. She was wearing a wide hat of grey straw, and a loose, swinging dress of nigger-grey velvet. She walked with slow inevitability. Albert faltered a little as he approached her. Then he saluted her, and his roguish, slightly withered skin flushed. She was staring straight into his face.

He fell in by her side, saying impudently:

'Not so nice for a walk as it was, is it?'

She only stared at him. He looked back at her.

'You've seen me before, you know,' he said, grinning slightly. 'Perhaps you never noticed me. Oh, I'm quite nice-looking, in a quiet way, you know. What—?'

But Miss Stokes did not speak: she only stared with large, icy blue eyes at him. He became self-conscious, lifted up his chin, walked with his nose in the air, and whistled at random. So they went down the quiet, deserted grey lane. He was whistling the air: 'I'm Gilbert, the filbert, the colonel of the nuts.'

At last she found her voice:

'Where's Joe?'

'He thought you'd like a change: they say variety's the salt of life – that's why I'm mostly in pickle.'

'Where is he?'

'Am I my brother's keeper? He's gone his own ways.'

'Where?'

'Nay, how am I to know? Not so far but he'll be back for supper.'

She stopped in the middle of the lane. He stopped facing her.

'Where's Joe?' she asked.

He struck a careless attitude, looked down the road this way and that, lifted his eyebrows, pushed his khaki cap on one side, and answered:

'He is not conducting the service tonight: he asked me if I'd officiate.'

'Why hasn't he come?'

'Didn't want to, I expect. I wanted to.'

She stared him up and down, and he felt uncomfortable in his spine, but maintained his air of nonchalance. Then she turned slowly on her heel, and started to walk back. The corporal went at her side.

'You're not going back, are you?' he pleaded. 'Why, me and you, we should get on like a house on fire.'

She took no heed, but walked on. He went uncomfortably at her side, making his funny remarks from time to time. But she was as if stone deaf. He glanced at her, and to his dismay saw the tears running down her cheeks. He stopped suddenly, and pushed back his cap.

'I say, you know—' he began.

But she was walking on like an automaton, and he had to hurry after her.

She never spoke to him. At the gate of her farm she walked straight in, as if he were not there. He watched her disappear. Then he turned on his heel, cursing silently, puzzled, lifting off his cap to scratch his head.

That night, when they were in bed, he remarked:

'Say, Joe, boy; strikes me you're well off without Monkey nuts. Gord love us, beans ain't in it.'

So they slept in amity. But they waited with some anxiety for the morrow.

It was a cold morning, a grey sky shifting in a cold wind, and threatening rain. They watched the wagon come up the road and through the yard gates. Miss Stokes was with her team as usual; her 'Whoa!' rang out like a war-whoop.

She faced up at the truck where the two men stood.

'Joe!' she called, to the averted figure which stood up in the wind.

'What?' he turned unwillingly.

She made a queer movement, lifting her head slightly in a sipping, half-inviting, half-commanding gesture. And Joe was crouching already to jump off the truck to obey her, when Albert put his hand on his shoulder.

'Half a minute, boy! Where are you off? Work's work, and nuts is nuts. You stop here.'

Joe slowly straightened himself.

'Joe?' came the woman's clear call from below.

Again Joe looked at her. But Albert's hand was on his shoulder, detaining him. He stood half averted, with his tail between his legs.

'Take your hand off him, you!' said Miss Stokes.

'Yes, Major,' retorted Albert satirically.

She stood and watched.

'Joe!' Her voice rang for the third time.

Joe turned and looked at her, and a slow, jeering smile gathered on his face.

'Monkey nuts!' he replied, in a tone mocking her call.

She turned white – dead white. The men thought she would fall. Albert began yelling to the porters up the line to come and help with the load. He could yell like any non-commissioned officer upon occasion.

Some way or other the wagon was unloaded, the girl was gone. Joe and his corporal looked at one another and smiled slowly. But they had a weight on their minds, they were afraid.

They were reassured, however, when they found that Miss Stokes came no more with the hay. As far as they were concerned, she had vanished into oblivion. And Joe felt more relieved even than he had felt when he heard the firing cease, after the news had come that the armistice was signed.

Fanny and Annie

FLAME-LURID his face as he turned among the throng of flame-lit and dark faces upon the platform. In the light of the furnace she caught sight of his drifting countenance, like a piece of floating fire. And the nostalgia, the doom of homecoming went through her veins like a drug. His eternal face, flame-lit now! The pulse and darkness of red fire from the furnace towers in the sky, lighting the desultory, industrial crowd on the wayside station, lit him and went out.

Of course he did not see her. Flame-lit and unseeing! Always the same, with his meeting eyebrows, his common cap, and his red-and-black scarf knotted round his throat. Not even a collar to meet her! The flames had sunk, there was shadow.

She opened the door of her grimy, branch-line carriage, and began to get down her bags. The porter was nowhere, of course, but there was Harry, obscure, on the outer edge of the little crowd, missing her, of course.

'Here! Harry!' she called, waving her umbrella in the twilight. He hurried forward.

'Tha's come, has ter?' he said, in a sort of cheerful welcome. She got down, rather flustered, and gave him a peck of a kiss.

'Two suit-cases!' she said.

Her soul groaned within her, as he clambered into the carriage after her bags. Up shot the fire in the twilight sky, from the great furnace behind the station. She felt the red flame go across her face. She had come back, she had come back for good.

And her spirit groaned dismally. She doubted if she could bear it.

There, on the sordid little station under the furnaces, she stood, tall and distinguished, in her well-made coat and skirt and her broad grey velour hat. She held her umbrella, her bead chatelaine, and a little leather case in her grey-gloved hands, while Harry staggered out of the ugly little train with her bags.

'There's a trunk at the back,' she said in her bright voice. But she was not feeling bright. The twin black cones of the iron foundry blasted their sky-high fires into the night. The whole scene was lurid. The train waited cheerfully. It would wait another ten minutes. She knew it. It was all so deadly familiar.

Let us confess it at once. She was a lady's maid, thirty years old, come back to marry her first-love, a foundry worker: after having kept him dangling, off and on, for a dozen years. Why had she come back? Did she love him? No. She didn't pretend to. She had loved her brilliant and ambitious cousin, who had jilted her, and who had died. She had had other affairs which had come to nothing. So here she was, come back suddenly to marry her first-love, who had waited – or remained single – all these years.

'Won't a porter carry those?' she said, as Harry strode with his workman's stride down the platform towards the guard's van.

'I can manage,' he said.

And with her umbrella, her chatelaine, and her little leather case, she followed him.

The trunk was there.

'We'll get Heather's greengrocer's cart to fetch it up,' he said.

'Isn't there a cab?' said Fanny, knowing dismally enough that there wasn't.

'I'll just put it aside o' the penny-in-the-slot, and Heather's greengrocers'll fetch it about half-past eight,' he said.

He seized the box by its two handles and staggered with it across the level-crossing, bumping his legs against it as he waddled. Then he dropped it by the red sweetmeats machine.

'Will it be safe there?' she said.

'Ay – safe as houses,' he answered. He returned for the two bags. Thus laden, they started to plod up the hill, under the great long black building of the foundry. She walked beside him – workman of workmen he was, trudging with that luggage. The red lights flared over the deepening darkness. From the foundry came the horrible, slow clang, clang, clang of iron, a great noise, with an interval just long enough to make it unendurable.

Compare this with the arrival at Gloucester: the carriage for her mistress, the dog-cart for herself with the luggage; the drive out past the river, the pleasant trees of the carriage-approach; and herself sitting beside Arthur, everybody so polite to her.

She had come home – for good! Her heart nearly stopped beating as she trudged up that hideous and interminable hill, beside the laden figure. What a come-down! What a come-down! She could not take it with her usual bright cheerfulness. She knew it all too well. It is easy to bear up against the unusual, but the deadly familiarity of an old stale past!

He dumped the bags down under a lamp-post, for a rest. There they stood, the two of them, in the lamp-light. Passers-by stared at her, and gave good night to Harry. Her they hardly knew, she had become a stranger.

'They're too heavy for you, let me carry one,' she said.

'They begin to weigh a bit by the time you've gone a mile,' he answered.

'Let me carry the little one,' she insisted.

'Tha can ha'e it for a minute, if ter's a mind,' he said, handing over the valise.

And thus they arrived in the streets of shops of the little ugly town on top of the hill. How everybody stared at her; my word, how they stared! And the cinema was just going in, and the queues were tailing down the road to the corner. And everybody took full stock of her. 'Night, Harry!' shouted the fellows, in an interested voice.

However, they arrived at her aunt's – a little sweet-shop in a side street. They 'pinged' the door-bell, and her aunt came running forward out of the kitchen.

'There you are, child! Dying for a cup of tea, I'm sure. How are you?'

Fanny's aunt kissed her, and it was all Fanny could do to refrain from bursting into tears, she felt so low. Perhaps it was her tea she wanted.

'You've had a drag with that luggage,' said Fanny's aunt to Harry.

'Ay – I'm not sorry to put it down,' he said, looking at his hand which was crushed and cramped by the bag handle.

Then he departed to see about Heather's greengrocery cart.

When Fanny sat at tea, her aunt, a grey-haired, fair-faced little woman, looked at her with an admiring heart, feeling bitterly sore for her. For Fanny was beautiful: tall, erect, finely coloured, with her delicately arched nose, her rich brown hair, her large lustrous-grey eyes. A passionate woman – a woman to be afraid of. So proud, so inwardly violent! She came of a violent race.

It needed a woman to sympathize with her. Men had not the courage. Poor Fanny! She was such a lady, and so straight and magnificent. And yet everything seemed to do her down. Every time she seemed to be doomed to humiliation and disappointment, this handsome, brilliantly sensitive woman, with her nervous, over-wrought laugh.

'So you've really come back, child?' said her aunt.

'I really have, Aunt,' said Fanny.

'Poor Harry! I'm not sure, you know, Fanny, that you're not taking a bit of an advantage of him.'

'Oh, Aunt, he's waited so long, he may as well have what he's waited for.' Fanny laughed grimly.

'Yes, child, he's waited so long, that I'm not sure it isn't a bit hard on him. You know, I *like* him, Fanny – though as you know quite well, I don't think he's good enough for you. And I think he thinks so himself, poor fellow.'

'Don't you be so sure of that, Aunt. Harry is common, but he's not humble. He wouldn't think the Queen was any too good for him, if he's a mind to her.'

'Well – it's as well if he has a proper opinion of himself.'

'It depends what you call proper,' said Fanny. 'But he's got his good points—'

'Oh, he's a nice fellow, and I like him, I do like him. Only, as I tell you, he's not good enough for you.'

'I've made up my mind, Aunt,' said Fanny grimly.

'Yes,' mused the aunt. 'They say all things come to him who waits—'

'More than he's bargained for, eh, Aunt?' laughed Fanny rather bitterly.

The poor aunt, this bitterness grieved her for her niece.

They were interrupted by the ping of the shop-bell, and Harry's call of 'Right!' But as he did not come in at once, Fanny, feeling solicitous for him presumably at the moment, rose and went into the shop. She saw a cart outside, and went to the door.

And the moment she stood in the doorway, she heard a woman's common vituperative voice crying from the darkness of the opposite side of the road:

'Tha'rt theer, are ter? I'll shame thee, Mester. I'll shame thee, see if I dunna.'

Startled, Fanny started across the darkness, and saw a woman in a black bonnet go under one of the lamps up the side street.

Harry and Bill Heather had dragged the trunk off the little dray, and she retreated before them as they came up the shop step with it.

'Wheer shal ha'e it?' asked Harry.

'Best take it upstairs,' said Fanny.

She went up first to light the gas.

When Heather had gone, and Harry was sitting down having tea and pork-pie, Fanny asked:

'Who was that woman shouting?'

'Nay, I canna tell thee. To somebody, I s'd think,' replied Harry. Fanny looked at him, but asked no more.

He was a fair-haired fellow of thirty-two, with a fair moustache. He was broad in his speech, and looked like a foundry-hand, which he was. But women always liked him. There was something of a mother's lad about him – something warm and playful and really sensitive.

He had his attractions even for Fanny. What she rebelled against so bitterly was that he had no sort of ambition. He was a moulder, but of very commonplace skill. He was thirty-two years old, and hadn't saved twenty pounds. She would have to provide the money for the home. He didn't care. He just didn't care. He had no initiative at all. He had no vices – no obvious ones. But he was just indifferent, spending as he went, and not caring. Yet he did not look happy. Sne remembered his face in the fire-glow: something haunted, abstracted about it. As he sat there eating his pork-pie, bulging his cheek out, she felt he was like a doom to her. And she raged against the doom of him. It wasn't that he was gross. His *way* was common, almost on purpose. But he himself wasn't really common. For instance, his food was not particularly important to him, he was not greedy. He had a charm, too, particularly for women, with his blondness and his sensitiveness and his way of making a woman feel that she was a higher being. But Fanny knew him, knew the peculiar obstinate limitedness of him, that would nearly send her mad.

He stayed till about half-past nine. She went to the door with him.

'When are you coming up?' he said, jerking his head in the direction, presumably, of his own home.

'I'll come tomorrow afternoon,' she said brightly. Between Fanny and Mrs Goodall, his mother, there was naturally no love lost.

Again she gave him an awkward little kiss, and said good night.

'You can't wonder, you know, child, if he doesn't seem so very keen,' said her aunt. 'It's your own fault.'

'Oh, Aunt, I couldn't stand him when he was keen. I can do with him a lot better as he is.'

The two women sat and talked far into the night. They understood each other. The aunt, too, had married as Fanny was marrying: a man who was no companion to her, a violent man, brother of Fanny's father. He was dead, Fanny's father was dead.

Poor Aunt Lizzie, she cried woefully over her bright niece, when she had gone to bed.

Fanny paid the promised visit to his people the next afternoon. Mrs Goodall was a large woman, with smooth-parted hair, a common, obstinate woman, who had spoiled her four lads and her one vixen of a married daughter. She was one of those old-fashioned powerful natures that couldn't do with looks or education or any form of showing-off. She fairly hated the sound of correct English. She *thee'd* and *tha'd* her prospective daughter-in-law, and said:

'I'm none as ormin' as I look, seest ta.'

Fanny did not think her prospective mother-in-law looked at all orming, so the speech was unnecessary.

'I towd him mysen,' said Mrs Goodall, ' 'Er's held back all this long, let 'er stop as 'er is. 'E'd none ha' had thee for *my* tellin' – tha hears. No, 'e's a fool, an' I know it. I says to him: "Tha looks a man, doesn't ter, at thy age, goin' an' openin' to her when her hears her scrat' at th' gate, after she's done galli-

vantin' round wherever she's a mind. That looks rare an' soft."
But it's no use o' any talking: he answered that letter o' thine
and made his own bad bargain.'

But in spite of the old woman's anger, she was also flattered
at Fanny's coming back to Harry. For Mrs Goodall was
impressed by Fanny – a woman of her own match. And more
than this, everybody knew that Fanny's Aunt Kate had left
her two hundred pounds: this apart from the girl's savings.

So there was high tea in Princes Street when Harry came
home black from work, and a rather acrid odour of cordiality,
the vixen Jinny darting in to say vulgar things. Of course Jinny
lived in a house whose garden end joined the paternal garden.
They were a clan who stuck together, these Goodalls.

It was arranged that Fanny should come to tea again on the
Sunday, and the wedding was discussed. It should take place
in a fortnight's time at Morley Chapel. Morley was a hamlet
on the edge of the real country, and in its little Congregational
Chapel Fanny and Harry had first met.

What a creature of habit he was! He was still in the choir
of Morley Chapel – not very regular. He belonged just because
he had a tenor voice, and enjoyed singing. Indeed, his solos
were only spoilt to local fame because when he sang he handled
his aitches so hopelessly.

> 'And I saw 'eaven hopened
> And be'old, a wite 'orse—'

This was one of Harry's classics, only surpassed by the fine
outburst of his heaving:

> 'Hangels – hever bright an' fair—'

It was a pity, but it was unalterable. He had a good voice,
and he sang with a certain lacerating fire, but his pronunciation
made it all funny. And *nothing* could alter him.

So he was never heard save at cheap concerts and in the little, poorer chapels. The others scoffed.

Now the month was September, and Sunday was Harvest Festival at Morley Chapel, and Harry was singing solos. So that Fanny was to go to service, and come home to a grand spread of Sunday tea with him. Poor Fanny! One of the most wonderful afternoons had been a Sunday afternoon service, with her cousin Luther at her side, Harvest Festival in Morley Chapel. Harry had sung solos then – ten years ago. She remembered his pale-blue tie, and the purple asters and the great vegetable marrows in which he was framed, and her cousin Luther at her side, young, clever, come down from London, where he was getting on well, learning his Latin and his French and German so brilliantly.

However, once again it was Harvest Festival at Morley Chapel, and once again, as ten years before, a soft, exquisite September day, with the last roses pink in the cottage gardens, the last dahlias crimson, the last sunflowers yellow. And again the little old chapel was a bower, with its famous sheaves of corn and corn-plaited pillars, its great bunches of grapes, dangling like tassels from the pulpit corners, its marrows and potatoes and pears and apples and damsons, its purple asters and yellow Japanese sunflowers. Just as before, the red dahlias round the pillars were dropping, weak-headed among the oats. The place was crowded and hot, the plates of tomatoes seemed balanced perilous on the gallery front, the Rev. Enderby was weirder than ever to look at, so long and emaciated and hairless.

The Rev. Enderby, probably forewarned, came and shook hands with her and welcomed her, in his broad northern, melancholy sing-song before he mounted the pulpit. Fanny was handsome in a gauzy dress and a beautiful lace hat. Being a little late, she sat in a chair in the side-aisle wedged in, right in front of the chapel. Harry was in the gallery above, and she could only see him from the eyes upwards. She noticed how his eyebrows met, blond and not very marked, over his nose. He was attractive, too: physically lovable, very. If only – if only her *pride* had not suffered! She felt he dragged her down.

> 'Come, ye thankful people, come,
> Raise the song of harvest-home.
> All is safely gathered in
> Ere the winter storms begin—'

Even the hymn was a falsehood, as the season had been wet, and half the crops were still out, and in a poor way.

Poor Fanny! She sang little, and looked beautiful through that inappropriate hymn. Above her stood Harry – mercifully in a dark suit and a dark tie, looking almost handsome. And his lacerating, pure tenor sounded well, when the words were drowned in the general commotion. Brilliant she looked, and brilliant she felt, for she was hot and angrily miserable and inflamed with a sort of fatal despair. Because there was about him a physical attraction which she really hated, but which she could not escape from. He was the first man who had ever kissed her. And his kisses, even while she rebelled from them, had lived in her blood and sent roots down into her soul. After all this time she had come back to them. And her soul groaned, for she felt dragged down, dragged down to earth, as a bird which some dog has got down in the dust. She knew her life would be unhappy. She knew that what she was doing was fatal. Yet it was her doom. She had to come back to him.

He had to sing two solos this afternoon: one before the 'address' from the pulpit and one after. Fanny looked at him, and wondered he was not too shy to stand up there in front of all the people. But no, he was not shy. He had even a kind of assurance on his face as he looked down from the choir gallery at her: the assurance of a common man deliberately entrenched in his commonness. Oh, such a rage went through her veins as

she saw the air of triumph, laconic, indifferent triumph which
sat so obstinately and recklessly on his eyelids as he looked
down at her. Ah, she despised him! But there he stood up in
that choir gallery like Balaam's ass in front of her, and she
could not get beyond him. A certain winsomeness also about
him. A certain physical winsomeness, and as if his flesh were
new and lovely to touch. The thorn of desire rankled bitterly
in her heart.

He, it goes without saying, sang like a canary, this particular
afternoon, with a certain defiant passion which pleasantly
crisped the blood of the congregation. Fanny felt the crisp
flames go through her veins as she listened. Even the curious
loud-mouthed vernacular had a certain fascination. But, oh,
also, it was so repugnant. He would triumph over her, obstinately he would drag her right back into the common people: a
doom, a vulgar doom.

The second performance was an anthem, in which Harry
sang the solo parts. It was clumsy, but beautiful, with lovely
words.

'They that sow in tears shall reap in joy,
He that goeth forth and weepeth, bearing precious seed
Shall doubtless come again with rejoicing, bringing his
    sheaves with him—'

'Shall doubtless come, Shall doubtless come—' softly intoned
the altos – 'Bringing his she-e-eaves with him,' the trebles
flourished brightly, and then again began the half-wistful
solo:

'They that sow in tears shall reap in joy—'

Yes, it was effective and moving.
But at the moment when Harry's voice sank carelessly down

to his close, and the choir, standing behind him, were opening their mouths for the final triumphant outburst, a shouting female voice rose up from the body of the congregation. The organ gave one startled trump, and went silent; the choir stood transfixed.

'You look well standing there, singing in God's holy house,' came the loud, angry female shout. Everybody turned electrified. A stoutish, red-faced woman in a black bonnet was standing up denouncing the soloist. Almost fainting with shock, the congregation realized it. 'You look well, don't you, standing there singing solos in God's holy house, you, Goodall. But I said I'd shame on you. You look well, bringing your young woman here with you, don't you? I'll let her know who she's dealing with. A scamp as won't take the consequences of what he's done.' The hard-faced, frenzied woman turned in the direction of Fanny. '*That's* what Harry Goodall is, if you want to know.'

And she sat down again in her seat. Fanny, startled like all the rest, had turned to look. She had gone white, and then a burning red, under the attack. She knew the woman: a Mrs Nixon, a devil of a woman, who beat her pathetic, drunken, red-nosed second husband, Bob, and her two lanky daughters, grown-up as they were. A notorious character. Fanny turned round again, and sat motionless as eternity in her seat.

There was a minute of perfect silence and suspense. The audience was open-mouthed and dumb; the choir stood like Lot's wife and Harry, with his music-sheet, stood there uplifted, looking down with a dumb sort of indifference on Mrs Nixon, his face naïve and faintly mocking. Mrs Nixon sat defiant in her seat, braving them all.

Then a rustle, like a wood when the wind suddenly catches the leaves. And then the tall, weird minister got to his feet, and in his strong, bell-like beautiful voice – the only beautiful thing about him – he said with infinite mournful pathos:

'Let us unite in singing the last hymn on the hymn-sheet; the last hymn on the hymn-sheet, number eleven.

"Fair waved the golden corn
In Canaan's pleasant land." '

The organ tuned up promptly. During the hymn the offertory was taken. And after the hymn, the prayer.

Mr Enderby came from Northumberland. Like Harry, he had never been able to conquer his accent, which was very broad. He was a little simple, one of God's fools, perhaps, an odd bachelor soul, emotional, ugly, but very gentle.

'And if, O our dear Lord, beloved Jesus, there should fall a shadow of sin upon our harvest, we leave it to Thee to judge, for Thou art judge. We lift our spirits and our sorrow, Jesus, to Thee, and our mouths are dumb. O Lord, keep us from froward speech, restrain us from foolish words and thoughts, we pray Thee, Lord Jesus, who knowest all and judgest all.'

Thus the minister said in his sad, resonant voice, washed his hands before the Lord. Fanny bent forward open-eyed during the prayer. She could see the roundish head of Harry, also bent forward. His face was inscrutable and expressionless. The shock left her bewildered. Anger perhaps was her dominating emotion.

The audience began to rustle to its feet, to ooze slowly and excitedly out of the chapel, looking with wildly interested eyes at Fanny, at Mrs Nixon, and at Harry. Mrs Nixon, shortish, stood defiant in her pew, facing the aisle, as if announcing that, without rolling her sleeves up, she was ready for anybody. Fanny sat quite still. Luckily the people did not have to pass her. And Harry, with red ears, was making his way sheepishly out of the gallery. The loud noise of the organ covered all the downstairs commotion of exit.

The minister sat silent and inscrutable in his pulpit, rather like a death's-head, while the congregation filed out. When the last lingerers had unwillingly departed, craning their necks to stare at the still seated Fanny, he rose, stalked in his hooked fashion down the little country chapel and fastened the door. Then he returned and sat down by the silent young woman.

'This is most unfortunate, most unfortunate!' he moaned. 'I am so sorry, I am so sorry, indeed, indeed, ah, indeed!' he sighed himself to a close.

'It's a sudden surprise, that's one thing,' said Fanny brightly.

'Yes – yes – indeed. Yes, a surprise, yes. I don't know the woman, I don't know her.'

'I know her,' said Fanny. 'She's a bad one.'

'Well! Well!' said the minister. 'I don't know her. I don't understand. I don't understand at all. But it is to be regretted, it is very much to be regretted. I am very sorry.'

Fanny was watching the vestry door. The gallery stairs communicated with the vestry, not with the body of the chapel. She knew the choir members had been peeping for information.

At last Harry came – rather sheepishly – with his hat in his hand.

'Well!' said Fanny, rising to her feet.

'We've had a bit of an extra,' said Harry.

'I should think so,' said Fanny.

'A most unfortunate circumstance – a most *unfortunate* circumstance. Do you understand it, Harry? I don't understand it at all.'

'Ay, I understand it. The daughter's goin' to have a childt, an' 'er lays it to me.'

'And has she no occasion to?' asked Fanny rather censorious.

'It's no more mine than it is some other chap's,' said Harry, looking aside.

There was a moment of pause.

'Which girl is it?' asked Fanny.

'Annie – the young one—'

There followed another silence.

'I don't think I know them, do I?' asked the minister.

'I shouldn't think so. Their name's Nixon – mother married old Bob for her second husband. She's a tanger, she's driven the gel to what she is. They live in Manners Road.'

'Why, what's amiss with the girl?' asked Fanny sharply. 'She was all right when I knew her.'

'Ay – she's all right. But she's always in an' out o' th' pubs, wi' th' fellows,' said Harry.

'A nice thing!' said Fanny.

Harry glanced towards the door. He wanted to get out.

'Most distressing, indeed!' the minister slowly shook his head.

'What about tonight, Mr Enderby?' asked Harry, in rather a small voice. 'Shall you want me?'

Mr Enderby looked up painedly, and put his hand to his brow. He studied Harry for some time, vacantly. There was the faintest sort of a resemblance between the two men.

'Yes,' he said. 'Yes, I think. I think we must take no notice and cause as little remark as possible.'

Fanny hesitated. Then she said to Harry:

'But *will* you come?'

He looked at her.

'Ay, I s'll come,' he said.

Then he turned to Mr Enderby.

'Well, good afternoon, Mr Enderby,' he said.

'Good afternoon, Harry, good afternoon,' replied the mournful minister. Fanny followed Harry to the door, and for some time they walked in silence through the late afternoon.

'And it's yours as much as anybody else's?' she said.

'Ay,' he answered shortly.

And they went without another word, for the long mile or

so, till they came to the corner of the street where Harry lived. Fanny hesitated. Should she go on to her aunt's? Should she? It would mean leaving all this, for ever. Harry stood silent.

Some obstinancy made her turn with him along the road to his own home. When they entered the house-place, the whole family was there, mother and father and Jinny, with Jinny's husband and children and Harry's two brothers.

'You've been having your ears warmed, they tell me,' said Mrs Goodall grimly.

'Who told thee?' asked Harry shortly.

'Maggie and Luke's both been in.'

'You look well, don't you!' said interfering Jinny.

Harry went and hung his hat up, without replying.

'Come upstairs and take your hat off,' said Mrs Goodall to Fanny, almost kindly. It would have annoyed her very much if Fanny had dropped her son at this moment.

'What's 'er say, then?' asked the father secretly of Harry, jerking his head in the direction of the stairs whence Fanny had disappeared.

'Nowt yet,' said Harry.

'Serve you right if she chucks you now,' said Jinny. 'I'll bet it's right about Annie Nixon an' you.'

'Tha bets so much,' said Harry.

'Yi – but you can't deny it,' said Jinny.

'I can if I've a mind.'

His father looked at him enquiringly.

'It's no more mine than it is Bill Bower's, or Ted Slaney's, or six or seven on 'em,' said Harry to his father.

And the father nodded silently.

'That'll not get you out of it, in court,' said Jinny.

Upstairs Fanny evaded all the thrusts made by his mother, and did not declare her hand. She tidied her hair, washed her hands, and put the tiniest bit of powder on her face, for coolness, there in front of Mrs Goodall's indignant gaze. It was like a declaration of independence. But the old woman said nothing.

They came down to Sunday tea, with sardines and tinned salmon and tinned peaches, besides tarts and cakes. The chatter was general. It concerned the Nixon family and the scandal.

'Oh, she's a foul-mouthed woman,' said Jinny of Mrs Nixon. 'She may well talk about God's holy house, *she* had. It's first time she's set foot in it, ever since she dropped off from being converted. She's a devil and she always was one. Can't you remember how she treated Bob's children, mother, when we lived down in the Buildings? I can remember when I was a little girl she used to bathe them in the yard, in the cold, so that they shouldn't splash the house. She'd half kill them if they made a mark on the floor, and the language she'd use! And one Saturday I can remember Garry, that was Bob's own girl, she ran off when her stepmother was going to bathe her – ran off without a rag of clothes on – can you remember, mother? And she hid in Smedley's closes – it was the time of mowing-grass – and nobody could find her. She hid out there all night, didn't she, mother? Nobody could find her. My word, there was a talk. They found her on Sunday morning—'

'Fred Coutts threatened to break every bone in the woman's body, if she touched the children again,' put in the father.

'Anyhow, they frightened her,' said Jinny. 'But she was nearly as bad with her own two. And anybody can see that she'd driven old Bob till he's gone soft.'

'Ah, soft as mush,' said Jack Goodall. ''E'd never addle a week's wages, nor yet a day's, if th' chaps didn't make it up to him.'

'My word, if he didn't bring her a week's wage, she'd pull his head off,' said Jinny.

'But a clean woman, and respectable, except for her foul mouth,' said Mr Goodall. 'Keeps to herself like a bulldog. Never lets anybody come near the house, and neighbours with nobody.'

'Wanted it thrashed out of her,' said Mr Goodall, a silent, evasive sort of man.

'Where Bob gets the money for his drink from is a mystery,' said Jinny.

'Chaps treats him,' said Harry.

'Well, he's got the pair of frightenedest rabbit-eyes you'd wish to see,' said Jinny.

'Ay, with a drunken man's murder in them, *I* think,' said Mrs Goodall.

So the talk went on after tea, till it was practically time to start off to the chapel again.

'You'll have to be getting ready, Fanny,' said Mrs Goodall.

'I'm not going tonight,' said Fanny abruptly. And there was a sudden halt in the family. 'I'll stop with *you* tonight, mother,' she added.

'Best you had, my gel,' said Mrs Goodall, flattered and assured.

You Touched Me

THE Pottery House was a square, ugly, brick house girt in by the wall that enclosed the whole grounds of the pottery itself. To be sure, a privet hedge partly masked the house and its ground from the pottery-yard and works: but only partly. Through the hedge could be seen the desolate yard, and the many-windowed, factory-like pottery, over the hedge could be seen the chimneys and the out-houses. But inside the hedge, a pleasant garden and lawn sloped down to a willow pool, which had once supplied the works.

The Pottery itself was now closed, the great doors of the yard permanently shut. No more the great crates with yellow straw showing through stood in stacks by the packing-shed. No more the drays drawn by great horses rolled down the hill with a high load. No more the pottery-lasses in their clay-coloured overalls, their faces and hair splashed with grey fine mud, shrieked and larked with the men. All that was over.

'We like it much better – oh, much better – quieter,' said Matilda Rockley.

'Oh, yes,' assented Emmie Rockley, her sister.

'I'm sure you do,' agreed the visitor.

But whether the two Rockley girls really liked it better, or whether they only imagined they did, is a question. Certainly their lives were much more grey and dreary now that the grey clay had ceased to spatter its mud and silt its dust over the premises. They did not quite realize how they missed the shrieking, shouting lasses, whom they had known all their lives and disliked so much.

Matilda and Emmie were already old maids. In a thorough industrial district, it is not easy for the girls who have expectations above the common to find husbands. The ugly industrial town was full of men, young men who were ready to marry. But they were all colliers or pottery-hands, mere workmen. The Rockley girls would have about ten thousand pounds each when their father died: ten thousand pounds' worth of profitable house-property. It was not to be sneezed at: they felt so themselves, and refrained from sneezing away such a fortune on any mere member of the proletariat. Consequently, bank-clerks or non-conformist clergymen or even school-teachers having failed to come forward, Matilda had begun to give up all idea of ever leaving the Pottery House.

Matilda was a tall, thin, graceful, fair girl, with a rather large nose. She was the Mary to Emmie's Martha: that is, Matilda loved painting and music, and read a good many novels, whilst Emmie looked after the housekeeping. Emmie was shorter, plumper than her sister, and she had no accomplishments. She looked up to Matilda; whose mind was naturally refined and sensible.

In their quiet, melancholy way, the two girls were happy. Their mother was dead. Their father was ill also. He was an intelligent man who had had some education, but preferred to remain as if he were one with the rest of the working people. He had a passion for music and played the violin pretty well. But now he was getting old, he was very ill, dying of a kidney disease. He had been rather a heavy whisky-drinker.

This quiet household, with one servant-maid, lived on year after year in the Pottery House. Friends came in, the girls went out, the father drank himself more and more ill. Outside in the street there was a continual racket of the colliers and their dogs and children. But inside the pottery wall was a deserted quiet.

In all this ointment there was one little fly. Ted Rockley, the father of the girls, had had four daughters, and no son. As his girls grew, he felt angry at finding himself always in a household of women. He went off to London and adopted a boy out of a Charity Institution. Emmie was fourteen years old, and Matilda sixteen, when their father arrived home with his prodigy, the boy of six, Hadrian.

Hadrian was just an ordinary boy from a Charity Home, with ordinary brownish hair and ordinary bluish eyes and of ordinary rather Cockney speech. The Rockley girls – there were three at home at the time of his arrival – had resented his being sprung on them. He, with his watchful, charity-institution instinct, knew this at once. Though he was only six years old, Hadrian had a subtle, jeering look on his face when he regarded the three young women. They insisted he should address them as Cousin: Cousin Flora, Cousin Matilda, Cousin Emmie. He complied, but there seemed a mockery in his tone.

The girls, however, were kind-hearted by nature. Flora married and left home. Hadrian did very much as he pleased with Matilda and Emmie, though they had certain strictnesses. He grew up in the Pottery House and about the Pottery premises, went to an elementary school, and was invariably called Hadrian Rockley. He regarded Cousin Matilda and Cousin Emmie with a certain laconic indifference, was quiet and reticent in his ways. The girls called him sly, but that was unjust. He was merely cautious, and without frankness. His uncle, Ted Rockley, understood him tacitly, their natures were somewhat akin. Hadrian and the elderly man had a real but unemotional regard for one another.

When he was thirteen years old the boy was sent to a High School in the County town. He did not like it. His Cousin Matilda had longed to make a little gentleman of him, but he refused to be made. He would give a little contemptuous curve to his lip, and take on a shy, charity-boy grin, when refinement was thrust upon him. He played truant from the High School, sold his books, his cap with its badge, even his very scarf and pocket-handkerchief, to his school-fellows, and went raking off heaven knows where with the money. So he spent two very unsatisfactory years.

When he was fifteen he announced that he wanted to leave England to go to the Colonies. He had kept touch with the Home. The Rockleys knew that, when Hadrian made a declaration, in his quiet, half-jeering manner, it was worse than useless to oppose him. So at last the boy departed, going to Canada under the protection of the Institution to which he had belonged. He said good-bye to the Rockleys, without a word of thanks, and parted, it seemed, without a pang. Matilda and Emmie wept often to think of how he left them: even on their father's face a queer look came. But Hadrian wrote fairly regularly from Canada. He had entered some electricity works near Montreal, and was doing well.

At last, however, the war came. In his turn, Hadrian joined up and came to Europe. The Rockleys saw nothing of him. They lived on, just the same, in the Pottery House. Ted Rockley was dying of a sort of dropsy, and in his heart he wanted to see the boy. When the Armistice was signed, Hadrian had a long leave, and wrote that he was coming home to the Pottery House.

The girls were terribly fluttered. To tell the truth, they were a little afraid of Hadrian. Matilda, tall and thin, was frail in her health, both girls were worn with nursing their father. To have Hadrian, a young man of twenty-one, in the house with them, after he had left them so coldly five years before, was a trying circumstance.

They were in a flutter. Emmie persuaded her father to have his bed made finally in the morning-room downstairs, whilst his room upstairs was prepared for Hadrian. This was done, and preparations were going on for the arrival, when, at ten o'clock in the morning, the young man suddenly turned up, quite unexpectedly. Cousin Emmie, with her hair bobbed up in absurd little bobs round her forehead, was busily polishing the stair-rods, while Cousin Matilda was in the kitchen washing the drawing-room ornaments in a lather, her sleeves rolled back on her thin arms, and her head tied up oddly and coquettishly in a duster.

Cousin Matilda blushed deep with mortification when the self-possessed young man walked in with his kit-bag, and put his cap on the sewing-machine. He was little and self-confident, with a curious neatness about him that still suggested the Charity Institution. His face was brown, he had a small moustache, he was vigorous enough in his smallness.

'*Well*, is it Hadrian!' exclaimed Cousin Matilda, wringing the lather off her hand. 'We didn't expect you till tomorrow.'

'I got off Monday night,' said Hadrian, glancing round the room.

'Fancy!' said Cousin Matilda. Then, having dried her hands, she went forward, held out her hand, and said:

'How are you?'

'Quite well, thank you,' said Hadrian.

'You're quite a man,' said Cousin Matilda.

Hadrian glanced at her. She did not look her best: so thin, so large-nosed, with that pink-and-white checked duster tied round her head. She felt her disadvantage. But she had had a good deal of suffering and sorrow, she did not mind any more.

The servant entered – one that did not know Hadrian.

'Come and see my father,' said Cousin Matilda.

In the hall they roused Cousin Emmie like a partridge from cover. She was on the stairs pushing the bright stair-rods into place. Instinctively her hand went to the little knobs, her front hair bobbed on her forehead.

'Why!' she exclaimed crossly. 'What have you come today for?'

'I got off a day earlier,' said Hadrian, and his man's voice so deep and unexpected was like a blow to Cousin Emmie.

'Well, you've caught us in the midst of it,' she said, with resentment. Then all three went into the middle room.

Mr Rockley was dressed – that is, he had on his trousers and socks – but he was resting on the bed, propped up just under the window, from whence he could see his beloved and resplendent garden, where tulips and apple trees were ablaze. He did not look as ill as he was, for the water puffed him up, and his face kept its colour. His stomach was much swollen.

He glanced round swiftly, turning his eyes without turning his head. He was the wreck of a handsome, well-built man.

Seeing Hadrian, a queer, unwilling smile went over his face. The young man greeted him sheepishly.

'You wouldn't make a life-guardsman,' he said. 'Do you want something to eat?'

Hadrian looked round – as if for the meal.

'I don't mind,' he said.

'What shall you have – egg and bacon?' asked Emmie shortly.

'Yes, I don't mind,' said Hadrian.

The sisters went down to the kitchen, and sent the servant to finish the stairs.

'Isn't he *altered*?' said Matilda, *sotto voce*.

'Isn't he!' said Cousin Emmie. '*What* a little man!'

They both made a grimace, and laughed nervously.

'Get the frying-pan,' said Emmie to Matilda.

'But he's as cocky as ever,' said Matilda, narrowing her eyes and shaking her head knowingly, as she handed the frying-pan.

'Mannie!' said Emmie sarcastically. Hadrian's new-fledged, cocksure manliness evidently found no favour in her eyes.

'Oh, he's not bad,' said Matilda. 'You don't want to be prejudiced against him.'

'I'm not prejudiced against him, I think he's all right for looks,' said Emmie, 'but there's too much of the little mannie about him.'

'Fancy catching us like this,' said Matilda.

'They've no thought for anything,' said Emmie with contempt. 'You go up and get dressed, our Matilda. I don't care about him. I can see to things, and you can talk to him. I shan't.'

'He'll talk to my father,' said Matilda, meaningful.

'*Sly*—!' exclaimed Emmie, with a grimace.

The sisters believed that Hadrian had been hoping to get something out of their father – hoping for a legacy. And they were not at all sure he would not get it.

Matilda went upstairs to change. She had thought it all out how she would receive Hadrian, and impress him. And he had caught her with her head tied up in a duster, and her thin arms in a basin of lather. But she did not care. She now dressed herself most scrupulously, carefully folded her long, beautiful, blonde hair, touched her pallor with a little rouge, and put her long string of exquisite crystal beads over her soft green dress. Now she looked elegant, like a heroine in a magazine illustration, and almost as unreal.

She found Hadrian and her father talking away. The young man was short of speech as a rule, but he could find his tongue with his 'uncle'. They were both sipping a glass of brandy, and smoking, and chatting like a pair of old cronies. Hadrian was telling about Canada. He was going back there when his leave was up.

'You wouldn't like to stop in England, then?' said Mr Rockley.

'No, I wouldn't stop in England,' said Hadrian.

'How's that? There's plenty of electricians here,' said Mr Rockley.

'Yes. But there's too much difference between the men and the employers over here – too much of that for me,' said Hadrian.

The sick man looked at him narrowly, with oddly smiling eyes.

'That's it, is it?' he replied.

Matilda heard and understood. 'So that's your big idea, is it, my little man,' she said to herself. She had always said of Hadrian that he had no proper *respect* for anybody or anything, that he was sly and *common*. She went down to the kitchen for a *sotto voce* confab with Emmie.

'He thinks a rare lot of himself!' she whispered.

'He's somebody, he is!' said Emmie with contempt.

'He thinks there's too much difference between masters and men over here,' said Matilda.

'Is it any different in Canada?' asked Emmie.

'Oh yes – democratic,' replied Matilda. 'He thinks they're all on a level over there.'

'Ay, well, he's over here now,' said Emmie dryly, 'so he can keep his place.'

As they talked they saw the young man sauntering down the garden, looking casually at the flowers. He had his hands in his pockets, and his soldier's cap neatly on his head. He looked quite at his ease, as if in possession. The two women, fluttered, watched him through the window.

'We know what he's come for,' said Emmie, churlishly. Matilda looked a long time at the neat khaki figure. It had something of the charity-box about it still; but now it was a man's figure, laconic, charged with plebeian energy. She thought of the derisive passion in his voice as he had declaimed against the propertied classes, to her father.

'You don't know, Emmie. Perhaps he's not come for that,' she rebuked her sister. They were both thinking of the money.

They were still watching the young soldier. He stood away at the bottom of the garden, with his back to them, his hands in his pockets, looking into the water of the willow pond. Matilda's dark blue eyes had a strange, full look in them, the lids, with the faint blue veins showing, dropped rather low. She carried her head light and high, but she had a look of pain. The young man at the bottom of the garden turned and looked up the path. Perhaps he saw them through the window. Matilda moved into shadow.

That afternoon their father seemed weak and ill. He was easily exhausted. The doctor came, and told Matilda that the sick man might die suddenly at any moment – but then he might not. They must be prepared.

So the day passed, and the next. Hadrian made himself at home. He went about in the morning in his brownish jersey and his khaki trousers, collarless, his bare neck showing. He explored the pottery premises, as if he had some secret purpose in so doing, he talked with Mr Rockley, when the sick man had strength. The two girls were always angry when the two men sat talking together like cronies. Yet it was chiefly a kind of politics they talked.

On the second day after Hadrian's arrival, Matilda sat with her father in the evening. She was drawing a picture which she wanted to copy. It was very still, Hadrian was gone out somewhere, no one knew where, and Emmie was busy. Mr Rockley reclined on his bed, looking out in silence over his evening-sunny garden.

'If anything happens to me, Matilda,' he said, 'you won't sell this house – you'll stop here—'

Matilda's eyes took their slightly haggard look as she stared at her father.

'Well, we couldn't do anything else,' she said.

'You don't know what you might do,' he said. 'Everything is left to you and Emmie, equally. You do as you like with it – only don't sell this house, don't part with it.'

'No,' she said.

'And give Hadrian my watch and chain, and a hundred pounds out of what's in the bank – and help him if he ever wants helping. I haven't put his name in the will.'

'Your watch and chain, and a hundred pounds – yes. But you'll be here when he goes back to Canada, father.'

'You never know what'll happen,' said her father.

Matilda sat and watched him, with her full, haggard eyes, for a long time, as if tranced. She saw that he knew he must go soon – she saw like a clairvoyant.

Later on she told Emmie what her father had said about the watch and chain and the money.

'What right has *he*' – *he* – meaning Hadrian – 'to my father's watch and chain – what has it to do with him? Let him have the money, and get off,' said Emmie. She loved her father.

That night Matilda sat late in her room. Her heart was anxious and breaking, her mind seemed entranced. She was too much entranced even to weep, and all the time she thought of her father, only her father. At last she felt she must go to him.

It was near midnight. She went along the passage and to his room. There was a faint light from the moon outside. She listened at his door. Then she softly opened and entered. The room was faintly dark. She heard a movement on the bed.

'Are you asleep?' she said softly, advancing to the side of the bed.

'Are you asleep?' she repeated gently, as she stood at the side of the bed. And she reached her hand in the darkness to touch his forehead. Delicately, her fingers met the nose and the eye-brows, she laid her fine, delicate hand on his brow. It seemed fresh and smooth – very fresh and smooth. A sort of surprise stirred her, in her entranced state. But it could not waken her. Gently, she leaned over the bed and stirred her fingers over the low-growing hair on his brow.

'Can't you sleep tonight?' she said.

There was a quick stirring in the bed. 'Yes, I can,' a voice answered. It was Hadrian's voice. She started away. Instantly she was wakened from her late-at-night trance. She remembered that her father was downstairs, that Hadrian had his room. She stood in the darkness as if stung.

'Is it you, Hadrian?' she said. 'I thought it was my father.' She was so startled, so shocked, that she could not move. The young man gave an uncomfortable laugh, and turned in his bed.

At last she got out of the room. When she was back in her own room, in the light, and her door was closed, she stood holding up her hand that had touched him, as if it were hurt. She was almost too shocked, she could not endure.

'Well,' said her calm and weary mind, 'it was only a mistake, why take any notice of it.'

But she could not reason her feelings so easily. She suffered, feeling herself in a false position. Her right hand, which she had laid so gently on his face, on his fresh skin, ached now, as if it were really injured. She could not forgive Hadrian for the mistake. It made her dislike him deeply.

Hadrian too slept badly. He had been awakened by the opening of the door, and had not realized what the question meant. But the soft, straying tenderness of her hand on his face startled something out of his soul. He was a charity boy, aloof and more or less at bay. The fragile exquisiteness of her caress startled him most, revealed unknown things to him.

In the morning she could feel the consciousness in his eyes, when she came downstairs. She tried to bear herself as if nothing at all had happened, and she succeeded. She had the calm self-control, self-indifference, of one who has suffered and borne her suffering. She looked at him from her darkish, almost drugged blue eyes, she met the spark of consciousness in his eyes, and quenched it. And with her long, fine hand she put the sugar in his coffee.

But she could not control him as she thought she could. He had a keen memory stinging his mind, a new set of sensations working in his consciousness. Something new was alert in him. At the back of his reticent, guarded mind he kept his secret alive and vivid. She was at his mercy, for he was unscrupulous, his standard was not her standard.

He looked at her curiously. She was not beautiful, her nose was too large, her chin was too small, her neck was too thin. But her skin was clear and fine, she had a high-bred sensitiveness. This queer, brave, high-bred quality she shared with her father. The charity boy could see it in her tapering fingers, which were white and ringed. The same glamour that he knew in the elderly man he now saw in the woman. And he wanted to possess himself of it, he wanted to make himself master of it. As he went about through the old pottery-yard, his secretive mind schemed and worked. To be master of that strange soft delicacy such as he had felt in her hand upon his face – this was what he set himself towards. He was secretly plotting.

He watched Matilda as she went about, and she became aware of his attention, as of some shadow following her. But her pride made her ignore it. When he sauntered near her, his hands in his pockets, she received him with that same commonplace kindliness which mastered him more than any contempt. Her superior breeding seemed to control him. She made herself feel towards him exactly as she had always felt: he was a young boy who lived in the house with them, but was a stranger. Only, she dared not remember his face under her hand. When she remembered that, she was bewildered. Her hand had offended her, she wanted to cut it off. And she wanted, fiercely, to cut off the memory in him. She assumed she had done so.

One day, when he sat talking with his 'uncle', he looked straight into the eyes of the sick man, and said:

'But I shouldn't like to live and die here in Rawsley.'

'No – well – you needn't,' said the sick man.

'Do you think Cousin Matilda likes it?'

'I should think so.'

'I don't call it much of a life,' said the youth. 'How much older is she than me, Uncle?'

The sick man looked at the young soldier.

'A good bit,' he said.

'Over thirty?' said Hadrian.

'Well, not so much. She's thirty-two.'

Hadrian considered a while.

'She doesn't look it,' he said.

Again the sick father looked at him.

'Do you think she'd like to leave here?' said Hadrian.

'Nay, I don't know,' replied the father, restive.

Hadrian sat still, having his own thoughts. Then in a small, quiet voice, as if he were speaking from inside himself, he said:

'I'd marry her if you wanted me to.'

The sick man raised his eyes suddenly and stared. He stared for a long time. The youth looked inscrutably out of the window.

'*You!*' said the sick man, mocking, with some contempt. Hadrian turned and met his eyes. The two men had an inexplicable understanding.

'If you wasn't against it,' said Hadrian.

'Nay,' said the father, turning aside, 'I don't think I'm against it. I've never thought of it. But – but Emmie's the youngest.'

He had flushed and looked suddenly more alive. Secretly he loved the boy.

'You might ask her,' said Hadrian.

The elder man considered.

'Hadn't you better ask her yourself?' he said.

'She'd take more notice of you,' said Hadrian.

They were both silent. Then Emmie came in.

For two days Mr Rockley was excited and thoughtful. Hadrian went about quietly, secretly, unquestioning. At last the father and daughter were alone together. It was very early morning, the father had been in much pain. As the pain abated, he lay still thinking.

'Matilda!' he said suddenly, looking at his daughter.

'Yes, I'm here,' she said.

'Ay! I want you to do something—'

She rose in anticipation.

'Nay, sit still. I want you to marry Hadrian—'

She thought he was raving. She rose, bewildered and frightened.

'Nay, sit you still, sit you still. You hear what I tell you.'

'But you don't know what you're saying, father.'

'Ay, I know well enough. I want you to marry Hadrian, I tell you.'

She was dumbfounded. He was a man of few words.

'You'll do what I tell you,' he said.

She looked at him slowly.

'What put such an idea in your mind?' she said proudly.

'He did.'

Matilda almost looked her father down, her pride was so offended.

'Why, it's disgraceful,' she said.

'Why?'

She watched him slowly.

'What do you ask me for?' she said. 'It's disgusting.'

'The lad's sound enough,' he replied testily.

'You'd better tell him to clear out,' she said coldly.

He turned and looked out of the window. She sat flushed and erect for a long time. At length her father turned to her, looking really malevolent.

'If you won't,' he said, 'you're a fool, and I'll make you pay for your foolishness, do you see?'

Suddenly a cold fear gripped her. She could not believe her senses. She was terrified and bewildered. She stared at her father, believing him to be delirious, or mad, or drunk. What could she do?

'I tell you,' he said. 'I'll send for Whittle tomorrow if you don't. You shall neither of you have anything of mine.'

Whittle was the solicitor. She understood her father well

enough: he would send for his solicitor, and make a will leaving all his property to Hadrian: neither she nor Emmie should have anything. It was too much. She rose and went out of the room, up to her own room, where she locked herself in.

She did not come out for some hours. At last, late at night, she confided in Emmie.

'The sliving demon, he wants the money,' said Emmie. 'My father's out of his mind.'

The thought that Hadrian merely wanted the money was another blow to Matilda. She did not love the impossible youth – but she had not yet learned to think of him as a thing of evil. He now became hideous to her mind.

Emmie had a little scene with her father next day.

'You don't mean what you said to our Matilda yesterday, do you, father?' she asked aggressively.

'Yes,' he replied.

'What, that you'll alter your will?'

'Yes.'

'You won't,' said his angry daughter.

But he looked at her with a malevolent little smile.

'Annie!' he shouted. 'Annie!'

He had still power to make his voice carry. The servant-maid came in from the kitchen.

'Put your things on, and go down to Whittle's office, and say I want to see Mr Whittle as soon as he can, and will he bring a will-form.'

The sick man lay back a little – he could not lie down. His daughter sat as if she had been struck. Then she left the room.

Hadrian was pottering about in the garden. She went straight down to him.

'Here,' she said. 'You'd better get off. You'd better take your things and go from here, quick.'

Hadrian looked slowly at the infuriated girl.

'Who says so?' he asked.

'We say so – get off, you've done enough mischief and damage.'

'Does Uncle say so?'

'Yes, he does.'

'I'll go and ask him.'

But like a fury Emmie barred his way.

'No, you needn't. You needn't ask him nothing at all. We don't want you, so you can go.'

'Uncle's boss here.'

'A man that's dying, and you crawling round and working on him for his money! – you're not fit to live.'

'Oh!' he said. 'Who says I'm working for his money?'

'I say. But my father told our Matilda, and she knows what you are. She knows what you're after. So you might as well clear out, for all you'll get – guttersnipe!'

He turned his back on her, to think. It had not occurred to him that they would think he was after the money. He did want the money – badly. He badly wanted to be an employer himself, not one of the employed. But he knew, in his subtle, calculating way, that it was not for money he wanted Matilda. He wanted both the money and Matilda. But he told himself the two desires were separate, not one. He could not do with Matilda, without the money. But he did not want her for the money.

When he got this clear in his mind, he sought for an opportunity to tell it her, lurking and watching. But she avoided him. In the evening, the lawyer came. Mr Rockley seemed to have a new access of strength – a will was drawn up, making the previous arrangements wholly conditional. The old will held good, if Matilda would consent to marry Hadrian. If she refused then at the end of six months the whole property passed to Hadrian.

Mr Rockley told this to the young man, with malevolent satisfaction. He seemed to have a strange desire, quite unreason-

able, for revenge upon the women who had surrounded him for
so long, and served him so carefully.

'Tell her in front of me,' said Hadrian.

So Mr Rockley sent for his daughters.

At last they came, pale, mute, stubborn. Matilda seemed to
have retired far off, Emmie seemed like a fighter ready to fight
to the death. The sick man reclined on the bed, his eyes bright,
his puffed hand trembling. But his face had again some of its
old, bright handsomeness. Hadrian sat quiet, a little aside: the
indomitable, dangerous charity boy.

'There's the will,' said their father, pointing them to the
paper.

The two women sat mute and immovable, they took no
notice.

'Either you marry Hadrian, or he has everything,' said the
father with satisfaction.

'Then let him have everything,' said Matilda coldly.

'He's not! He's not!' cried Emmie fiercely. 'He's not going to
have it. The guttersnipe!'

An amused look came on her father's face.

'You hear that, Hadrian,' he said.

'I didn't offer to marry Cousin Matilda for the money,' said
Hadrian, flushing and moving on his seat.

Matilda looked at him slowly, with her dark blue, drugged
eyes. He seemed a strange little monster to her.

'Why, you liar, you know you did,' cried Emmie.

The sick man laughed. Matilda continued to gaze strangely at
the young man.

'She knows I didn't,' said Hadrian.

He too had his courage, as a rat has indomitable courage in
the end. Hadrian had some of the neatness, the reserve, the
underground quality of the rat. But he had perhaps the ultimate
courage, the most unquenched courage of all.

Emmie looked at her sister.

'Oh, well,' she said. 'Matilda – don't you bother. Let him have everything, we can look after ourselves.'

'I know he'll take everything,' said Matilda, abstractedly.

Hadrian did not answer. He knew in fact that if Matilda refused him he would take everything, and go off with it.

'A clever little mannie—!' said Emmie, with a jeering grimace. The father laughed noiselessly to himself. But he was tired. . . .

'Go on, then,' he said. 'Go on, let me be quiet.'

Emmie turned and looked at him.

'You deserve what you've got,' she said to her father bluntly.

'Go on,' he answered mildly. 'Go on.'

Another night passed – a night nurse sat up with Mr Rockley. Another day came. Hadrian was there as ever, in his woollen jersey and coarse khaki trousers and bare neck. Matilda went about, frail and distant, Emmie black-browed in spite of her blondness. They were all quiet, for they did not intend the mystified servant to learn anything.

Mr Rockley had very bad attacks of pain, he could not breathe. The end seemed near. They all went about quiet and stoical, all unyielding. Hadrian pondered within himself. If he did not marry Matilda he could go to Canada with twenty thousand pounds. This was itself a very satisfactory prospect. If Matilda consented he would have nothing – she would have her own money.

Emmie was the one to act. She went off in search of the solicitor and brought him home with her. There was an interview, and Whittle tried to frighten the youth into withdrawal – but without avail. The clergyman and relatives were summoned – but Hadrian stared at them and took no notice. It made him angry, however.

He wanted to catch Matilda alone. Many days went by, and he was not successful: she avoided him. At last, lurking, he surprised her one day as she came to pick gooseberries, and he cut off her retreat. He came to the point at once.

'You don't want me, then?' he said, in his subtle, insinuating voice.

'I don't want to speak to you,' she said, averting her face.

'You put your hand on me, though,' he said. 'You shouldn't have done that, and then I should never have thought of it. You shouldn't have touched me.'

'If you were anything decent, you'd know that was a mistake, and forget it,' she said.

'I know it was a mistake – but I shan't forget it. If you wake a man up, he can't go to sleep again because he's told to.'

'If you had any decent feeling in you, you'd have gone away,' she replied.

'I didn't want to,' he replied.

She looked away into the distance. At last she asked:

'What do you persecute me for, if it isn't for the money? I'm old enough to be your mother. In a way I've been your mother.'

'Doesn't matter,' he said. 'You've been no mother to me. Let us marry and go out to Canada – you might as well – you've touched me.'

She was white and trembling. Suddenly she flushed with anger.

'It's so *indecent*,' she said.

'How?' he retorted. 'You touched me.'

But she walked away from him. She felt as if he had trapped her. He was angry and depressed, he felt again despised.

That same evening she went into her father's room.

'Yes,' she said suddenly. 'I'll marry him.'

Her father looked up at her. He was in pain, and very ill.

'You like him now, do you?' he said, with a faint smile.

She looked down into his face, and saw death not far off. She turned and went coldly out of the room.

The solicitor was sent for, preparations were hastily made. In all the interval Matilda did not speak to Hadrian, never answered him if he addressed her. He approached her in the morning.

'You've come round to it, then?' he said, giving her a pleasant look from his twinkling, almost kindly eyes. She looked down at him and turned aside. She looked down on him both literally and figuratively. Still he persisted, and triumphed.

Emmie raved and wept, the secret flew abroad. But Matilda was silent and unmoved, Hadrian was quiet and satisfied, and nipped with fear also. But he held out against his fear. Mr Rockley was very ill, but unchanged.

On the third day the marriage took place. Matilda and Hadrian drove straight home from the registrar, and went straight into the room of the dying man. His face lit up with a clear twinkling smile.

'Hadrian – you've got her?' he said, a little hoarsely.

'Yes,' said Hadrian, who was pale round the gills.

'Ay, my lad, I'm glad you're mine,' replied the dying man. Then he turned his eyes closely on Matilda.

'Let's look at you, Matilda,' he said. Then his voice went strange and unrecognizable. 'Kiss me,' he said.

She stooped and kissed him. She had never kissed him before, not since she was a tiny child. But she was quiet, very still.

'Kiss him,' the dying man said.

Obediently, Matilda put forward her mouth and kissed the young husband.

'That's right! That's right!' murmured the dying man.

The Man who loved Islands

I

THERE was a man who loved islands. He was born on one, but it didn't suit him, as there were too many other people on it, besides himself. He wanted an island all of his own: not necessarily to be alone on it, but to make it a world of his own.

An island, if it is big enough, is no better than a continent. It has to be really quite small, before it *feels* like an island; and this story will show how tiny it has to be, before you can presume to fill it with your own personality.

Now circumstances so worked out that this lover of islands, by the time he was thirty-five, actually acquired an island of his own. He didn't own it as freehold property, but he had a ninety-nine years' lease of it, which, as far as a man and an island are concerned, is as good as everlasting. Since, if you are like Abraham, and want your offspring to be numberless as the sands of the sea-shore, you don't choose an island to start breeding on. Too soon there would be over-population, over-crowding, and slum conditions. Which is a horrid thought, for one who loves an island for its insulation. No, an island is a nest which holds one egg, and one only. This egg is the islander himself.

The island acquired by our potential islander was not in the remote oceans. It was quite near at home, no palm trees nor boom of surf on the reef, nor any of that kind of thing; but a good solid dwelling house, rather gloomy, above the landing-place, and beyond, a small farmhouse with sheds, and a few out-lying fields. Down on the little landing-bay were three cottages in a row, like coastguards' cottages, all neat and whitewashed.

What could be more cosy and home-like? It was four miles if you walked all round your island, through the gorse and the blackthorn bushes, above the steep rocks of the sea and down in the little glades where the primroses grew. If you walked straight over the two humps of hills, the length of it, through the rocky fields where the cows lay chewing, and through the rather sparse oats, on into the gorse again, and so to the low cliffs' edge, it took you only twenty minutes. And when you came to the edge, you could see another, bigger island lying beyond. But the sea was between you and it. And as you returned over the turf where the short, downland cowslips nodded, you saw to the east still another island, a tiny one this time, like the calf of the cow. This tiny island also belonged to the islander.

Thus it seems that even islands like to keep each other company.

Our islander loved his island very much. In early spring, the little ways and glades were a snow of blackthorn, a vivid white among the Celtic stillness of close green and grey rock, black-birds calling out in the whiteness their first long, triumphant calls. After the blackthorn and the nestling primroses came the blue apparition of hyacinths, like elfin lakes and slipping sheets of blue, among the bushes and under the glade of trees. And many birds with nests you could peep into, on the island all your own. Wonderful what a great world it was!

Followed summer, and the cowslips gone, the wild roses faintly fragrant through the haze. There was a field of hay, the foxgloves stood looking down. In a little cove, the sun was on the pale granite where you bathed, and the shadow was in the rocks. Before the mist came stealing, you went home through the ripening oats, the glare of the sea fading from the high air as the fog-horn started to moo on the other island. And then the sea-fog went, it was autumn, the oat-sheaves lying prone, the great moon, another island, rose golden out of the sea, and rising higher, the world of the sea was white.

So autumn ended with rain, and winter came, dark skies and dampness and rain, but rarely frost. The island, your island, cowered dark, holding away from you. You could feel, down in the wet, sombre hollows, the resentful spirit coiled upon itself, like a wet dog coiled in gloom, or a snake that is neither asleep nor awake. Then in the night, when the wind left off blowing in great gusts and volleys, as at sea, you felt that your island was a universe, infinite and old as the darkness; not an island at all, but an infinite dark world where all the souls from all the other bygone nights lived on, and the infinite distance was near.

Strangely, from your little island in space, you were gone forth into the dark, great realms of time, where all the souls that never die veer and swoop on their vast, strange errands. The little earthly island has dwindled, like a jumping-off place, into nothingness, for you have jumped off, you know not how, into the dark wide mystery of time, where the past is vastly alive, and the future is not separated off.

This is the danger of becoming an islander. When, in the city, you wear your white spats and dodge the traffic with the fear of death down your spine, then you are quite safe from the terrors of infinite time. The moment is your little islet in time, it is the spatial universe that careers round you.

But once isolate yourself on a little island in the sea of space, and the moment begins to heave and expand in great circles, the solid earth is gone, and your slippery, naked dark soul finds herself out in the timeless world, where the chariots of the so-called dead dash down the old streets of centuries, and souls crowd on the footways that we, in the moment, call bygone years. The souls of all the dead are alive again, and pulsating actively around you. You are out in the other infinity.

Something of this happened to our islander. Mysterious 'feelings' came upon him that he wasn't used to; strange awarenesses of old, far-gone men, and other influences; men of Gaul, with big moustaches, who had been on his island, and had vanished from the face of it, but not out of the air of night. They were there still, hurtling their big, violent, unseen bodies through the night. And there were priests with a crucifix; then pirates with murder on the sea.

Our islander was uneasy. He didn't believe, in the day-time, in any of this nonsense. But at night it just was so. He had reduced himself to a single point in space, and, a point being that which has neither length nor breadth, he had to step off it into somewhere else. Just as you must step into the sea, if the waters wash your foothold away, so he had, at night, to step off into the other worlds of undying time.

He was uncannily aware, as he lay in the dark, that the black-thorn grove that seemed a bit uncanny even in the realm of space and day, at night was crying with old men of an invisible race, around the altar stone. What was a ruin under the horn-beam trees by day, was a moaning of blood-stained priests with crucifixes, on the ineffable night. What was a cave and a hidden beach between coarse rocks, became in the invisible dark the purple-lipped imprecation of pirates.

To escape any more of this sort of awareness, our islander daily concentrated upon his material island. Why should it not be the Happy Isle at last? Why not the last small isle of the Hesperides, the perfect place, all filled with his own gracious, blossom-like spirit? A minute world of pure perfection, made by man himself.

He began, as we begin all our attempts to regain Paradise, by spending money. The old, semi-feudal dwelling-house he restored, let in more light, put clear lovely carpets on the floor, clear, flower-petal curtains at the sullen windows, and wines in the cellars of rock. He brought over a buxom housekeeper from the world, and a soft-spoken, much-experienced butler. These two were to be islanders.

In the farmhouse he put a bailiff, with two farm-hands. There were Jersey cows tinkling a slow bell, among the gorse. There was a call to meals at midday, and the peaceful smoking of chimneys at evening, when rest descended.

A jaunty sailing-boat with a motor accessory rode in the shelter of the bay, just below the row of three white cottages. There was also a little yawl, and two row-boats drawn up on the sand. A fishing-net was drying on its supports, a boat-load of new white planks stood criss-cross, a woman was going to the well with a bucket.

In the end cottage lived the skipper of the yacht, and his wife and son. He was a man from the other, large island, at home on this sea. Every fine day he went out fishing, with his son, every fair day there was fresh fish in the island.

In the middle cottage lived an old man and wife, a very faithful couple. The old man was a carpenter, and man of many jobs. He was always working, always the sound of his plane or his saw; lost in his work, he was another kind of islander.

In the third cottage was a mason, a widower with a son and two daughters. With the help of his boy, this man dug ditches and built fences, raised buttresses and erected a new outbuilding, and hewed stone from the little quarry. One daughter worked at the big house.

It was a quiet, busy little world. When the islander brought you over as his guest, you met first the dark-bearded, thin, smiling skipper, Arnold, then his boy Charles. At the house, the smooth-lipped butler who had lived all over the world valeted you, and created that curious creamy-smooth, disarming sense of luxury around you which only a perfect and rather untrustworthy servant can create. He disarmed you and had you at his mercy. The buxom housekeeper smiled and treated you with the subtly respectful familiarity that is only dealt out to the true gentry. And the rosy maid threw a glance at you, as if you were very wonderful, coming from the great outer world. Then you met the smiling but watchful bailiff, who came from Cornwall, and the shy farm-hand from Berkshire, with his clean wife and two little children: then the rather sulky farm-hand from Suffolk. The mason, a Kent man, would talk to you by the yard if you let him. Only the old carpenter was gruff and elsewhere absorbed.

Well then, it was a little world to itself, and everybody feeling very safe, and being very nice to you, as if you were really something special. But it was the islander's world, not yours. He was the Master. The special smile, the special attention was to the Master. They all knew how well off they were. So the islander was no longer Mr So-and-so. To everyone on the island, even to you yourself, he was 'the Master'.

Well, it was ideal. The Master was no tyrant. Ah, no! He was a delicate, sensitive, handsome Master, who wanted everything perfect and everybody happy. Himself, of course, to be the fount of this happiness and perfection.

But in his way, he was a poet. He treated his guests royally, his servants liberally. Yet he was shrewd, and very wise. He never came the boss over his people. Yet he kept his eye on everything, like a shrewd, blue-eyed young Hermes. And it was amazing what a lot of knowledge he had at hand. Amazing what he knew about Jersey cows, and cheese-making, ditching and fencing, flowers and gardening, ships and the sailing of ships. He was a fount of knowledge about everything, and this knowledge he imparted to his people in an odd, half-ironical, half-portentous fashion, as if he really belonged to the quaint, half-real world of the gods.

They listened to him with their hats in their hands. He loved white clothes; or creamy white; and cloaks, and broad hats. So, in fine weather, the bailiff would see the elegant tall figure in creamy-white serge coming like some bird over the fallow, to look at the weeding of the turnips. Then there would be a doffing of hats, and a few minutes of whimsical, shrewd, wise talk, to which the bailiff answered admiringly, and the farm-hands listened in silent wonder, leaning on their hoes. The bailiff was almost tender, to the Master.

Or, on a windy morning, he would stand with his cloak blowing in the sticky sea-wind, on the edge of the ditch that was being dug to drain a little swamp, talking in the teeth of the wind to the man below, who looked up at him with steady and inscrutable eyes.

Or at evening in the rain he would be seen hurrying across the yard, the broad hat turned against the rain. And the farm-wife would hurriedly exclaim: 'The Master! Get up, John, and clear him a space on the sofa.' And then the door opened, and it was a cry of: 'Why, of all things, if it isn't the Master! Why, have ye turned out then, of a night like this, to come across to the like of we?' And the bailiff took his cloak, and the farm-wife his hat, the two farm-hands drew their chairs to the back, he sat on the sofa and took a child up near him. He was wonderful with children, talked to them simply wonderful, made you think of Our Saviour Himself, said the woman.

He was always greeted with smiles, and the same peculiar deference, as if he were a higher, but also frailer being. They handled him almost tenderly, and almost with adulation. But when he left, or when they spoke of him, they had often a subtle, mocking smile on their faces. There was no need to be afraid of 'the Master'. Just let him have his own way. Only the old carpenter was sometimes sincerely rude to him; so he didn't care for the old man.

It is doubtful whether any of them really liked him, man to man, or even woman to man. But then it is doubtful if he really liked any of them, as man to man, or man to woman. He wanted them to be happy, and the little world to be perfect. But anyone who wants the world to be perfect must be careful not to have real likes or dislikes. A general goodwill is all you can afford.

The sad fact is, alas, that general goodwill is always felt as something of an insult, by the mere object of it; and so it breeds a quite special brand of malice. Surely general goodwill is a form of egoism, that it should have such a result!

Our islander, however, had his own resources. He spent long hours in his library, for he was compiling a book of references to all the flowers mentioned in the Greek and Latin authors. He was not a great classical scholar; the usual public-school equipment. But there are such excellent translations nowadays. And it was so lovely, tracing flower after flower as it blossomed in the ancient world.

So the first year on the island passed by. A great deal had been done. Now the bills flooded in, and the Master, conscientious in all things, began to study them. The study left him pale and breathless. He was not a rich man. He knew he had been making a hole in his capital to get the island into running order. When he came to look, however, there was hardly anything left but hole. Thousands and thousands of pounds had the island swallowed into nothingness.

But surely the bulk of the spending was over! Surely the island would now begin to be self-supporting, even if it made no profit! Surely he was safe. He paid a good many of the bills, and took a little heart. But he had had a shock, and the next year, the coming year, there must be economy, frugality. He told his people so in simple and touching language. And they said: 'Why, surely! Surely!'

So, while the wind blew and the rain lashed outside, he would sit in his library with the bailiff over a pipe and pot of beer, discussing farm projects. He lifted his narrow, handsome face, and his blue eyes became dreamy. '*What* a wind!' It blew like cannon-shots. He thought of his island, lashed with foam, and inaccessible, and he exulted. . . . No, he must not lose it. He turned back to the farm projects with the zest of genius, and his hands flicked white emphasis, while the bailiff intoned: 'Yes, sir! Yes, sir! You're right, Master!'

But the man was hardly listening. He was looking at the Master's blue lawn shirt and curious pink tie with the fiery red stone, at the enamel sleeve-links, and at the ring with the peculiar scarab. The brown searching eyes of the man of the soil glanced repeatedly over the fine, immaculate figure of the Master, with a sort of slow, calculating wonder. But if he happened to catch the Master's bright, exalted glance, his own eye lit up with a careful cordiality and deference, as he bowed his head slightly.

Thus between them they decided what crops should be sown, what fertilizers should be used in different places, which breed of pigs should be imported, and which line of turkeys. That is to say, the bailiff, by continually cautiously agreeing with the Master, kept out of it, and let the young man have his own way.

The Master knew what he was talking about. He was brilliant at grasping the gist of a book, and knowing how to apply his knowledge. On the whole, his ideas were sound. The bailiff even knew it. But in the man of the soil there was no answering enthusiasm. The brown eyes smiled their cordial deference, but the thin lips never changed. The Master pursed his own flexible mouth in a boyish versatility, as he cleverly sketched in his ideas to the other man, and the bailiff made eyes of admiration, but in his heart he was not attending, he was only watching the Master as he would have watched a queer, caged animal, quite without sympathy, not implicated.

So, it was settled, and the Master rang for Elvery, the butler, to bring a sandwich. He, the Master, was pleased. The butler saw it, and came back with anchovy and ham sandwiches, and a newly opened bottle of vermouth. There was always a newly opened bottle of something.

It was the same with the mason. The Master and he discussed the drainage of a bit of land, and more pipes were ordered, more special bricks, more this, more that.

Fine weather came at last; there was a little lull in the hard work on the island. The Master went for a short cruise in his yacht. It was not really a yacht, just a little bit of a thing. They sailed along the coast of the mainland, and put in at the ports. At every port some friend turned up, the butler made elegant little meals in the cabin. Then the Master was invited to villas and hotels, his people disembarked him as if he were a prince.

And oh, how expensive it turned out! He had to telegraph to the bank for money. And he went home again to economize.

The marsh-marigolds were blazing in the little swamp where the ditches were being dug for drainage. He almost regretted, now, the work in hand. The yellow beauties would not blaze again.

Harvest came, and a bumper crop. There must be a harvest-home supper. The long barn was now completely restored and added to. The carpenter had made long tables. Lanterns hung from the beams of the high-pitched roof. All the people of the island were assembled. The bailiff presided. It was a gay scene.

Towards the end of the supper the Master, in a velvet jacket, appeared with his guests. Then the bailiff rose and proposed 'The Master! Long life and health to the Master!' All the people drank the health with great enthusiasm and cheering. The Master replied with a little speech: They were on an island in a little world of their own. It depended on them all to make this world a world of true happiness and content. Each must do his part. He hoped he himself did what he could, for his heart was in his island, and with the people of his island.

The butler responded: As long as the island had such a Master, it could not help but be a little heaven for all the people on it. This was seconded with virile warmth by the bailiff and the mason, the skipper was beside himself. Then there was dancing, the old carpenter was fiddler.

But under all this, things were not well. The very next morning came the farm-boy to say that a cow had fallen over the cliff. The Master went to look. He peered over the not very high declivity, and saw her lying dead on a green ledge under a bit of late-flowering broom. A beautiful, expensive creature, already looking swollen. But what a fool, to fall so unnecessarily!

It was a question of getting several men to haul her up the bank, and then of skinning and burying her. No one would eat the meat. How repulsive it all was!

This was symbolic of the island. As sure as the spirits rose in the human breast, with a movement of joy, an invisible hand struck malevolently out of the silence. There must not be any joy, nor even any quiet peace. A man broke a leg, another was crippled with rheumatic fever. The pigs had some strange disease. A storm drove the yacht on a rock. The mason hated the butler, and refused to let his daughter serve at the house.

Out of the very air came a stony, heavy malevolence. The island itself seemed malicious. It would go on being hurtful and evil for weeks at a time. Then suddenly again one morning it would be fair, lovely as a morning in Paradise, everything beautiful and flowing. And everybody would begin to feel a great relief, and a hope for happiness.

Then as soon as the Master was opened out in spirit like an open flower, some ugly blow would fall. Somebody would send him an anonymous note, accusing some other person on the island. Somebody else would come hinting things against one of his servants.

'Some folks think they've got an easy job out here, with all the pickings they make!' the mason's daughter screamed at the suave butler, in the Master's hearing. He pretended not to hear.

'My man says this island is surely one of the lean kine of Egypt, it would swallow a sight of money, and you'd never get anything back out of it,' confided the farm-hand's wife to one of the Master's visitors.

The people were not contented. They were not islanders. 'We feel we're not doing right by the children,' said those who had children. 'We feel we're not doing right by ourselves,' said those who had no children. And the various families fairly came to hate one another.

Yet the island was so lovely. When there was a scent of honey-suckle and the moon brightly flickering down on the sea, then even the grumblers felt a strange nostalgia for it. It set you yearning, with a wild yearning; perhaps for the past, to be far back in the mysterious past of the island, when the blood had a different throb. Strange floods of passion came over you, strange violent lusts and imaginations of cruelty. The blood and the passion and the lust which the island had known. Uncanny dreams, half-dreams, half-evoked yearnings.

The Master himself began to be a little afraid of his island. He felt here strange, violent feelings he had never felt before, and lustful desires that he had been quite free from. He knew quite well now that his people didn't love him at all. He knew that their spirits were secretly against him, malicious, jeering, envious, and lurking to down him. He became just as wary and secretive with regard to them.

But it was too much. At the end of the second year, several departures took place. The housekeeper went. The Master always blamed self-important women most. The mason said he wasn't going to be monkeyed about any more, so he took his departure, with his family. The rheumatic farm-hand left.

And then the year's bills came in, the Master made up his accounts. In spite of good crops, the assets were ridiculous, against the spending. The island had again lost, not hundreds but thousands of pounds. It was incredible. But you simply couldn't believe it! Where had it all gone?

The Master spent gloomy nights and days going through accounts in the library. He was thorough. It became evident, now the housekeeper had gone, that she had swindled him. Probably everybody was swindling him. But he hated to think it, so he put the thought away.

He emerged, however, pale and hollow-eyed from his balancing of unbalanceable accounts, looking as if something had kicked him in the stomach. It was pitiable. But the money had gone, and there was an end of it. Another great hole in his capital. How could people be so heartless?

It couldn't go on, that was evident. He would soon be bankrupt. He had to give regretful notice to his butler. He was afraid to find out how much his butler had swindled him. Because the man was such a wonderful butler, after all. And the farm bailiff had to go. The Master had no regrets in that quarter. The losses on the farm had almost embittered him.

The third year was spent in rigid cutting down of expenses. The island was still mysterious and fascinating. But it was also treacherous and cruel, secretly, fathomlessly malevolent. In spite of all its fair show of white blossom and bluebells, and the lovely dignity of foxgloves bending their rose-red bells, it was your implacable enemy.

With reduced staff, reduced wages, reduced splendour, the third year went by. But it was fighting against hope. The farm still lost a good deal. And once more there was a hole in that remnant of capital. Another hole in that which was already a mere remnant round the old holes. The island was mysterious in this also: it seemed to pick the very money out of your pocket, as if it were an octopus with invisible arms stealing from you in every direction.

Yet the Master still loved it. But with a touch of rancour now.

He spent, however, the second half of the fourth year intensely working on the mainland, to be rid of it. And it was amazing how difficult he found it, to dispose of an island. He had thought that everybody was pining for such an island as his; but not at all. Nobody would pay any price for it. And he wanted now to get rid of it, as a man who wants a divorce at any cost.

It was not till the middle of the fifth year that he transferred it, at a considerable loss to himself, to an hotel company who were willing to speculate in it. They were to turn it into a handy honeymoon-and-golf island.

There, take that, island which didn't know when it was well off. Now be a honeymoon-and-golf island!

II

THE SECOND ISLAND

The islander had to move. But he was not going to the main-land. Oh, no! He moved to the smaller island, which still belonged to him. And he took with him the faithful old car-penter and wife, the couple he never really cared for; also a widow and daughter, who had kept house for him the last year; also an orphan lad, to help the old man.

The small island was very small; but being a hump of rock in the sea, it was bigger than it looked. There was a little track among the rocks and bushes, winding and scrambling up and down around the islet, so that it took you twenty minutes to do the circuit. It was more than you would have expected.

Still, it was an island. The islander moved himself, with all his books, into the commonplace six-roomed house up to which you had to scramble from the rocky landing-place. There were also two joined-together cottages. The old carpenter lived in one, with his wife and the lad, the widow and daughter lived in the other.

At last all was in order. The Master's books filled two rooms. It was already autumn, Orion lifting out of the sea. And in the dark nights, the Master could see the lights on his late island, where the hotel company were entertaining guests who would advertise the new resort for honeymoon-golfers.

On his lump of rock, however, the Master was still master. He explored the crannies, the odd hand-breadths of grassy level, the steep little cliffs where the last harebells hung and the seeds of summer were brown above the sea, lonely and untouched. He peered down the old well. He examined the stone pen where the pig had been kept. Himself, he had a goat.

Yes, it was an island. Always, always underneath among the rocks the Celtic sea sucked and washed and smote its feathery greyness. How many different noises of the sea! Deep explosions, rumblings, strange long sighs and whistling noises; then voices, real voices of people clamouring as if they were in a market, under the waters: and again, the far-off ringing of a bell, surely an actual bell! Then a tremendous trilling noise, very long and alarming, and an undertone of hoarse gasping.

On this island there were no human ghosts, no ghosts of any ancient race. The sea, and the spume and the weather, had washed them out, washed them out so there was only the sound of the sea itself, its own ghost, myriad-voiced, communing and plotting and shouting all winter long. And only the smell of the sea, with a few bristly bushes of gorse and coarse tufts of heather, among the grey, pellucid rocks, in the grey, more-pellucid air. The coldness, the greyness, even the soft, creeping fog of the sea, and the islet of rock humped up in it all, like the last point in space.

Green star Sirius stood over the sea's rim. The island was a shadow. Out at sea a ship showed small lights. Below, in the rocky cove, the row-boat and the motor-boat were safe. A light shone in the carpenter's kitchen. That was all.

Save, of course, that the lamp was lit in the house, where the widow was preparing supper, her daughter helping. The islander went in to his meal. Here he was no longer the Master, he was an islander again and he had peace. The old carpenter, the widow and daughter were all faithfulness itself. The old man worked while ever there was light to see, because he had a passion for work. The widow and her quiet, rather delicate daughter of thirty-three worked for the Master, because they loved looking

after him, and they were infinitely grateful for the haven he
provided them. But they didn't call him 'the Master'. They gave
him his name: 'Mr Cathcart, sir!' softly and reverently. And
he spoke back to them also softly, gently, like people far from
the world, afraid to make a noise.

The island was no longer a 'world'. It was a sort of refuge.
The islander no longer struggled for anything. He had no need.
It was as if he and his few dependants were a small flock of
sea-birds alighted on this rock, as they travelled through space,
and keeping together without a word. The silent mystery of
travelling birds.

He spent most of his day in his study. His book was coming
along. The widow's daughter could type out his manuscript
for him, she was not uneducated. It was the one strange sound
on the island, the typewriter. But soon even its spattering fitted
in with the sea's noises, and the wind's.

The months went by. The islander worked away in his study,
the people of the island went quietly about their concerns. The
goat had a little black kid with yellow eyes. There were mackerel
in the sea. The old man went fishing in the row-boat with the
lad, when the weather was calm enough; they went off in the
motor-boat to the biggest island for the post. And they brought
supplies, never a penny wasted. And the days went by, and the
nights, without desire, without ennui.

The strange stillness from all desire was a kind of wonder
to the islander. He didn't want anything. His soul at last was
still in him, his spirit was like a dim-lit cave under water,
where strange sea-foliage expands upon the watery atmosphere,
and scarcely sways, and a mute fish shadowily slips in and
slips away again. All still and soft and uncrying, yet alive as
rooted seaweed is alive.

The islander said to himself: 'Is this happiness?' He said to
himself: 'I am turned into a dream. I feel nothing, or I don't
know what I feel. Yet it seems to me I am happy.'

Only he had to have something upon which his mental activity could work. So he spent long, silent hours in his study, working not very fast, nor very importantly, letting the writing spin softly from him as if it were drowsy gossamer. He no longer fretted whether it were good or not, what he produced. He slowly, softly spun it like gossamer, and if it were to melt away as gossamer in autumn melts, he would not mind. It was only the soft evanescence of gossamy things which now seemed to him permanent. The very mist of eternity was in them. Whereas stone buildings, cathedrals for example, seemed to him to howl with temporary resistance, knowing they must fall at last; the tension of their long endurance seemed to howl forth from them all the time.

Sometimes he went to the mainland and to the city. Then he went elegantly, dressed in the latest style, to his club. He sat in a stall at the theatre, he shopped in Bond Street. He discussed terms for publishing his book. But over his face was that gossamy look of having dropped out of the race of progress, which made the vulgar city people feel they had won it over him, and made him glad to go back to his island.

He didn't mind if he never published his book. The years were blending into a soft mist, from which nothing obtruded. Spring came. There was never a primrose on his island, but he found a winter-aconite. There were two little sprayed bushes of blackthorn, and some wind-flowers. He began to make a list of the flowers of his islet, and that was absorbing. He noted a wild currant bush and watched for the elder flowers on a stunted little tree, then for the first yellow rags of the broom, and wild roses. Bladder campion, orchids, stitchwort, celandine, he was prouder of them than if they had been people on his island. When he came across the golden saxifrage, so inconspicuous in a damp corner, he crouched over it in a trance, he knew not for how long, looking at it. Yet it was nothing to look at. As the widow's daughter found, when he showed it her.

He had said to her in real triumph:

'I found the golden saxifrage this morning.'

The name sounded splendid. She looked at him with fascinated brown eyes, in which was a hollow ache that frightened him a little.

'Did you, sir? Is it a nice flower?'

He pursed his lips and tilted his brows.

'Well – not showy exactly. I'll show it you if you like.'

'I should like to see it.'

She was so quiet, so wistful. But he sensed in her a persistency which made him uneasy. She said she was so happy: really happy. She followed him quietly, like a shadow, on the rocky track where there was never room for two people to walk side by side. He went first, and could feel her there, immediately behind him, following so submissively, gloating on him from behind.

It was a kind of pity for her which made him become her lover: though he never realized the extent of the power she had gained over him, and how *she* willed it. But the moment he had fallen, a jangling feeling came upon him, that it was all wrong. He felt a nervous dislike of her. He had not wanted it. And it seemed to him, as far as her physical self went, she had not wanted it either. It was just her will. He went away, and climbed at the risk of his neck down to a ledge near the sea. There he sat for hours, gazing all jangled at the sea, and saying miserably to himself: 'We didn't want it. We didn't really want it.'

It was the automatism of sex that had caught him again. Not that he hated sex. He deemed it, as the Chinese do, one of the great life-mysteries. But it had become mechanical, automatic, and he wanted to escape that. Automatic sex shattered him, and filled him with a sort of death. He thought he had come through, to a new stillness of desirelessness. Perhaps beyond that there was a new fresh delicacy of desire, an unentered frail communion of two people meeting on untrodden ground.

Be that as it might, this was not it. This was nothing new or fresh. It was automatic, and driven from the will. Even she, in her true self, hadn't wanted it. It was automatic in her.

When he came home, very late, and saw her face white with fear and apprehension of his feeling against her, he pitied her, and spoke to her delicately, reassuringly. But he kept himself remote from her.

She gave no sign. She served him with the same silence, the same hidden hunger to serve him, to be near where he was. He felt her love following him with strange, awful persistency. She claimed nothing. Yet now, when he met her bright, brown, curiously vacant eyes, he saw in them the mute question. The question came direct at him, with a force and a power of will he never realized.

So he succumbed, and asked her again.

'Not,' she said, 'if it will make you hate me.'

'Why should it?' he replied, nettled. 'Of course not.'

'You know I would do anything on earth for you.'

It was only afterwards, in his exasperation, he remembered what she said, and was more exasperated. Why should she pretend to do this *for him*? Why not herself? But in his exasperation, he drove himself deeper in. In order to achieve some sort of satisfaction, which he never did achieve, he abandoned himself to her. Everybody on the island knew. But he did not care.

Then even what desire he had left him, and he felt only shattered. He felt that only with her will had she wanted him. Now he was shattered and full of self-contempt. His island was smirched and spoiled. He had lost his place in the rare, desireless levels of Time to which he had at last arrived, and he had fallen right back. If only it had been true, delicate desire between them, and a delicate meeting on the third rare place where a man might meet a woman, when they were both true to the frail, sensitive, crocus-flame of desire in them. But it had been no such thing: automatic, an act of will, not of true desire, it left him feeling humiliated.

He went away from the islet, in spite of her mute reproach. And he wandered about the continent, vainly seeking a place where he could stay. He was out of key; he did not fit in the world any more.

There came a letter from Flora – her name was Flora – to say she was afraid she was going to have a child. He sat down as if he were shot, and he remained sitting. But he replied to her: 'Why be afraid? If it is so, it is so, and we should rather be pleased than afraid.'

At this very moment, it happened there was an auction of islands. He got the maps, and studied them. And at the auction he bought, for very little money, another island. It was just a few acres of rock away in the north, on the outer fringe of the isles. It was low, it rose low out of the great ocean. There was not a building, not even a tree on it. Only northern sea-turf, a pool of rain-water, a bit of sedge, rock, and sea-birds. Nothing else. Under the weeping wet western sky.

He made a trip to visit his new possession. For several days, owing to the seas, he could not approach it. Then, in a light sea-mist, he landed, and saw it hazy, low, stretching apparently a long way. But it was illusion. He walked over the wet, springy turf, and dark-grey sheep tossed away from him, spectral, bleating hoarsely. And he came to the dark pool, with the sedge. Then on in the dampness, to the grey sea sucking angrily among the rocks.

This was indeed an island.

So he went home to Flora. She looked at him with guilty fear, but also with a triumphant brightness in her uncanny eyes. And again he was gentle, he reassured her, even he wanted her again, with that curious desire that was almost like toothache. So he took her to the mainland, and they were married, since she was going to have his child.

They returned to the island. She still brought in his meals, her own along with them. She sat and ate with him. He would have it so. The widowed mother preferred to stay in the kitchen. And Flora slept in the guest-room of his house, mistress of his house.

His desire, whatever it was, died in him with nauseous finality. The child would still be months coming. His island was hateful to him, vulgar, a suburb. He himself had lost all his finer distinction. The weeks passed in a sort of prison, in humiliation. Yet he stuck it out, till the child was born. But he was meditating escape. Flora did not even know.

A nurse appeared, and ate at table with them. The doctor came sometimes, and, if the sea were rough, he too had to stay. He was cheery over his whisky.

They might have been a young couple in Golders Green.

The daughter was born at last. The father looked at the baby, and felt depressed, almost more than he could bear. The mill-stone was tied round his neck. But he tried not to show what he felt. And Flora did not know. She still smiled with a kind of half-witted triumph in her joy, as she got well again. Then she began again to look at him with those aching, suggestive, somehow impudent eyes. She adored him so.

This he could not stand. He told her that he had to go away for a time. She wept, but she thought she had got him. He told her he had settled the best part of his property on her, and wrote down for her what income it would produce. She hardly listened, only looked at him with those heavy, adoring, impudent eyes. He gave her a cheque-book, with the amount of her credit duly entered. This did arouse her interest. And he told her, if she got tired of the island, she could choose her home wherever she wished.

She followed him with those aching, persistent brown eyes, when he left, and he never even saw her weep.

He went straight north, to prepare his third island.

III

THE THIRD ISLAND

The third island was soon made habitable. With cement and the big pebbles from the shingle beach, two men built him a hut, and roofed it with corrugated iron. A boat brought over a bed and table, and three chairs, with a good cupboard, and a few books. He laid in a supply of coal and paraffin and food – he wanted so little.

The house stood near the flat shingle bay where he landed, and where he pulled up his light boat. On a sunny day in August the men sailed away and left him. The sea was still and pale blue. On the horizon he saw the small mail-steamer slowly passing northwards, as if she were walking. She served the outer isles twice a week. He could row out to her if need be, in calm weather, and he could signal her from a flagstaff behind his cottage.

Half a dozen sheep still remained on the island, as company; and he had a cat to rub against his legs. While the sweet, sunny days of the northern autumn lasted, he would walk among the rocks, and over the springy turf of his small domain, always coming to the ceaseless, restless sea. He looked at every leaf, that might be different from another, and he watched the endless expansion and contraction of the water-tossed seaweed. He had never a tree, not even a bit of heather to guard. Only the turf, and tiny turf-plants, and the sedge by the pool, the seaweed in the ocean. He was glad. He didn't want trees or bushes. They stood up like people, too assertive. His bare, low-pitched island in the pale blue sea was all he wanted.

He no longer worked at his book. The interest had gone. He liked to sit on the low elevation of his island, and see the sea; nothing but the pale, quiet sea. And to feel his mind turn soft and hazy, like the hazy ocean. Sometimes, like a mirage, he would see the shadow of land rise hovering to northwards. It was a big island beyond. But quite without substance.

He was soon almost startled when he perceived the steamer on the near horizon, and his heart contracted with fear, lest it were going to pause and molest him. Anxiously he watched it go, and not till it was out of sight did he feel truly relieved, himself again. The tension of waiting for human approach was cruel. He did not want to be approached. He did not want to hear voices. He was shocked by the sound of his own voice, if he inadvertently spoke to his cat. He rebuked himself for having broken the great silence. And he was irritated when his cat would look up at him and mew faintly, plaintively. He frowned at her. And she knew. She was becoming wild, lurking in the rocks, perhaps fishing.

But what he disliked most was when one of the lumps of sheep opened its mouth and baa-ed its hoarse, raucous baa. He watched it, and it looked to him hideous and gross. He came to dislike the sheep very much.

He wanted only to hear the whispering sound of the sea, and the sharp cries of the gulls, cries that came out of another world to him. And best of all, the great silence.

He decided to get rid of the sheep when the boat came. They were accustomed to him now, and stood and stared at him with yellow or colourless eyes, in an insolence that was almost cold ridicule. There was a suggestion of cold indecency about them. He disliked them very much. And when they jumped with staccato jumps off the rocks, and their hoofs made the dry, sharp hit, and the fleece flopped on their square backs, he found them repulsive, degrading.

The fine weather passed, and it rained all day. He lay a great deal on his bed, listening to the water trickling from his roof into the zinc water-butt, looking through the open door at the rain, the dark rocks, the hidden sea. Many gulls were on the island now: many sea-birds of all sorts. It was another world of life. Many of the birds he had never seen before. His old impulse came over him, to send for a book, to know their names. In a flicker of the old passion, to know the name of everything he saw, he decided to row out to the steamer. The names of these birds! He must know their names, otherwise he had not got them, they were not quite alive to him.

But the desire left him, and he merely watched the birds as they wheeled or walked around him, watched them vaguely, without discrimination. All interest had left him. Only there was one gull, a big, handsome fellow, who would walk back and forth, back and forth in front of the open door of the cabin, as if he had some mission there. He was big, and pearl-grey, and his roundnesses were as smooth and lovely as a pearl. Only the folded wings had shut black pinions, and on the closed black feathers were three very distinct white dots, making a pattern. The islander wondered very much, why this bit of trimming on the bird out of the far, cold seas. And as the gull walked back and forth, back and forth in front of the cabin, strutting on pale-dusky gold feet, holding up his pale yellow beak, that was curved at the tip, with curious alien importance, the man wondered over him. He was portentous, he had a meaning.

Then the bird came no more. The island, which had been full of sea-birds, the flash of wings, the sound and cut of wings and sharp eerie cries in the air, began to be deserted again. No longer they sat like living eggs on the rocks and turf, moving their heads, but scarcely rising into flight round his feet. No longer they ran across the turf among the sheep, and lifted themselves upon low wings. The host had gone. But some remained, always.

The days shortened, and the world grew eerie. One day the boat came: as if suddenly, swooping down. The islander found it a violation. It was torture to talk to those two men, in their homely clumsy clothes. The air of familiarity around them was very repugnant to him. Himself, he was neatly dressed, his cabin was neat and tidy. He resented any intrusion, the clumsy homeliness, the heavy-footedness of the two fishermen was really repulsive to him.

The letters they had brought he left lying unopened in a little box. In one of them was his money. But he could not bear to open even that one. Any kind of contact was repulsive to him. Even to read his name on an envelope. He hid the letters away.

And the hustle and horror of getting the sheep caught and tied and put in the ship made him loathe with profound repulsion the whole of the animal creation. What repulsive god invented animals and evil-smelling men? To his nostrils, the fishermen and the sheep alike smelled foul; an uncleanness on the fresh earth.

He was still nerve-racked and tortured when the ship at last lifted sail and was drawing away, over the still sea. And sometimes, days after, he would start with repulsion, thinking he heard the munching of sheep.

The dark days of winter drew on. Sometimes there was no real day at all. He felt ill, as if he were dissolving, as if dissolution had already set in inside him. Everything was twilight, outside, and in his mind and soul. Once, when he went to the door, he saw black heads of men swimming in his bay. For some moments he swooned unconscious. It was the shock, the horror of unexpected human approach. The horror in the twilight! And not till the shock had undermined him and left him disembodied, did he realize that the black heads were the heads of seals swimming in. A sick relief came over him. But he was barely conscious, after the shock. Later on, he sat and wept with gratitude, because they were not men. But he never realized that he wept. He was too dim. Like some strange, ethereal animal, he no longer realized what he was doing.

Only he still derived his single satisfaction from being alone, absolutely alone, with the space soaking into him. The grey sea alone, and the footing of his sea-washed island. No other contact. Nothing human to bring its horror into contact with him. Only space, damp, twilit, sea-washed space! This was the bread of his soul.

For this reason, he was most glad when there was a storm, or when the sea was high. Then nothing could get at him. Nothing could come through to him from the outer world. True, the terrific violence of the wind made him suffer badly. At the same time, it swept the world utterly out of existence for him. He always liked the sea to be heavily rolling and tearing. Then no boat could get at him. It was like eternal ramparts round his island.

He kept no track of time, and no longer thought of opening a book. The print, the printed letters, so like the depravity of speech, looked obscene. He tore the brass label from his paraffin stove. He obliterated any bit of lettering in his cabin.

His cat had disappeared. He was rather glad. He shivered at her thin, obtrusive call. She had lived in the coal-shed. And each morning he had put her a dish of porridge, the same as he ate. He washed her saucer with repulsion. He did not like her writhing about. But he fed her scrupulously. Then one day she did not come for her porridge; she always mewed for it. She did not come again.

He prowled about his island in the rain, in a big oilskin coat, not knowing what he was looking at, nor what he went out to see. Time had ceased to pass. He stood for long spaces, gazing from a white, sharp face, with those keen, far-off blue eyes of his, gazing fiercely and almost cruelly at the dark sea under the dark sky. And if he saw the labouring sail of a fishing-boat away on the cold waters, a strange malevolent anger passed over his features.

Sometimes he was ill. He knew he was ill, because he staggered as he walked, and easily fell down. Then he paused to think what it was. And he went to his stores and took out dried milk and malt, and ate that. Then he forgot again. He ceased to register his own feelings.

The days were beginning to lengthen. All winter the weather had been comparatively mild, but with much rain, much rain. He had forgotten the sun. Suddenly, however, the air was very cold, and he began to shiver. A fear came over him. The sky was level and grey, and never a star appeared at night. It was very cold. More birds began to arrive. The island was freezing. With trembling hands he made a fire in his grate. The cold frightened him.

And now it continued, day after day, a dull, deathly cold. Occasional crumblings of snow were in the air. The days were greyly longer, but no change in the cold. Frozen grey daylight. The birds passed away, flying away. Some he saw lying frozen. It was as if all life were drawing away, contracting away from the north, contracting southwards. 'Soon,' he said to himself, 'it will all be gone, and in all these regions nothing will be alive.' He felt a cruel satisfaction in the thought.

Then one night there seemed to be a relief; he slept better, did not tremble half-awake, and writhe so much, half-conscious. He had become so used to the quaking and writhing of his body, he hardly noticed it. But when for once it slept deep, he noticed that.

He woke in the morning to a curious whiteness. His window was muffled. It had snowed. He got up and opened his door, and shuddered. Ugh! How cold! All white, with a dark leaden sea, and black rocks curiously speckled with white. The foam was no longer pure. It seemed dirty. And the sea ate at the whiteness of the corpse-like land. Crumbles of snow were silting down the dead air.

On the ground the snow was a foot deep, white and smooth and soft, windless. He took a shovel to clear round his house and shed. The pallor of morning darkened. There was a strange rumbling of far-off thunder in the frozen air, and through the newly-falling snow, a dim flash of lightning. Snow now fell steadily down in the motionless obscurity.

He went out for a few minutes. But it was difficult. He stumbled and fell in the snow, which burned his face. Weak, faint, he toiled home. And when he recovered, took the trouble to make hot milk.

It snowed all the time. In the afternoon again there was a muffled rumbling of thunder, and flashes of lightning blinking reddish through the falling snow. Uneasy, he went to bed and lay staring fixedly at nothingness.

Morning seemed never to come. An eternity long he lay and waited for one alleviating pallor on the night. And at last it seemed the air was paler. His house was a cell faintly illuminated with white light. He realized the snow was walled outside his window. He got up, in the dead cold. When he opened his door, the motionless snow stopped him in a wall as high as his breast. Looking over the top of it, he felt the dead wind slowly driving, saw the snow-powder lift and travel like a funeral train. The blackish sea churned and champed, seeming to bite at the snow, impotent. The sky was grey, but luminous.

He began to work in a frenzy, to get at his boat. If he was to be shut in, it must be by his own choice, not by the mechanical power of the elements. He must get to the sea. He must be able to get at his boat.

But he was weak, and at times the snow overcame him. It fell on him, and he lay buried and lifeless. Yet every time he struggled alive before it was too late, and fell upon the snow with the energy of fever. Exhausted, he would not give in. He crept indoors and made coffee and bacon. Long since he had cooked so much. Then he went at the snow once more. He must conquer the snow, this new, white brute force which had accumulated against him.

He worked in the awful, dead wind, pushing the snow aside, pressing it with his shovel. It was cold, freezing hard in the wind, even when the sun came out for a while and showed him his white, lifeless surroundings, the black sea rolling sullen, flecked with dull spume, away to the horizons. Yet the sun had power on his face. It was March.

He reached the boat. He pushed the snow away, then sat down under the lee of the boat, looking at the sea, which swirled nearly to his feet, in the high tide. Curiously natural the pebbles looked, in a world gone all uncanny. The sun shone no more. Snow was falling in hard crumbs, that vanished as if by a miracle as they touched the hard blackness of the sea. Hoarse waves rang in the shingle, rushing up at the snow. The wet rocks were brutally black. And all the time the myriad swooping crumbs of snow, demonish, touched the dark sea and disappeared.

During the night there was a great storm. It seemed to him he could hear the vast mass of snow striking all the world with a ceaseless thud; and over it all, the wind roared in strange hollow volleys, in between which came a jump of blindfold lightning, then the low roll of thunder heavier than the wind. When at last the dawn faintly discoloured the dark, the storm had more or less subsided, but a steady wind drove on. The snow was up to the top of his door.

Sullenly, he worked to dig himself out. And he managed through sheer persistency to get out. He was in the tail of a great drift, many feet high. When he got through, the frozen snow was not more than two feet deep. But his island was gone. Its shape was all changed, great heaping white hills rose where no hills had been, inaccessible, and they fumed like volcanoes, but with snow powder. He was sickened and overcome.

His boat was in another, smaller drift. But he had not the strength to clear it. He looked at it helplessly. The shovel slipped from his hands, and he sank in the snow, to forget. In the snow itself, the sea resounded.

Something brought him to. He crept to his house. He was almost without feeling. Yet he managed to warm himself, just that part of him which leaned in snow-sleep over the coal fire. Then again he made hot milk. After which, carefully, he built up the fire.

The wind dropped. Was it night again? In the silence, it seemed he could hear the panther-like dropping of infinite snow. Thunder rumbled nearer, crackled quick after the bleared reddened lightning. He lay in bed in a kind of stupor. The elements! The elements! His mind repeated the word dumbly. You can't win against the elements.

How long it went on, he never knew. Once, like a wraith, he got out and climbed to the top of a white hill on his unrecognizable island. The sun was hot. 'It is summer,' he said to himself, 'and the time of leaves.' He looked stupidly over the whiteness of his foreign island, over the waste of the lifeless sea. He pretended to imagine he saw the wink of a sail. Because he knew too well there would never again be a sail on that stark sea.

As he looked, the sky mysteriously darkened and chilled. From far off came the mutter of the unsatisfied thunder, and he knew it was the signal of the snow rolling over the sea. He turned, and felt its breath on him.

Things

THEY were true idealists from New England. But that is
some time ago: before the war. Several years before the
war, they met and married; he a tall, keen-eyed young
man from Connecticut, she a smallish, demure, Puritan-looking
young woman from Massachusetts. They both had a little
money. Not much, however. Even added together, it didn't make
three thousand dollars a year. Still – they were free. Free!

Ah! Freedom! To be free to live one's own life! To be
twenty-five and twenty-seven, a pair of true idealists with a
mutual love of beauty, and an inclination towards 'Indian
thought' – meaning, alas, Mrs Besant – and an income a little
under three thousand dollars a year! But what is money? All
one wishes to do is to live a full and beautiful life. In Europe,
of course, right at the fountain-head of tradition. It might possibly be done in America: in New England, for example. But at
a forfeiture of a certain amount of 'beauty'. True beauty takes
a long time to mature. The baroque is only half-beautiful, half-
matured. No, the real silver bloom, the real golden-sweet
bouquet of beauty had its roots in the Renaissance, not in any
later or shallower period.

Therefore the two idealists, who were married in New Haven,
sailed at once to Paris: Paris of the old days. They had a studio
apartment on the Boulevard Montparnasse, and they became
real Parisians, in the old, delightful sense, not in the modern,
vulgar. It was the shimmer of the pure impressionists, Monet

and his followers, the world seen in terms of pure light, light broken and unbroken. How lovely! How lovely the nights, the river, the mornings in the old streets and by the flower-stalls and the book-stalls, the afternoons up on Montmartre or in the Tuileries, the evenings on the boulevards!

They both painted, but not desperately. Art had not taken them by the throat, and they did not take Art by the throat. They painted: that's all. They knew people – nice people, if possible, though one had to take them mixed. And they were happy.

Yet it seems as if human beings must set their claws in *something*. To be 'free', to be 'living a full and beautiful life', you must, alas, be attached to something. A 'full and beautiful life' means a tight attachment to *something* – at least, it is so for all idealists – or else a certain boredom supervenes; there is a certain waving of loose ends upon the air, like the waving, yearning tendrils of the vine that spread and rotate, seeking something to clutch, something up which to climb towards the necessary sun. Finding nothing, the vine can only trail, half-fulfilled, upon the ground. Such is freedom! – a clutching of the right pole. And human beings are all vines. But especially the idealist. He is a vine, and he needs to clutch and climb. And he despises the man who is a mere *potato*, or turnip, or lump of wood.

Our idealists were frightfully happy, but they were all the time reaching out for something to cotton on to. At first, Paris was enough. They explored Paris *thoroughly*. And they learned French till they almost felt like French people, they could speak it so glibly.

Still, you know, you never talk French with your *soul*. It can't be done. And though it's very thrilling, at first, talking in French to clever Frenchmen – they seem *so* much cleverer than oneself – still, in the long run, it is not satisfying. The endlessly clever *materialism* of the French leaves you cold, in the end, gives a sense of barrenness and incompatibility with true New England depth. So our two idealists felt.

They turned away from France – but ever so gently. France had disappointed them. 'We've loved it, and we've got a great deal out of it. But after a while, after a considerable while, several years, in fact, Paris leaves one feeling disappointed. It hasn't quite got what one wants.'

'But Paris isn't France.'

'No, perhaps not. France is quite different from Paris. And France is lovely – quite lovely. But *to us*, though we love it, it doesn't say a great deal.'

So, when the war came, the idealists moved to Italy. And they loved Italy. They found it beautiful, and more poignant than France. It seemed much nearer to the New England conception of beauty: something pure, and full of sympathy, without the *materialism* and the *cynicism* of the French. The two idealists seemed to breathe their own true air in Italy.

And in Italy, much more than in Paris, they felt they could thrill to the teachings of the Buddha. They entered the swelling stream of modern Buddhistic emotion, and they read the books, and they practised meditation, and they deliberately set themselves to eliminate from their own souls greed, pain, and sorrow. They did not realize – yet – that Buddha's very eagerness to free himself from pain and sorrow is in itself a sort of greed. No, they dreamed of a perfect world, from which all greed, and nearly all pain, and a great deal of sorrow, were eliminated.

But America entered the war, so the two idealists had to help. They did hospital work. And though their experience made them realize more than ever that greed, pain, and sorrow *should* be eliminated from the world, nevertheless the Buddhism, or the theosophy, didn't emerge very triumphant from the long crisis. Somehow, somewhere, in some part of themselves, they felt that greed, pain, and sorrow would never be eliminated, because most people don't care about eliminating them, and never will care. Our idealists were far too Western to think of abandoning all the world to damnation, while they saved their two selves. They were far too unselfish to sit tight under a bho tree and reach Nirvana in a mere couple.

It was more than that, though. They simply hadn't enough *Seitzfleisch* to squat under a bho tree and get to Nirvana by contemplating anything, least of all their own navel. If the whole wide world was not going to be saved, they, personally, were not so very keen on being saved just by themselves. No, it would be so lonesome. They were New Englanders, so it must be all or nothing. Greed, pain, and sorrow must either be eliminated from *all the world*, or else, what was the use of eliminating them from oneself? No use at all! One was just a victim.

And so, although they still *loved* 'Indian thought', and felt very tender about it: well, to go back to our metaphor, the pole up which the green and anxious vines had clambered so far now proved dry-rotten. It snapped, and the vines came slowly subsiding to earth again. There was no crack and crash. The vines held themselves up by their own foliage, for a while. But they subsided. The beanstalk of 'Indian thought' had given way before Jack and Jill had climbed off the tip of it to a further world.

They subsided with a slow rustle back to earth again. But they made no outcry. They were again 'disappointed'. But they never admitted it. 'Indian thought' had let them down. But they never complained. Even to one another, they never said a word. They were disappointed, faintly but deeply disillusioned, and they both knew it. But the knowledge was tacit.

And they still had so much in their lives. They still had Italy – dear Italy. And they still had freedom, the priceless treasure. And they still had so much 'beauty'. About the fullness of their lives they were not quite so sure. They had one little boy, whom they loved as parents should love their children, but whom they wisely refrained from fastening upon, to build their lives on him. No, no, they must live their own lives! They still had strength of mind to know that.

But they were now no longer very young. Twenty-five and twenty-seven had become thirty-five and thirty-seven. And though they had had a very wonderful time in Europe, and though they still loved Italy – dear Italy! – yet: they were disappointed. They had got a lot out of it: oh, a very great deal indeed! Still, it hadn't given them quite, not *quite*, what they had expected. Europe was lovely, but it was dead. Living in Europe, you were living in the past. And Europeans, with all their superficial charm, were not *really* charming. They were materialistic, they had no *real* soul. They just did not understand the inner urge of the spirit, because the inner urge was dead in them, they were all survivals. There, that was the truth about Europeans: they were survivals, with no more getting ahead in them.

It was another bean-pole, another vine-support crumbled under the green life of the vine. And very bitter it was, this time. For up the old tree-trunk of Europe the green vine had been clambering silently for more than ten years, ten hugely important years, the years of real living. The two idealists had *lived* in Europe, lived on Europe and on European life and European things as vines in an everlasting vineyard.

They had made their home here: a home such as you could never make in America. Their watchword had been 'beauty'. They had rented, the last four years, the second floor of an old palazzo on the Arno, and here they had all their 'things'. And they derived a profound, profound satisfaction from their apartment: the lofty, silent, ancient rooms with windows on the river, with glistening, dark-red floors, and the beautiful furniture that the idealists had 'picked up'.

Yes, unknown to themselves, the lives of the idealists had

been running with a fierce swiftness horizontally, all the time.
They had become tense, fierce, hunters of 'things' for their
home. While their souls were climbing up to the sun of old
European culture or old Indian thought, their passions were
running horizontally, clutching at 'things'. Of course they did
not buy the things for the things' sakes, but for the sake of
'beauty'. They looked upon their home as a place entirely furn-
ished by loveliness, not by 'things' at all. Valerie had some very
lovely curtains at the windows of the long *salotto*, looking on
the river: curtains of queer ancient material that looked like
finely-knitted silk, most beautifully faded down from vermilion
and orange, and gold, and black, down to a sheer soft glow.
Valerie hardly ever came into the *salotto* without mentally falling on her knees before the curtains. 'Chartres!' she said. 'To
me they are Chartres!' And Melville never turned and looked at
his sixteenth-century Venetian bookcase, with its two or three
dozen of choice books, without feeling his marrow stir in his
bones. The holy of holies!

The child silently, almost sinisterly, avoided any rude contact
with these ancient monuments of furniture, as if they had been
nests of sleeping cobras, or that 'thing' most perilous to the
touch, the Ark of the Covenant. His childish awe was silent and
cold, but final.

Still, a couple of New England idealists cannot live merely
on the bygone glory of their furniture. At least, one couple
could not. They got used to the marvellous Bologna cupboard,
they got used to the wonderful Venetian bookcase, and the
books, and the Siena curtains and bronzes, and the lovely sofas
and side-tables and chairs they had 'picked up' in Paris. Oh,
they had been picking things up since the first day they landed
in Europe. And they were still at it. It is the last interest Europe
can offer to an outsider: or to an insider either.

When people came, and were thrilled by the Melville interior,
then Valerie and Erasmus felt they had not lived in vain: that

they still were living. But in the long mornings, when Erasmus was desultorily working at Renaissance Florentine literature, and Valerie was attending to the apartment: and in the long hours after lunch; and in the long, usually very cold and oppressive evenings in the ancient palazzo: then the halo died from around the furniture, and the things became things, lumps of matter that just stood there or hung there, *ad infinitum*, and said nothing; and Valerie and Erasmus almost hated them. The glow of beauty, like every other glow, dies down unless it is fed. The idealists still dearly loved their things. But they had got them. And the sad fact is, things that glow vividly while you're getting them, go almost quite cold after a year or two. Unless, of course, people envy them very much, and the museums are pining for them. And the Melvilles' 'things', though very good, were not quite so good as that.

So, the glow gradually went out of everything, out of Europe, out of Italy – 'the Italians are *dears*' – even out of that marvellous apartment on the Arno. 'Why, if I had this apartment, I'd never, never even want to go out of doors! It's too lovely and perfect.' That was something, of course – to hear that.

And yet Valerie and Erasmus went out of doors: they even went out to get away from its ancient, cold-floored, stone-heavy silence and dead dignity. 'We're living on the past, you know, Dick,' said Valerie to her husband. She called him Dick.

They were grimly hanging on. They did not like to give in. They did not like to own up that they were through. For twelve years, now, they had been 'free' people living a 'full and beautiful life'. And America for twelve years had been their anathema, the Sodom and Gomorrah of industrial materialism.

It wasn't easy to own that you were 'through'. They hated to admit that they wanted to go back. But at last, reluctantly, they decided to go, 'for the boy's sake'. – 'We can't *bear* to leave Europe. But Peter is an American, so he had better look at America while he's young.' The Melvilles had an entirely

English accent and manner; almost; a little Italian and French here and there.

They left Europe behind, but they took as much of it along with them as possible. Several van-loads, as a matter of fact. All those adorable and irreplaceable 'things'. And all arrived in New York, idealists, child, and the huge bulk of Europe they had lugged along.

Valerie had dreamed of a pleasant apartment, perhaps on Riverside Drive, where it was not so expensive as east of Fifth Avenue, and where all their wonderful things would look marvellous. She and Erasmus house-hunted. But alas! their income was quite under three thousand dollars a year. They found – well, everybody knows what they found. Two small rooms and a kitchenette, and don't let us unpack a *thing*!

The chunk of Europe which they had bitten off went into a warehouse, at fifty dollars a month. And they sat in two small rooms and a kitchenette, and wondered why they'd done it.

Erasmus, of course, ought to get a job. This was what was written on the wall, and what they both pretended not to see. But it had been the strange, vague threat that the Statue of Liberty had always held over them: 'Thou shalt get a job!' Erasmus had the tickets, as they say. A scholastic career was still possible for him. He had taken his exams brilliantly at Yale, and had kept up his 'researches' all the time he had been in Europe.

But both he and Valerie shuddered. A scholastic career! The scholastic world! The *American* scholastic world! Shudder upon shudder! Give up their freedom, their full and beautiful life? Never! Never! Erasmus would be forty next birthday.

The 'things' remained in warehouse. Valerie went to look at them. It cost her a dollar an hour, and horrid pangs. The 'things', poor things, looked a bit shabby and wretched, in that warehouse.

However, New York was not all America. There was the great clean West. So the Melvilles went West, with Peter, but without the things. They tried living the simple life, in the mountains. But doing their own chores became almost a nightmare. 'Things' are all very well to look at, but it's awful handling them, even when they're beautiful. To be the slave of hideous things, to keep a stove going, cook meals, wash dishes, carry water and clean floors: pure horror of sordid anti-life!

In the cabin on the mountains, Valerie dreamed of Florence, the lost apartment; and her Bologna cupboard and Louis-Quinze chairs, above all, her 'Chartres' curtains, stood in New York and costing fifty dollars a month.

A millionaire friend came to the rescue, offering them a cottage on the Californian coast – California! Where the new soul is to be born in man. With joy the idealists moved a little farther west, catching at new vine-props of hope.

And finding them straws! The millionaire cottage was perfectly equipped. It was perhaps as labour-savingly perfect as is possible: electric heating and cooking, a white-and-pearl-enamelled kitchen, nothing to make dirt except the human being himself. In an hour or so the idealists had got through their chores. They were 'free' – free to hear the great Pacific pounding the coast, and to feel a new soul filling their bodies.

Alas! the Pacific pounded the coast with hideous brutality, brute force itself! And the new soul, instead of sweetly stealing into their bodies, seemed only meanly to gnaw the old soul out of their bodies. To feel you are under the fist of the most blind and crunching brute force: to feel that your cherished idealist's soul is being gnawed out of you, and only irritation left in place of it: well, it isn't good enough.

After about nine months, the idealists departed from the Californian west. It had been a great experience, they were glad to have had it. But, in the long run, the West was not the place for them, and they knew it. No, the people who wanted new souls had better get them. They, Valerie and Erasmus Melville, would like to develop the old soul a little further. Anyway, they had not felt any influx of new soul on the Californian coast. On the contrary.

So, with a slight hole in their material capital, they returned to Massachusetts and paid a visit to Valerie's parents, taking the boy along. The grandparents welcomed the child – poor expatriated boy – and were rather cold to Valerie, but really cold to Erasmus. Valerie's mother definitely said to Valerie, one day, that Erasmus ought to take a job, so that Valerie could live decently. Valerie haughtily reminded her mother of the beautiful apartment on the Arno, and the 'wonderful' things in store in New York, and of the 'marvellous and satisfying life' she and Erasmus had led. Valerie's mother said that she didn't think her daughter's life looked so very marvellous at present: homeless, with a husband idle at the age of forty, a child to educate, and a dwindling capital: looked the reverse of marvellous to *her*. Let Erasmus take some post in one of the universities.

'What post? What university?' interrupted Valerie.

'That could be found, considering your father's connections and Erasmus's qualifications,' replied Valerie's mother. 'And you could get all your valuable things out of store, and have a really lovely home, which everybody in America would be proud to visit. As it is, your furniture is eating up your income, and you are living like rats in a hole, with nowhere to go.'

This was very true. Valerie was beginning to pine for a home, with her 'things'. Of course, she could have sold her furniture for a substantial sum. But nothing would have induced her to. Whatever else passed away, religions, cultures, continents, and hopes, Valerie would *never* part from the 'things' which she and Erasmus had collected with such passion. To these she was nailed.

But she and Erasmus still would not give up that freedom, that full and beautiful life they had so believed in. Erasmus cursed America. He did not *want* to earn a living. He panted for Europe.

Leaving the boy in charge of Valerie's parents, the two idealists once more set off for Europe. In New York they paid two dollars and looked for a brief, bitter hour at their 'things'. They sailed 'student class' – that is, third. Their income now was less than two thousand dollars instead of three. And they made straight for Paris – cheap Paris.

They found Europe, this time, a complete failure. 'We have returned like dogs to our vomit,' said Erasmus; 'but the vomit has staled in the meantime.' He found he couldn't stand Europe. It irritated every nerve in his body. He hated America too. But America at least was a darn sight better than this miserable, dirt-eating continent; which was by no means cheap any more, either.

Valerie, with her heart on her things – she had really burned to get them out of the warehouse, where they had stood now for three years, eating up two thousand dollars – wrote to her mother she thought Erasmus would come back if he could get some suitable work in America. Erasmus, in a state of frustration bordering on rage and insanity, just went round Italy in a poverty-stricken fashion, his coat-cuffs frayed, hating everything with intensity. And when a post was found for him in Cleveland University, to teach French, Italian, and Spanish literature, his eyes grew more beady, and his long, queer face grew sharper and more rat-like with utter baffled fury. He was forty, and the job was upon him.

'I think you'd better accept, dear. You don't care for Europe any longer. As you say, it's dead and finished. They offer us a house on the college lot, and mother says there's room in it for all our things. I think we'd better cable "Accept".'

He glowered at her like a cornered rat. One almost expected to see rat's whiskers twitching at the sides of the sharp nose.

'Shall I send the cablegram?' she asked.

'Send it!' he blurted.

And she went out and sent it.

He was a changed man, quieter, much less irritable. A load was off him. He was inside the cage.

But when he looked at the furnaces of Cleveland, vast and like the greatest of black forests, with red and white-hot cascades of gushing metal, and tiny gnomes of men, and terrific noises, gigantic, he said to Valerie:

'Say what you like, Valerie, this is the biggest thing the modern world has to show.'

And when they were in their up-to-date little house on the college lot of Cleveland University, and that woebegone débris of Europe: Bologna cupboard, Venice book-shelves, Ravenna bishop's chair, Louis-Quinze side-tables, 'Chartres' curtains, Siena bronze lamps, all were arrayed, and looked perfectly out of keeping, and therefore very impressive; and when the idealists had had a bunch of gaping people in, and Erasmus had showed off in his best European manner, but still quite cordial and American; and Valerie had been most ladylike, but for all that, 'we prefer America'; then Erasmus said, looking at her with queer, sharp eyes of a rat :

'Europe's the mayonnaise all right, but America supplies the good old lobster – what?'

'Every time!' she said, with satisfaction.

And he peered at her. He was in the cage: but it was safe inside. And she, evidently, was her real self at last. She had got the goods. Yet round his nose was a queer, evil scholastic look of pure scepticism. But he liked lobster.

Daughters of the Vicar

I

M R L I N D L E Y was the first vicar of Aldecross. The
cottages of this tiny hamlet had nestled in peace since
their beginning, and the country folk had crossed the
lanes and farm-land, two or three miles, to the parish church
at Greymeed, on the bright Sunday mornings.

But when the pits were sunk, blank rows of dwellings started
up beside the high roads, and a new population, skimmed from
the floating scum of workmen, was filled in, the cottages and
the country people almost obliterated.

To suit the convenience of these new collier-inhabitants, a
church must be built at Aldecross. There was not too much
money. And so the little building crouched like a humped
stone-and-mortar mouse, with two little turrets at the west
corners for ears, in the fields near the cottages and the apple
trees, as far as possible from the dwellings down the high road.
It had an uncertain, timid look about it. And so they planted
big-leaved ivy, to hide its shrinking newness. So that now the
little church stands buried in its greenery, stranded and sleeping among the fields, while the brick houses elbow nearer and
nearer, threatening to crush it down. It is already obsolete.

The Reverend Ernest Lindley, aged twenty-seven, and newly
married, came from his curacy in Suffolk to take charge of his
church. He was just an ordinary young man, who had been
to Cambridge and taken orders. His wife was a self-assured

young woman, daughter of a Cambridgeshire rector. Her father had spent the whole of his thousand a year, so that Mrs Lindley had nothing of her own. Thus the young married people came to Aldecross to live on a stipend of about a hundred and twenty pounds, and to keep up a superior position.

They were not very well received by the new, raw, disaffected population of colliers. Being accustomed to farm labourers, Mr Lindley had considered himself as belonging indisputably to the upper or ordering classes. He had to be humble to the county families, but still, he was of their kind, whilst the common people were something different. He had no doubts of himself.

He found, however, that the collier population refused to accept this arrangement. They had no use for him in their lives, and they told him so, callously. The women merely said: 'they were throng', or else: 'Oh, it's no good you coming here, we're Chapel.' The men were quite good-humoured so long as he did not touch them too nigh, they were cheerfully contemptuous of him, with a preconceived contempt he was powerless against.

At last, passing from indignation to silent resentment, even, if he dared have acknowledged it, to conscious hatred of the majority of the flock, and unconscious hatred of himself, he confined his activities to a narrow round of cottages, and he had to submit. He had no particular character, having always depended on his position in society to give him position among men. Now he was so poor, he had no social standing even among the common vulgar tradespeople of the district, and he had not the nature nor the wish to make his society agreeable to them, nor the strength to impose himself where he would have liked to be recognized. He dragged on, pale and miserable and neutral.

At first his wife raged with mortification. She took on airs and used a high hand. But her income was too small, the wrestling with tradesmen's bills was too pitiful, she only met with general, callous ridicule when she tried to be impressive.

Wounded to the quick of her pride, she found herself isolated in an indifferent, callous population. She raged indoors and out. But soon she learned that she must pay too heavily for her outdoor rages, and then she only raged within the walls of the rectory. There her feeling was so strong that she frightened herself. She saw herself hating her husband, and she knew that, unless she were careful, she would smash her form of life and bring catastrophe upon him and upon herself. So in very fear she went quiet. She hid, bitter and beaten by fear, behind the only shelter she had in the world, her gloomy, poor parsonage.

Children were born one every year; almost mechanically, she continued to perform her maternal duty, which was forced upon her. Gradually, broken by the suppressing of her violent anger and misery and disgust, she became an invalid and took to her couch.

The children grew up healthy, but unwarmed and rather rigid. Their father and mother educated them at home, made them very proud and very genteel, put them definitely and cruelly in the upper classes, apart from the vulgar around them. So they lived quite isolated. They were good-looking, and had that curiously clean, semi-transparent look of the genteel, isolated and poor.

Gradually Mr and Mrs Lindley lost all hold on life, and spent their hours, weeks and years merely haggling to make ends meet, and bitterly repressing and pruning their children into gentility, urging them to ambition, weighting them with duty. On Sunday morning the whole family, except the mother, went down the lane to church, the long-legged girls in skimpy frocks, the boys in black coats and long, grey, unfitting trousers. They passed by their father's parishioners with mute clear faces, childish mouths closed in pride that was like a doom to them, and childish eyes already unseeing. Miss Mary, the eldest, was the leader. She was a long, slim thing with a fine profile and a proud, pure look of submission to a high fate. Miss Louisa, the second, was short and plump and obstinate-looking. She had more enemies than ideals. She looked after the lesser children, Miss Mary after the elder. The collier children watched the pale, distinguished procession of the vicar's family pass mutely by, and they were impressed by the air of gentility and distance, they made mock of the trousers of the small sons, they felt inferior in themselves, and hate stirred their hearts.

In her time, Miss Mary received as governess a few little daughters of tradesmen; Miss Louisa managed the house and went among her father's church-goers, giving lessons on the piano to the colliers' daughters at thirteen shillings for twenty-six lessons.

II

One winter morning, when his daughter Mary was about twenty years old, Mr Lindley, a thin, unobtrusive figure in his black overcoat and his wideawake, went down into Aldecross with a packet of white papers under his arm. He was delivering the parish almanacs.

A rather pale, neutral man of middle age, he waited while the train thumped over the level-crossing, going up to the pit which rattled busily just along the line. A wooden-legged man hobbled to open the gate, Mr Lindley passed on. Just at his left hand, below the road and the railway, was the red roof of a cottage, showing through the bare twigs of apple trees. Mr Lindley passed round the low wall, and descended the worn steps that led from the highway down to the cottage which crouched darkly and quietly away below the rumble of passing trains and the clank of coal-carts, in a quiet little underworld of its own. Snowdrops with tight-shut buds were hanging very still under the bare currant bushes.

The clergyman was just going to knock when he heard a clinking noise, and turning saw through the open door of a black shed just behind him an elderly woman in a black lace cap stooping among reddish big cans, pouring a very bright liquid into a tundish. There was a smell of paraffin. The woman put down her can, took the tundish and laid it on a shelf, then rose with a tin bottle. Her eyes met those of the clergyman.

'Oh, is it you, Mr Lin'ley!' she said, in a complaining tone. 'Go in.'

The minister entered the house. In the hot kitchen sat a big, elderly man with a great grey beard, taking snuff. He grunted in a deep, muttering voice, telling the minister to sit down, and then took no more notice of him, but stared vacantly into the fire. Mr Lindley waited.

The woman came in, the ribbons of her black lace cap, or bonnet, hanging on her shawl. She was of medium stature, everything about her was tidy. She went up a step out of the kitchen, carrying the paraffin-tin. Feet were heard entering the room up the step. It was a little haberdashery shop, with parcels on the shelves of the walls, a big, old-fashioned sewing-machine with tailor's work lying round it, in the open space. The woman went behind the counter, gave the child who had entered the paraffin-bottle, and took from her a jug.

'My mother says shall yer put it down,' said the child, and she was gone. The woman wrote in a book, then came into the kitchen with her jug. The husband, a very large man, rose and brought more coal to the already hot fire. He moved slowly and sluggishly. Already he was going dead; being a tailor, his large form had become an encumbrance to him. In his youth he had been a great dancer and boxer. Now he was taciturn, and inert. The minister had nothing to say, so he sought for his phrases. But John Durant took no notice, existing silent and dull.

Mrs Durant spread the cloth. Her husband poured himself beer into a mug, and began to smoke and drink.

'Shall you have some?' he growled through his beard at the clergyman, looking slowly from the man to the jug, capable of this one idea.

'No, thank you,' replied Mr Lindley, though he would have liked some beer. He must set the example in a drinking parish.

'We need a drop to keep us going,' said Mrs Durant.

She had rather a complaining manner. The clergyman sat on uncomfortably while she laid the table for the half-past ten lunch. Her husband drew up to eat. She remained in her little round arm-chair by the fire.

She was a woman who would have liked to be easy in her life, but to whose lot had fallen a rough and turbulent family, and a slothful husband who did not care what became of himself or anybody. So, her rather good-looking square face was peevish, she had that air of having been compelled all her life to serve unwillingly, and to control where she did not want to control. There was about her, too, that masterful aplomb of a woman who has brought up and ruled her sons: but even them she had ruled unwillingly. She had enjoyed managing her little haberdashery shop, riding in the carrier's cart to Nottingham, going through the big warehouses to buy her goods. But the fret of managing her sons she did not like. Only she loved her youngest boy, because he was her last, and she saw herself free.

This was one of the houses the clergyman visited occasionally. Mrs Durant, as part of her regulation, had brought up all her sons in the Church. Not that she had any religion. Only, it was what she was used to. Mr Durant was without religion. He read the fervently evangelical *Life of John Wesley* with a curious pleasure, getting from it a satisfaction as from the warmth of the fire, or a glass of brandy. But he cared no more about John Wesley, in fact, than about John Milton, of whom he had never heard.

Mrs Durant took her chair to the table.

'I don't feel like eating,' she sighed.

'Why – aren't you well?' asked the clergyman, patronizing.

'It isn't that,' she sighed. She sat with shut, straight mouth. 'I don't know what's going to become of us.'

But the clergyman had ground himself down so long that he could not easily sympathize.

'Have you any trouble?' he asked.

'Ay, have I any trouble!' cried the elderly woman. 'I shall end my days in the workhouse.'

The minister waited unmoved. What could she know of poverty in her little house of plenty!

'I hope not,' he said.

'And the one lad as I wanted to keep by me—' she lamented.

The minister listened without sympathy, quite neutral.

'And the lad as would have been a support to my old age! What is going to become of us?' she said.

The clergyman, justly, did not believe in the cry of poverty, but wondered what had become of the son.

'Has anything happened to Alfred?' he asked.

'We've got word he's gone for a Queen's sailor,' she said sharply.

'He has joined the Navy!' exclaimed Mr Lindley. 'I think he could scarcely have done better – to serve his Queen and country on the sea . . .'

'He is wanted to serve *me*,' she cried. 'And I wanted my lad at home.'

Alfred was her baby, her last, whom she had allowed herself the luxury of spoiling.

'You will miss him,' said Mr Lindley, 'that is certain. But this is no regrettable step for him to have taken – on the contrary.'

'That's easy for you to say, Mr Lindley,' she replied tartly. 'Do you think I want my lad climbing ropes at another man's bidding, like a monkey—'

'There is no *dishonour*, surely, in serving in the Navy?'

'Dishonour this dishonour that,' cried the angry old woman. 'He goes and makes a slave of himself, and he'll rue it.'

Her angry, scornful impatience nettled the clergyman, and silenced him for some moments.

'I do not see,' he retorted at last, white at the gills and inadequate, 'that the Queen's service is any more to be called slavery than working in a mine.'

'At home he was at home, and his own master. *I* know he'll find a difference.'

'It may be the making of him,' said the clergyman. 'It will take him away from bad companionship and drink.'

Some of the Durants' sons were notorious drinkers, and Alfred was not quite steady.

'And why indeed shouldn't he have his glass?' cried the mother. 'He picks no man's pocket to pay for it!'

The clergyman stiffened at what he thought was an allusion to his own profession, and his unpaid bills.

'With all due consideration, I am glad to hear he has joined the Navy,' he said.

'Me with my old age coming on, and his father working very little! I'd thank you to be glad about something else besides that, Mr Lindley.'

The woman began to cry. Her husband, quite impassive, finished his lunch of meat-pie, and drank some beer. Then he turned to the fire, as if there were no one in the room but himself.

'I shall respect all men who serve God and their country on the sea, Mrs Durant,' said the clergyman stubbornly.

'That is all very well, when they're not your sons who are doing the dirty work. It makes a difference,' she replied tartly.

'I should be proud if one of my sons were to enter the Navy.'

'Ay – well – we're not all of us made alike—'

The minister rose. He put down a large folded paper.

'I've brought the almanac,' he said.

Mrs Durant unfolded it.

'I do like a bit of colour in things,' she said, petulantly.

The clergyman did not reply.

'There's that envelope for the organist's fund—' said the old woman, and rising, she took the thing from the mantelpiece, went into the shop, and returned sealing it up.

'Which is all I can afford,' she said.

Mr Lindley took his departure, in his pocket the envelope containing Mrs Durant's offering for Miss Louisa's services. He went from door to door delivering the almanacs, in dull routine. Jaded with the monotony of the business, and with the repeated effort of greeting half-known people, he felt barren and rather irritable. At last he returned home.

In the dining-room was a small fire. Mrs Lindley, growing very stout, lay on her couch. The vicar carved the cold mutton: Miss Louisa, short and plump and rather flushed, came in from the kitchen; Miss Mary, dark, with a beautiful white brow and grey eyes, served the vegetables; the children chattered a little, but not exuberantly. The very air seemed starved.

'I went to the Durants,' said the vicar, as he served out small portions of mutton; 'it appears Alfred has run away to join the Navy.'

'Do him good,' came the rough voice of the invalid.

Miss Louisa, attending to the youngest child, looked up in protest.

'Why has he done that?' asked Mary's low, musical voice.

'He wanted some excitement, I suppose,' said the vicar. 'Shall we say grace?'

The children were arranged, all bent their heads, grace was pronounced, at the last word every face was being raised to go on with the interesting subject.

'He's just done the right thing, for once,' came the rather deep voice of the mother; 'save him from becoming a drunken sot, like the rest of them.'

'They're not *all* drunken, mama,' said Miss Louisa, stubbornly.

'It's no fault of their upbringing if they're not. Walter Durant is a standing disgrace.'

'As I told Mrs Durant,' said the vicar, eating hungrily, 'it is the best thing he could have done. It will take him away from temptation during the most dangerous years of his life – how old is he – nineteen?'

'Twenty,' said Miss Louisa.

'Twenty!' repeated the vicar. 'It will give him wholesome discipline and set before him some sort of standard of duty and honour – nothing could have been better for him. But—'

'We shall miss him from the choir,' said Miss Louisa, as if taking opposite sides to her parents.

'That is as may be,' said the vicar. 'I prefer to know he is safe in the Navy than running the risk of getting into bad ways here.'

'Was he getting into bad ways?' asked the stubborn Miss Louisa.

'You know, Louisa, he wasn't quite what he used to be,' said Miss Mary gently and steadily. Miss Louisa shut her rather heavy jaw sulkily. She wanted to deny it, but she knew it was true.

For her he had been a laughing, warm lad, with something kindly and something rich about him. He had made her feel warm. It seemed the days would be colder since he had gone.

'Quite the best thing he could do,' said the mother with emphasis.

'I think so,' said the vicar. 'But his mother was almost abusive because I suggested it.'

He spoke in an injured tone.

'What does she care for her children's welfare?' said the invalid. 'Their wages is all her concern.'

'I suppose she wanted him at home with her,' said Miss Louisa.

'Yes, she did – at the expense of his learning to be a drunkard like the rest of them,' retorted her mother.

'George Durant doesn't drink,' defended her daughter.

'Because he got burned so badly when he was nineteen – in the pit – and that frightened him. The Navy is a better remedy than that, at least.'

'Certainly,' said the vicar. 'Certainly.'

And to this Miss Louisa agreed. Yet she could not but feel angry that he had gone away for so many years. She herself was only nineteen.

III

It happened when Miss Mary was twenty-three years old that Mr Lindley was very ill. The family was exceedingly poor at the time, such a lot of money was needed, so little was forthcoming. Neither Miss Mary nor Miss Louisa had suitors. What chance had they? They met no eligible young men in Aldecross. And what they earned was a mere drop in a void. The girls' hearts were chilled and hardened with fear of this perpetual, cold penury, this narrow struggle, this horrible nothingness of their lives.

A clergyman had to be found for the church work. It so happened the son of an old friend of Mr Lindley's was waiting three months before taking up his duties. He would come and officiate, for nothing. The young clergyman was keenly expected. He was not more than twenty-seven, a Master of Arts of Oxford, had written his thesis on Roman Law. He came of an old Cambridgeshire family, had some private means, was going to take a church in Northamptonshire with a good stipend, and was not married. Mrs Lindley incurred new debts, and scarcely regretted her husband's illness.

But when Mr Massy came there was a shock of disappointment in the house. They had expected a young man with a pipe and a deep voice, but with better manners than Sidney, the eldest of the Lindleys. There arrived instead a small, *chétif* man, scarcely larger than a boy of twelve, spectacled, timid in the extreme, without a word to utter at first; yet with a certain inhuman self-sureness.

'What a little abortion!' was Mrs Lindley's exclamation to herself on first seeing him, in his buttoned-up clerical coat. And for the first time for many days she was profoundly thankful to God that all her children were decent specimens.

He had not normal powers of perception. They soon saw that he lacked the full range of human feelings, but had rather a strong philosophical mind, from which he lived. His body was almost unthinkable, in intellect he was something definite. The conversation at once took a balanced, abstract tone when he participated. There was no spontaneous exclamation, no violent assertion or expression of personal conviction, but all cold, reasonable assertion. This was very hard on Mrs Lindley. The little man would look at her, after one of her pronouncements, and then give, in his thin voice, his own calculated version, so that she felt as if she were tumbling into thin air through a hole in the flimsy floor on which their conversation stood. It was she who felt a fool. Soon she was reduced to a hardy silence.

Still, at the back of her mind, she remembered that he was an unattached gentleman, who would shortly have an income altogether of six or seven hundred a year. What did the man matter, if there were pecuniary ease! The man was a trifle thrown in. After twenty-two years her sentimentality was ground away, and only the millstone of poverty mattered to her. So she supported the little man as a representative of a decent income.

His most irritating habit was that of a sneering little giggle, all on his own, which came when he perceived or related some illogical absurdity on the part of another person. It was the only form of humour he had. Stupidity in thinking seemed to him exquisitely funny. But any novel was unintelligibly meaningless and dull, and to an Irish sort of humour he listened curiously, examining it like mathematics, or else simply not hearing. In normal human relationship he was not there. Quite unable to take part in simple everyday talk, he padded silently round the house, or sat in the dining-room looking nervously from side to side, always apart in a cold, rarefied little world of his own. Sometimes he made an ironic remark, that did not seem humanly relevant, or he gave his little laugh, like a sneer. He had to defend himself and his own insufficiency. And he answered questions grudgingly, with a yes or no, because he did not see their import and was nervous. It seemed to Miss Louisa he scarcely distinguished one person from another, but that he liked to be near to her, or to Miss Mary, for some sort of contact which stimulated him unknown.

Apart from all this, he was the most admirable workman. He was unremittingly shy, but perfect in his sense of duty: as far as he could conceive Christianity, he was a perfect Christian. Nothing that he realized he could do for anyone did he leave undone, although he was so incapable of coming into contact with another being that he could not proffer help. Now he attended assiduously to the sick man, investigated all the affairs of the parish or the church which Mr Lindley had in control, straightened out accounts, made lists of the sick and needy, padded round with help and to see what he could do. He heard of Mrs Lindley's anxiety about her sons, and began to investigate means of sending them to Cambridge. His kindness almost frightened Miss Mary. She honoured it so, and yet she shrank from it. For, in it all, Mr Massy seemed to have no sense of any person, any human being whom he was helping: he only realized a kind of mathematical working out, solving of given situations, a calculated well-doing. And it was as if he had accepted the

Christian tenets as axioms. His religion consisted in what his scrupulous, abstract mind approved of.

Seeing his acts, Miss Mary must respect and honour him. In consequence she must serve him. To this she had to force herself, shuddering and yet desirous, but he did not perceive it. She accompanied him on his visiting in the parish, and whilst she was cold with admiration for him, often she was touched with pity for the little padding figure with bent shoulders, buttoned up to the chin in his overcoat. She was a handsome, calm girl, tall, with a beautiful repose. Her clothes were poor, and she wore a black silk scarf, having no furs. But she was a lady. As the people saw her walking down Aldecross beside Mr Massy they said:

'My word, Miss Mary's got a catch. Did you ever see such a sickly little shrimp!'

She knew they were talking so, and it made her heart grow hot against them, and she drew herself as it were protectively towards the little man beside her. At any rate, she could see and give honour to his genuine goodness.

He could not walk fast, or far.

'You have not been well?' she asked, in her dignified way.

'I have an internal trouble.'

He was not aware of her slight shudder. There was silence, whilst she bowed to recover her composure, to resume her gentle manner towards him.

He was fond of Miss Mary. She had made it a rule of hospitality that he should always be escorted by herself or by her sister on his visits in the parish, which were not many. But some mornings she was engaged. Then Miss Louisa took her place. It was no good Miss Louisa's trying to adopt to Mr Massy an attitude of queenly service. She was unable to regard him save with aversion. When she saw him from behind, thin and bent-shouldered, looking like a sickly lad of thirteen, she disliked him exceedingly, and felt a desire to put him out of existence. And yet a deeper justice in Mary made Louisa humble before her sister.

They were going to see Mr Durant, who was paralysed and not expected to live. Miss Louisa was crudely ashamed at being admitted to the cottage in company with the little clergyman.

Mrs Durant was, however, much quieter in the face of her real trouble.

'How is Mr Durant?' asked Louisa.

'He is no different – and we don't expect him to be,' was the reply. The little clergyman stood looking on.

They went upstairs. The three stood for some time looking at the bed, at the grey head of the old man on the pillow, the grey beard over the sheet. Miss Louisa was shocked and afraid.

'It is so dreadful,' she said, with a shudder.

'It is how I always thought it would be,' replied Mrs Durant.

Then Miss Louisa was afraid of her. The two women were uneasy, waiting for Mr Massy to say something. He stood, small and bent, too nervous to speak.

'Has he any understanding?' he asked at length.

'Maybe,' said Mrs Durant. 'Can you hear, John?' she asked loudly. The dull blue eye of the inert man looked at her feebly.

'Yes, he understands,' said Mrs Durant to Mr Massy. Except for the dull look in his eyes, the sick man lay as if dead. The three stood in silence. Miss Louisa was obstinate but heavy-hearted under the load of unlivingness. It was Mr Massy who kept her there in discipline. His non-human will dominated them all.

Then they heard a sound below, a man's footsteps, and a man's voice called subduedly:

'Are you upstairs, mother?'

Mrs Durant started and moved to the door. But already a quick, firm step was running up the stairs.

'I'm a bit early, mother,' a troubled voice said, and on the landing they saw the form of the sailor. His mother came and clung to him. She was suddenly aware that she needed something to hold on to. He put his arms round her, and bent over her, kissing her.

'He's not gone, mother?' he asked anxiously, struggling to control his voice.

Miss Louisa looked away from the mother and son who stood together in the gloom on the landing. She could not bear it that she and Mr Massy should be there. The latter stood nervously, as if ill at ease before the emotion that was running. He was a witness nervous, unwilling, but dispassionate. To Miss Louisa's hot heart it seemed all, all wrong that they should be there.

Mrs Durant entered the bedroom, her face wet.

'There's Miss Louisa and the vicar,' she said, out of voice and quavering.

Her son, red-faced and slender, drew himself up to salute. But Miss Louisa held out her hand. Then she saw his hazel eyes recognize her for a moment, and his small white teeth showed in a glimpse of the greeting she used to love. She was covered with confusion. He went round to the bed; his boots clicked on the plaster floor, he bowed with dignity.

'How are you, dad?' he said, laying his hand on the sheet, faltering. But the old man stared fixedly and unseeing. The son stood perfectly still for a few minutes, then slowly recoiled. Miss Louisa saw the fine outline of his breast, under the sailor's blue blouse, as his chest began to heave.

'He doesn't know me,' he said, turning to his mother. He gradually went white.

'No, my boy!' cried the mother, pitiful, lifting her face. And suddenly she put her face against his shoulder, he was stooping down to her, holding her against him, and she cried aloud for a moment or two. Miss Louisa saw his sides heaving, and heard the sharp hiss of his breath. She turned away, tears streaming down her face. The father lay inert upon the white bed, Mr Massy looked queer and obliterated, so little now that the sailor with his sun-burned skin was in the room. He stood waiting. Miss Louisa wanted to die, she wanted to have done. She dared not turn round again to look.

'Shall I offer a prayer?' came the frail voice of the clergyman, and all kneeled down.

Miss Louisa was frightened of the inert man upon the bed. Then she felt a flash of fear of Mr Massy, hearing his thin, detached voice. And then, calmed, she looked up. On the far side of the bed were the heads of the mother and son, the one in the black lace cap, with the small white nape of the neck beneath, the other, with brown, sun-scorched hair too close and wiry to allow of a parting, and neck tanned firm, bowed as if unwillingly. The great grey beard of the old man did not move, the prayer continued. Mr Massy prayed with a pure lucidity that they all might conform to the higher Will. He was like something that dominated the bowed heads, something dispassionate that governed them inexorably. Miss Louisa was afraid of him. And she was bound, during the course of the prayer, to have a little reverence for him. It was like a foretaste of inexorable, cold death, a taste of pure justice.

That evening she talked to Mary of the visit. Her heart, her veins were possessed by the thought of Alfred Durant as he held his mother in his arms; then the break in his voice, as she remembered it again and again, was like a flame through her; and she wanted to see his face more distinctly in her mind, ruddy with the sun, and his golden-brown eyes, kind and careless, strained now with a natural fear, the fine nose tanned hard by the sun, the mouth that could not help smiling at her. And it went through her with pride, to think of his figure, a fine jet of life.

'He is a handsome lad,' said she to Miss Mary, as if he had not been a year older than herself. Underneath was the deeper dread, almost hatred, of the inhuman being of Mr Massy. She felt she must protect herself and Alfred from him.

'When I felt Mr Massy there,' she said, 'I almost hated him. What right had he to be there!'

'Surely he has all right,' said Miss Mary after a pause. 'He is *really* a Christian.'

'He seems to me nearly an imbecile,' said Miss Louisa.

Miss Mary, quiet and beautiful, was silent for a moment:

'Oh, no,' she said. 'Not *imbecile*—'

'Well then – he reminds me of a six months' child – or a five months' child – as if he didn't have time to get developed enough before he was born.'

'Yes,' said Miss Mary, slowly. 'There is something lacking. But there is something wonderful in him: and he is really *good*—'

'Yes,' said Miss Louisa, 'it doesn't seem right that he should be. What right has *that* to be called goodness!'

'But it *is* goodness,' persisted Mary. Then she added, with a laugh: 'And come, you wouldn't deny that as well.'

There was a doggedness in her voice. She went about very quietly. In her soul, she knew what was going to happen. She knew that Mr Massy was stronger than she, and that she must submit to what he was. Her physical self was prouder, stronger than he, her physical self disliked and despised him. But she was in the grip of his moral, mental being. And she felt the days allotted out to her. And her family watched.

IV

A few days after, old Mr Durant died. Miss Louisa saw Alfred once more, but he was stiff before her now, treating her not like a person, but as if she were some sort of will in command and he a separate, distinct will waiting in front of her. She had never felt such utter steel-plate separation from anyone. It puzzled her and frightened her. What had become of him? And she hated the military discipline – she was antagonistic to it. Now he was not himself. He was the will which obeys set over against the will which commands. She hesitated over accepting this. He had put himself out of her range. He had ranked himself inferior, subordinate to her. And that was how he could get away from her, that was how he would avoid all connection with her: by fronting her impersonally from the opposite camp, by taking up the abstract position of an inferior.

She went brooding steadily and sullenly over this, brooding and brooding. Her fierce, obstinate heart could not give way. It clung to its own rights. Sometimes she dismissed him. Why should he, her inferior, trouble her?

Then she relapsed to him, and almost hated him. It was his way of getting out of it. She felt the cowardice of it, his calmly placing her in a superior class, and placing himself inaccessibly apart, in an inferior, as if she, the sentient woman who was fond of him, did not count. But she was not going to submit. Dogged in her heart she held on to him.

V

In six months' time Miss Mary had married Mr Massy. There had been no love-making, nobody had made any remark. But everybody was tense and callous with expectation. When one day Mr Massy asked for Mary's hand, Mr Lindley started and trembled from the thin, abstract voice of the little man. Mr Massy was very nervous, but so curiously absolute.

'I shall be very glad,' said the vicar, 'but of course the decision lies with Mary herself.' And his still feeble hand shook as he moved a Bible on his desk.

The small man, keeping fixedly to his idea, padded out of the room to find Miss Mary. He sat a long time by her, while she made some conversation, before he had readiness to speak. She was afraid of what was coming, and sat stiff in apprehension. She felt as if her body would rise and fling him aside. But her spirit quivered and waited. Almost in expectation she waited, almost wanting him. And then she knew he would speak.

'I have already asked Mr Lindley,' said the clergyman, while suddenly she looked with aversion at his little knees, 'if he would consent to my proposal.' He was aware of his own disadvantage, but his will was set.

She went cold as she sat, and impervious, almost as if she had become stone. He waited a moment nervously. He would not persuade her. He himself had never even heard persuasion, but pursued his own course. He looked at her, sure of himself, unsure of her, and said:

'Will you become my wife, Mary?'

Still her heart was hard and cold. She sat proudly.

'I should like to speak to mama first,' she said.

'Very well,' replied Mr Massy. And in a moment he padded away.

Mary went to her mother. She was cold and reserved.

'Mr Massy has asked me to marry him, mama,' she said. Mrs Lindley went on staring at her book. She was cramped in her feeling.

'Well, and what did you say?'

They were both keeping calm and cold.

'I said I would speak to you before answering him.'

This was equivalent to a question. Mrs Lindley did not want to reply to it. She shifted her heavy form irritably on the couch. Miss Mary sat calm and straight, with closed mouth.

'Your father thinks it would not be a bad match,' said the mother, as if casually.

Nothing more was said. Everybody remained cold and shut-off. Miss Mary did not speak to Miss Louisa, the Reverend Ernest Lindley kept out of sight.

At evening Miss Mary accepted Mr Massy.

'Yes, I will marry you,' she said, with even a little movement of tenderness towards him. He was embarrassed, but satisfied. She could see him making some movement towards her, could feel the male in him, something cold and triumphant, asserting itself. She sat rigid, and waited.

When Miss Louisa knew, she was silent with bitter anger against everybody, even against Mary. She felt her faith wounded. Did the real things to her not matter after all? She wanted to get away. She thought of Mr Massy. He had some curious power, some unanswerable right. He was a will that they could not controvert. Suddenly a flush started in her. If he had come to her she would have flipped him out of the room. He was never going to touch *her*. And she was glad. She was glad that her blood would rise and exterminate the little man, if he came too near to her, no matter how her judgment was paralysed by him, no matter how he moved in abstract goodness. She thought she was perverse to be glad, but glad she was. 'I would just flip him out of the room,' she said, and she derived great satisfaction from the open statement. Nevertheless, perhaps she ought still to feel that Mary, on her plane, was a higher being than herself. But then Mary was Mary, and she was Louisa, and that also was inalterable.

Mary, in marrying him, tried to become a pure reason such as he was, without feeling or impulse. She shut herself up, she shut herself rigid against the agonies of shame and the terror of violation which came at first. She *would* not feel, and she *would* not feel. She was a pure will acquiescing to him. She elected a certain kind of fate. She would be good and purely just, she would live in a higher freedom than she had ever known, she would be free of mundane care, she was a pure will towards right. She had sold herself, but she had a new freedom. She had got rid of her body. She had sold a lower thing, her body, for a higher thing, her freedom from material things. She considered that she paid for all she got from her husband. So, in kind of independence, she moved proud and free. She had paid with her body: that was henceforward out of consideration. She was glad to be rid of it. She had bought her position in the world – that henceforth was taken for granted. There remained only the direction of her activity towards charity and high-minded living.

She could scarcely bear other people to be present with her and her husband. Her private life was her shame. But then, she could keep it hidden. She lived almost isolated in the rectory of the tiny village miles from the railway. She suffered as if it were an insult to her own flesh, seeing the repulsion which some people felt for her husband, or the special manner they had of treating him, as if he were a 'case'. But most people were uneasy before him, which restored her pride.

If she had let herself, she would have hated him, hated his padding round the house, his thin voice devoid of human understanding, his bent little shoulders and rather incomplete face that reminded her of an abortion. But rigorously she kept her position. She took care of him and was just to him. There was also a deep, craven fear of him, something slave-like.

There was not much fault to be found with his behaviour. He was scrupulously just and kind according to his lights. But the male in him was cold and self-complete, and utterly domineering. Weak, insufficient little thing as he was, she had not expected this of him. It was something in the bargain she had not understood. It made her hold her head, to keep still. She knew, vaguely, that she was murdering herself. After all, her body was not quite so easy to get rid of. And this manner of disposing of it – ah, sometimes she felt she must rise and bring about death, lift her hand for utter denial of everything, by a general destruction.

He was almost unaware of the conditions about him. He did not fuss in the domestic way, she did as she liked in the house. Indeed, she was a great deal free of him. He would sit obliterated for hours. He was kind, and almost anxiously considerate. But when he considered he was right, his will was just blindly male, like a cold machine. And on most points he was logically right, or he had with him the right of the creed they both accepted. It was so. There was nothing for her to go against.

Then she found herself with child, and felt for the first time horror, afraid before God and man. This also she had to go through – it was the right. When the child arrived, it was a bonny, healthy lad. Her heart hurt in her body, as she took the baby between her hands. The flesh that was trampled and silent in her must speak again in the boy. After all, she had to live – it was not so simple after all. Nothing was finished completely. She looked and looked at the baby, and almost hated it, and suffered an anguish of love for it. She hated it because it made her live again in the flesh, when she *could* not live in the flesh, she could not. She wanted to trample her flesh down, down, extinct, to live in the mind. And now there was this child. It was too cruel, too racking. For she must love the child. Her purpose was broken in two again. She had to become amorphous, purposeless, without real being. As a mother, she was a fragmentary, ignoble thing.

Mr Massy, blind to everything else in the way of human feeling, became obsessed by the idea of his child. When it arrived, suddenly it filled the whole world of feeling for him. It was his obsession, his terror was for its safety and well-being. It was something new, as if he himself had been born a naked infant, conscious of his own exposure, and full of apprehension. He who had never been aware of anyone else, all his life, now was aware of nothing but the child. Not that he ever played with it, or kissed it, or tended it. He did nothing for it. But it dominated him, it filled, and at the same time emptied his mind. The world was all baby for him.

This his wife must also bear, his question: 'What is the reason that he cries?' – his reminder, at the first sound: 'Mary, that is the child,' – his restlessness if the feeding-time were five minutes past. She had bargained for this – now she must stand by her bargain.

VI

Miss Louisa, at home in the dingy vicarage, had suffered a great deal over her sister's wedding. Having once begun to cry out against it, during the engagement, she had been silenced by Mary's quiet: 'I don't agree with you about him, Louisa, I *want* to marry him.' Then Miss Louisa had been angry deep in her heart, and therefore silent. This dangerous state started the change in her. Her own revulsion made her recoil from the hitherto undoubted Mary.

'I'd beg the streets barefoot first,' said Miss Louisa, thinking of Mr Massy.

But evidently Mary could perform a different heroism. So she, Louisa the practical, suddenly felt that Mary, her ideal, was questionable after all. How could she be pure – one cannot be dirty in act and spiritual in being. Louisa distrusted Mary's high spirituality. It was no longer genuine for her. And if Mary were spiritual and misguided, why did not her father protect her? Because of the money. He disliked the whole affair, but he backed away, because of the money. And the mother frankly did not care: her daughters could do as they liked. Her mother's pronouncement:

'Whatever happens to *him*, Mary is safe for life,' – so evidently and shallowly a calculation, incensed Louisa.

'I'd rather be safe in the workhouse,' she cried.

'Your father will see to that,' replied her mother brutally. This speech, in its directness, so injured Miss Louisa that she hated her mother deep, deep in her heart, and almost hated herself. It was a long time resolving itself out, this hate. But it worked and worked, and at last the young woman said:

'They are wrong – they are all wrong. They have ground out their souls for what isn't worth anything, and there isn't a grain of love in them anywhere. And I *will* have love. They want us to deny it. They've never found it, so they want to say it doesn't exist. But I *will* have it. I *will* love – it is my birthright. I will love the man I marry – that is all I care about.'

So Miss Louisa stood isolated from everybody. She and Mary had parted over Mr Massy. In Louisa's eyes, Mary was degraded, married to Mr Massy. She could not bear to think of her lofty, spiritual sister degraded in the body like this. Mary was wrong, wrong, wrong: she was not superior, she was flawed, incomplete. The two sisters stood apart. They still loved each other, they would love each other as long as they lived. But they had parted ways. A new solitariness came over the obstinate Louisa, and her heavy jaw set stubbornly. She was going on her own way. But which way? She was quite alone, with a blank world before her. How could she be said to have any way? Yet she had her fixed will to love, to have the man she loved.

VII

When her boy was three years old, Mary had another baby, a girl. The three years had gone by monotonously. They might have been an eternity, they might have been brief as a sleep. She did not know. Only, there was always a weight on top of her, something that pressed down her life. The only thing that had happened was that Mr Massy had had an operation. He was always exceedingly fragile. His wife had soon learned to attend to him mechanically, as part of her duty.

But this third year, after the baby girl had been born, Mary felt oppressed and depressed. Christmas drew near: the gloomy, unleavened Christmas of the rectory, where all the days were of the same dark fabric. And Mary was afraid. It was as if the darkness were coming upon her.

'Edward, I should like to go home for Christmas,' she said, and a certain terror filled her as she spoke.

'But you can't leave baby,' said her husband, blinking.

'We can all go.'

He thought, and stared in his collective fashion.

'Why do you wish to go?' he asked.

'Because I need a change. A change would do me good, and it would be good for the milk.'

He heard the will in his wife's voice, and was at a loss. Her language was unintelligible to him. But somehow he felt that Mary was set upon it. And while she was breeding, either about to have a child, or nursing, he regarded her as a special sort of being.

'Wouldn't it hurt baby to take her by the train?' he said.

'No,' replied the mother, 'why should it?'

They went. When they were in the train it began to snow. From the window of his first-class carriage the little clergyman watched the big flakes sweep by, like a blind drawn across the country. He was obsessed by thought of the baby, and afraid of the draughts of the carriage.

'Sit right in the corner,' he said to his wife, 'and hold baby close back.'

She moved at his bidding, and stared out of the window. His eternal presence was like an iron weight on her brain. But she was going partially to escape for a few days.

'Sit on the other side, Jack,' said the father. 'It is less draughty. Come to this window.'

He watched the boy in anxiety. But his children were the only beings in the world who took not the slightest notice of him.

'Look, mother, look!' cried the boy. 'They fly right in my face' – he meant the snowflakes.

'Come into this corner,' repeated his father, out of another world.

'He's jumped on this one's back, mother, an' they're riding to the bottom!' cried the boy, jumping with glee.

'Tell him to come on this side,' the little man bade his wife.

'Jack, kneel on this cushion,' said the mother, putting her white hand on the place.

The boy slid over in silence to the place she indicated, waited still for a moment, then almost deliberately, stridently cried:

'Look at all those in the corner, mother, making a heap,' and he pointed to the cluster of snowflakes with finger pressed dramatically on the pane, and he turned to his mother a bit ostentatiously.

'All in a heap!' she said.

He had seen her face, and had her response, and he was somewhat assured. Vaguely uneasy, he was reassured if he could win her attention.

They arrived at the vicarage at half-past two, not having had lunch.

'How are you, Edward?' said Mr Lindley, trying on his side to be fatherly. But he was always in a false position with his son-in-law, frustrated before him, therefore, as much as possible, he shut his eyes and ears to him. The vicar was looking thin and pale and ill-nourished. He had gone quite grey. He was, however, still haughty; but, since the growing-up of his children, it was a brittle haughtiness, that might break at any moment and leave the vicar only an impoverished, pitiable figure. Mrs Lindley took all the notice of her daughter, and of the children. She ignored her son-in-law. Miss Louisa was clucking and laughing and rejoicing over the baby. Mr Massy stood aside, a bent, persistent little figure.

'Oh a pretty! – a little pretty! oh a cold little pretty come in a railway train!' Miss Louisa was cooing to the infant, crouching on the hearth-rug, opening the white woollen wraps and exposing the child to the fireglow.

'Mary,' said the little clergyman, 'I think it would be better to give baby a warm bath; she may take cold.'

'I think it is not necessary,' said the mother, coming and closing her hand judiciously over the rosy feet and hands of the mite. 'She is not chilly.'

'Not a bit,' cried Miss Louisa. 'She's not caught cold.'

'I'll go and bring her flannels,' said Mr Massy, with one idea.

'I can bath her in the kitchen then,' said Mary, in an altered, cold tone.

'You can't, the girl is scrubbing there,' said Miss Louisa. 'Besides, she doesn't want a bath at this time of day.'

'She'd better have one,' said Mary, quietly, out of submission. Miss Louisa's gorge rose, and she was silent. When the little man padded down with the flannels on his arm, Mrs Lindley asked:

'Hadn't *you* better take a hot bath, Edward?'

But the sarcasm was lost on the little clergyman. He was absorbed in the preparations round the baby.

The room was dull and threadbare, and the snow outside seemed fairy-like by comparison, so white on the lawn and tufted on the bushes. Indoors the heavy pictures hung obscurely on the walls, everything was dingy with gloom.

Except in the fireglow, where they had laid the bath on the hearth. Mrs Massy, her black hair always smoothly coiled and queenly, kneeled by the bath, wearing a rubber apron, and holding the kicking child. Her husband stood holding the towels and the flannels to warm. Louisa, too cross to share in the joy of the baby's bath, was laying the table. The boy was hanging on the door-knob, wrestling with it to get out. His father looked round.

'Come away from the door, Jack,' he said ineffectually. Jack tugged harder at the knob as if he did not hear. Mr Massy blinked at him.

'He must come away from the door, Mary,' he said. 'There will be a draught if it is opened.'

'Jack, come away from the door, dear,' said the mother, dexterously turning the shiny wet baby on to her towelled knee, then glancing round: 'Go and tell Auntie Louisa about the train.'

Louisa, also afraid to open the door, was watching the scene on the hearth. Mr Massy stood holding the baby's flannel, as if assisting at some ceremonial. If everybody had not been subduedly angry, it would have been ridiculous.

'I want to see out of the window,' Jack said. His father turned hastily.

'Do *you* mind lifting him on to a chair, Louisa,' said Mary hastily. The father was too delicate.

When the baby was flannelled, Mr Massy went upstairs and returned with four pillows, which he set in the fender to warm. Then he stood watching the mother feed her child, obsessed by the idea of his infant.

Louisa went on with her preparations for the meal. She could not have told why she was so sullenly angry. Mrs Lindley, as usual, lay silently watching.

Mary carried her child upstairs, followed by her husband with the pillows. After a while he came down again.

'What is Mary doing? Why doesn't she come down to eat?' asked Mrs Lindley.

'She is staying with the baby. The room is rather cold. I will ask the girl to put in a fire.' He was going absorbedly to the door.

'But Mary has had nothing to eat. It is *she* who will catch cold,' said the mother, exasperated.

Mr Massy seemed as if he did not hear. Yet he looked at his mother-in-law, and answered:

'I will take her something.'

He went out. Mrs Lindley shifted on her couch with anger. Miss Louisa glowered. But no one said anything, because of the money that came to the vicarage from Mr Massy.

Louisa went upstairs. Her sister was sitting by the bed, reading a scrap of paper.

'Won't you come down and eat?' the younger asked.

'In a moment or two,' Mary replied, in a quiet, reserved voice, that forbade anyone to approach her.

It was this that made Miss Louisa most furious. She went downstairs, and announced to her mother:

'I am going out. I may not be home to tea.'

VIII

No one remarked on her exit. She put on her fur hat, that the village people knew so well, and the old Norfolk jacket. Louisa was short and plump and plain. She had her mother's heavy jaw, her father's proud brow, and her own grey, brooding eyes that were very beautiful when she smiled. It was true, as the people said, that she looked sulky. Her chief attraction was her glistening, heavy, deep-blonde hair, which shone and gleamed with a richness that was not entirely foreign to her.

'Where am I going?' she said to herself, when she got outside in the snow. She did not hesitate, however, but by mechanical walking found herself descending the hill towards Old Aldecross. In the valley that was black with trees, the colliery breathed in stertorous pants, sending out high conical columns of steam that remained upright, whiter than the snow on the hills, yet shadowy, in the dead air. Louisa would not acknowledge to herself whither she was making her way, till she came to the railway crossing. Then the bunches of snow in the twigs of the apple tree that leaned towards the fence told her she must go and see Mrs Durant. The tree was in Mrs Durant's garden.

Alfred was now at home again, living with his mother in the cottage below the road. From the highway hedge, by the railway crossing, the snowy garden sheered down steeply, like the side of a hole, then dropped straight in a wall. In this depth the house was snug, its chimney just level with the road. Miss Louisa descended the stone stairs, and stood below in the little back-yard, in the dimness and the semi-secrecy. A big tree leaned overhead, above the paraffin-hut. Louisa felt secure from all the world down there. She knocked at the open door, then looked round. The tongue of garden narrowing in from the quarry bed was white with snow: she thought of the thick fringes of snowdrops it would show beneath the currant bushes in a month's time. The ragged fringe of pinks hanging over the garden brim behind her was whitened now with snowflakes, that in summer held white blossom to Louisa's face. It was pleasant, she thought, to gather flowers that stooped to one's face from above.

She knocked again. Peeping in, she saw the scarlet glow of the kitchen, red firelight falling on the brick floor and on the bright chintz cushions. It was alive and bright as a peep-show. She crossed the scullery, where still an almanac hung. There was no one about. 'Mrs Durant,' called Louisa softly, 'Mrs Durant.'

She went up the brick step into the front room, that still had its little shop counter and its bundles of goods, and she called from the stair-foot. Then she knew Mrs Durant was out.

She went into the yard, to follow the old woman's footsteps up the garden path.

She emerged from the bushes and raspberry canes. There was the whole quarry bed, a wide garden white and dimmed, brindled with dark bushes, lying half submerged. On the left, overhead, the little colliery train rumbled by. Right away at the back was a mass of trees.

Louisa followed the open path, looking from right to left, and then she gave a cry of concern. The old woman was sitting rocking slightly among the ragged snowy cabbages. Louisa ran to her, found her whimpering with little, involuntary cries.

'Whatever have you done?' cried Louisa, kneeling in the snow.

'I've – I've— I was pulling a brussel-sprout stalk – and – oh-h! – something tore inside me. I've had a pain,' the old woman wept from shock and suffering, gasping between her whimpers, – 'I've had a pain there – a long time – and now – oh – oh!' She panted, pressed her hand on her side, leaned as if she would faint, looking yellow against the snow. Louisa supported her.

'Do you think you could walk now?' she asked.

'Yes,' gasped the old woman.

Louisa helped her to her feet.

'Get the cabbage – I want it for Alfred's dinner,' panted Mrs Durant. Louisa picked up the stalk of brussel-sprouts, and with difficulty got the old woman indoors. She gave her brandy, laid her on the couch, saying:

'I'm going to send for a doctor – wait just a minute.'

The young woman ran up the steps to the public-house a few yards away. The landlady was astonished to see Miss Louisa.

'Will you send for a doctor at once to Mrs Durant,' she said, with some of her father in her commanding tone.

'Is something the matter?' fluttered the landlady in concern.

Louisa, glancing out up the road, saw the grocer's cart driving to Eastwood. She ran and stopped the man, and told him.

Mrs Durant lay on the sofa, her face turned away, when the young woman came back.

'Let me put you to bed,' Louisa said. Mrs Durant did not resist.

Louisa knew the ways of working people. In the bottom drawer of the dresser she found dusters and flannels. With the old pit-flannel she snatched out the oven shelves, wrapped them up, and put them in the bed. From the son's bed she took a blanket, and, running down, set it before the fire. Having undressed the little old woman, Louisa carried her upstairs.

'You'll drop me, you'll drop me!' cried Mrs Durant.

Louisa did not answer, but bore her burden quickly. She could not light a fire, because there was no fire-place in the bedroom. And the floor was plaster. So she fetched the lamp, and stood it lighted in one corner.

'It will air the room,' she said.

'Yes,' moaned the old woman.

Louisa ran with more hot flannels, replacing those from the oven shelves. Then she made a bran-bag and laid it on the woman's side. There was a big lump on the side of the abdomen.

'I've felt it coming a long time,' moaned the old lady, when the pain was easier, 'but I've not said anything; I didn't want to upset our Alfred.'

Louisa did not see why 'our Alfred' should be spared.

'What time is it?' came the plaintive voice.

'A quarter to four.'

'Oh!' wailed the old lady, 'he'll be here in half an hour, and no dinner ready for him.'

'Let me do it?' said Louisa, gently.

'There's that cabbage – and you'll find the meat in the pantry – and there's an apple-pie you can hot up. But *don't you* do it—!'

'Who will, then?' asked Louisa.

'I don't know,' moaned the sick woman, unable to consider.

Louisa did it. The doctor came and gave serious examination. He looked very grave.

'What is it, doctor?' asked the old lady, looking up at him with old, pathetic eyes in which already hope was dead.

'I think you've torn the skin in which a tumour hangs,' he replied.

'Ay!' she murmured, and she turned away.

'You see, she may die any minute – and it *may* be swaled away,' said the old doctor to Louisa.

The young woman went upstairs again.

'He says the lump may be swaled away, and you may get quite well again,' she said.

'Ay!' murmured the old lady. It did not deceive her. Presently she asked:

'Is there a good fire?'

'I think so,' answered Louisa.

'He'll want a good fire,' the mother said. Louisa attended to it.

Since the death of Durant, the widow had come to church occasionally, and Louisa had been friendly to her. In the girl's heart the purpose was fixed. No man had affected her as Alfred Durant had done, and to that she kept. In her heart, she adhered to him. A natural sympathy existed between her and his rather hard, materialistic mother.

Alfred was the most lovable of the old woman's sons. He had grown up like the rest, however, headstrong and blind to everything but his own will. Like the other boys, he had insisted on going into the pit as soon as he left school, because that was the only way speedily to become a man, level with all the other men. This was a great chagrin to his mother, who would have liked to have this last of her sons a gentleman.

But still he remained constant to her. His feeling for her was deep and unexpressed. He noticed when she was tired, or when she had a new night-cap. And he bought little things for her occasionally. She was not wise enough to see how much he lived by her.

At the bottom he did not satisfy her, he did not seem manly enough. He liked to read books occasionally, and better still he liked to play the piccolo. It amused her to see his head nod over the instrument as he made an effort to get the right note. It made her fond of him, with tenderness, almost pity, but not with respect. She wanted a man to be fixed, going his own way without knowledge of women. Whereas she knew Alfred depended on her. He sang in the choir because he liked singing.

In the summer he worked in the garden, attended to the fowls and pigs. He kept pigeons. He played on Saturday in the cricket or football team. But to her he did not seem the man, the independent man her other boys had been. He was her baby – and whilst she loved him for it, she was a little bit contemptuous of him.

There grew up a little hostility between them. Then he began to drink, as the others had done; but not in their blind, oblivious way. He was a little self-conscious over it. She saw this, and she pitied it in him. She loved him most, but she was not satisfied with him because he was not free of her. He could not quite go his own way.

Then at twenty he ran away and served his time in the Navy. This had made a man of him. He had hated it bitterly, the service, the subordination. For years he fought with himself under the military discipline, for his own self-respect, struggling through blind anger and shame and a cramping sense of inferiority. Out of humiliation and self-hatred he rose into a sort of inner freedom. And his love for his mother, whom he idealized, remained the fact of hope and of belief.

He came home again, nearly thirty years old, but naïve and inexperienced as a boy, only with a silence about him that was new: a sort of dumb humility before life, a fear of living. He was almost quite chaste. A strong sensitiveness had kept him from women. Sexual talk was all very well among men, but somehow it had no application to living women. There were two things for him, the *idea* of women, with which he sometimes debauched himself, and real women, before whom he felt a deep uneasiness, and a need to draw away. He shrank and defended himself from the approach of any woman. And then he felt ashamed. In his innermost soul he felt he was not a man, he was less than the normal man. In Genoa he went with an under-officer to a drinking-house where the cheaper sort of girl came in to look for lovers. He sat there with his glass, the girls looked at him, but they never came to him. He knew that if they did come he could only pay for food and drink for them, because he felt a pity for them, and was anxious lest they lacked good necessities. He could not have gone with one of them; he knew it, and was ashamed, looking with curious envy at the swaggering, easy-passionate Italian whose body went to a woman by instinctive impersonal attraction. They were men, he was not a man. He sat feeling short, feeling like a leper. And he went away, imagining sexual scenes between himself and a woman, walking wrapt in this indulgence. But when the ready woman presented herself, the very fact that she was a palpable woman made it impossible for him to touch her. And this incapacity was like a core of rottenness in him.

So several times he went, drunk, with his companions, to the licensed prostitute-houses abroad. But the sordid insignificance of the experience appalled him. It had not been anything really: it meant nothing. He felt as if he were, not physically, but spiritually impotent: not actually impotent, but intrinsically so.

He came home with this secret, never-changing burden of his unknown, unbestowed self torturing him. His Navy training left him in perfect physical condition. He was sensible of, and proud of his body. He bathed and used dumb-bells, and kept himself fit. He played cricket and football. He read books and began to hold fixed ideas which he got from the Fabians. He played his piccolo, and was considered an expert. But at the bottom of his soul was always this canker of shame and incompleteness: he was miserable beneath all his healthy cheerfulness, he was uneasy and felt despicable among all his confidence and superiority of ideas. He would have changed with any mere brute, just to be free of himself, to be free of this shame of self-consciousness. He saw some collier lurching straight forward without misgiving, pursuing his own satisfactions, and he envied him. Anything, he would have given for this spontaneity and this blind stupidity which went to its own satisfaction direct.

IX

He was not unhappy in the pit. He was admired by the men, and well enough liked. It was only he himself who felt the difference between himself and the others. He seemed to hide his own stigma. But he was never sure that the others did not really despise him for a ninny, as being less a man than they were. Only he pretended to be more manly, and was surprised by the ease with which they were deceived. And, being naturally cheerful, he was happy at work. He was sure of himself there. Naked to the waist, hot and grimy with labour, they squatted on their heels for a few minutes and talked, seeing each other dimly by the light of the safety lamps, while the black coal rose jutting round them, and the props of wood stood like little pillars in the low, black, very dark temple. Then the pony came and the gang-lad with a message from Number 7, or with a bottle of water from the horse-trough or some news of the world above. The day passed pleasantly enough. There was an ease, a go-as-you-please about the day underground, a delightful camaraderie of men shut off alone from the rest of the world, in a dangerous place. and a variety of labour, holing, loading, timbering, and a glamour of mystery and adventure in the atmosphere, that made the pit not unattractive to him when he had again got over his anguish of desire for the open air and the sea.

This day there was much to do and Durant was not in humour to talk. He went on working in silence through the afternoon.

'Loose-all' came, and they tramped to the bottom. The white-washed underground office shone brightly. Men were putting out their lamps. They sat in dozens round the bottom of the shaft, down which black, heavy drops of water fell continuously into the sump. The electric lights shone away down the main underground road.

'Is it raining?' asked Durant.

'Snowing,' said an old man, and the younger was pleased. He liked to go up when it was snowing.

'It'll just come right for Christmas?' said the old man.

'Ay,' replied Durant.

'A green Christmas, a fat churchyard,' said the other sententiously.

Durant laughed, showing his small, rather pointed teeth.

The cage came down, a dozen men lined on. Durant noticed tufts of snow on the perforated, arched roof of the chain, and he was pleased. He wondered how it liked its excursion underground. But already it was getting soppy with black water.

He liked things about him. There was a little smile on his face. But underlying it was the curious consciousness he felt in himself.

The upper world came almost with a flash, because of the glimmer of snow. Hurrying along the bank, giving up his lamp at the office, he smiled to feel the open about him again, all glimmering round him with snow. The hills on either hand were pale blue in the dusk, and the hedges looked savage and dark. The snow was trampled between the railway lines. But far ahead, beyond the black figures of miners moving home, it became smooth again, spreading right up to the dark wall of the coppice.

To the west there was a pinkness, and a big star hovered half revealed. Below, the lights of the pit came out crisp and yellow among the darkness of the buildings, and the lights of Old Aldecross twinkled in rows down the bluish twilight.

Durant walked glad with life among the miners, who were

all talking animatedly because of the snow. He liked their company, he liked the white dusky world. It gave him a little thrill to stop at the garden gate and see the light of home down below, shining on the silent blue snow.

X

By the big gate of the railway, in the fence, was a little gate, that he kept locked. As he unfastened it, he watched the kitchen light that shone on to the bushes and the snow outside. It was a candle burning till night set in, he thought to himself. He slid down the steep path to the level below. He liked making the first marks in the smooth snow. Then he came through the bushes to the house. The two women heard his heavy boots ring outside on the scraper, and his voice as he opened the door:

'How much worth of oil do you reckon to save by that candle, mother?' He liked a good light from the lamp.

He had just put down his bottle and snap-bag and was hanging his coat behind the scullery door, when Miss Louisa came upon him. He was startled, but he smiled.

His eyes began to laugh – then his face went suddenly straight, and he was afraid.

'Your mother's had an accident,' she said.

'How?' he exclaimed.

'In the garden,' she answered. He hesitated with his coat in his hands. Then he hung it up and turned to the kitchen.

'Is she in bed?' he asked.

'Yes,' said Miss Louisa, who found it hard to deceive him. He was silent. He went into the kitchen, sat down heavily in his father's old chair, and began to pull off his boots. His head was small, rather finely shapen. His brown hair, close and crisp, would look jolly whatever happened. He wore heavy, moleskin trousers that gave off the stale, exhausted scent of the pit. Having put on his slippers, he carried his boots into the scullery.

'What is it?' he asked, afraid.

'Something internal,' she replied.

He went upstairs. His mother kept herself calm for his coming. Louisa felt his tread shake the plaster floor of the bedroom above.

'What have you done?' he asked.

'It's nothing, my lad,' said the old woman, rather hard. 'It's nothing. You needn't fret, my boy, it's nothing more the matter with me than I had yesterday, or last week. The doctor said I'd done nothing serious.'

'What were you doing?' asked her son.

'I was pulling up a cabbage, and I suppose I pulled too hard; for, oh – there was such a pain—'

Her son looked at her quickly. She hardened herself.

'But who doesn't have a sudden pain sometimes, my boy? We all do.'

'And what's it done?'

'I don't know,' she said, 'but I don't suppose it's anything.'

The big lamp in the corner was screened with a dark green screen, so that he could scarcely see her face. He was strung tight with apprehension and many emotions. Then his brow knitted.

'What did you go pulling your inside out at cabbages for, he asked, 'and the ground frozen? You'd go on dragging and dragging, if you killed yourself.'

'Somebody's got to get them,' she said.

'You needn't do yourself harm.'

But they had reached futility.

Miss Louisa could hear plainly downstairs. Her heart sank. It seemed so hopeless between them.

'Are you sure it's nothing much, mother?' he asked, appealing, after a little silence.

'Ay, it's nothing,' said the old woman, rather bitter.

'I don't want you to – to – to be badly – you know.'

'Go an' get your dinner,' she said. She knew she was going to die: moreover, the pain was torture just then. 'They're only cosseting me up a bit because I'm an old woman. Miss Louisa's very good – and she'll have got your dinner ready, so you'd better go and eat it.'

He felt stupid and ashamed. His mother put him off. He had to turn away. The pain burned in his bowels. He went downstairs. The mother was glad he was gone, so that she could moan with pain.

He had resumed the old habit of eating before he washed himself. Miss Louisa served his dinner. It was strange and exciting to her. She was strung up tense, trying to understand him and his mother. She watched him as he sat. He was turned away from his food, looking in the fire. Her soul watched him, trying to see what he was. His black face and arms were uncouth, he was foreign. His face was masked black with coal-dust. She could not see him, she could not know him. The brown eyebrows, the steady eyes, the coarse, small moustache above the closed mouth – these were the only familiar indications. What was he, as he sat there in his pit-dirt? She could not see him, and it hurt her.

She ran upstairs, presently coming down with flannels and the bran-bag, to heat them, because the pain was on again.

He was half-way through his dinner. He put down the fork, suddenly nauseated.

'They will soothe the wrench,' she said. He watched, useless and left out.

'Is she bad?' he asked.

'I think she is,' she answered.

It was useless for him to stir or comment. Louisa was busy. She went upstairs. The poor old woman was in a white, cold sweat of pain. Louisa's face was sullen with suffering as she went about to relieve her. Then she sat and waited. The pain passed gradually, the old woman sank into a state of coma. Louisa still sat silent by the bed. She heard the sound of water downstairs. Then came the voice of the old mother, faint but unrelaxing:

'Alfred's washing himself – he'll want his back washing—'

Louisa listened anxiously, wondering what the sick woman wanted.

'He can't bear if his back isn't washed—' the old woman persisted, in a cruel attention to his needs. Louisa rose and wiped the sweat from the yellowish brow.

'I will go down,' she said soothingly.

'If you would,' murmured the sick woman.

Louisa waited a moment. Mrs Durant closed her eyes, having discharged her duty. The young woman went downstairs. Herself, or the man, what did they matter? Only the suffering woman must be considered.

Alfred was kneeling on the hearth-rug, stripped to the waist, washing himself in a large panchion of earthenware. He did so every evening, when he had eaten his dinner; his brothers had done so before him. But Miss Louisa was strange in the house.

He was mechanically rubbing the white lather on his head, with a repeated, unconscious movement, his hand every now and then passing over his neck. Louisa watched. She had to brace herself to this also. He bent his head into the water, washed it free of soap, and pressed the water out of his eyes.

'Your mother said you would want your back washing,' she said.

Curious how it hurt her to take part in their fixed routine of life! Louisa felt the almost repulsive intimacy being forced upon her. It was all so common, so like herding. She lost her own distinctness.

He ducked his face round, looking up at her in what was a very comical way. She had to harden herself.

'How funny he looks with his face upside down,' she thought. After all, there was a difference between her and the common people. The water in which his arms were plunged was quite black, the soap-froth was darkish. She could scarcely conceive him as human. Mechanically, under the influence of habit, he groped in the black water, fished out soap and flannel, and handed them backward to Louisa. Then he remained rigid and submissive, his two arms thrust straight in the panchion, supporting the weight of his shoulders. His skin was beautifully white and unblemished, of an opaque, solid whiteness. Gradually Louisa saw it: this also was what he was. It fascinated her. Her feelings of separateness passed away: she ceased to draw back from contact with him and his mother. There was this living centre. Her heart ran hot. She had reached some goal in this beautiful, clean, male body. She loved him in a white, impersonal heat. But the sun-burnt, reddish neck and ears: they were more personal, more curious. A tenderness rose in her, she loved even his queer ears. A person – an intimate being he was to her. She put down the towel and went upstairs again, troubled in her heart. She had only seen one human being in her life – and that was Mary. All the rest were strangers. Now her soul was going to open, she was going to see another. She felt strange and pregnant.

'He'll be more comfortable,' murmured the sick woman abstractedly, as Louisa entered the room. The latter did not answer. Her own heart was heavy with its own responsibility. Mrs Durant lay silent awhile, then she murmured plaintively:

'You mustn't mind, Miss Louisa.'

'Why should I?' replied Louisa, deeply moved.

'It's what we're used to,' said the old woman.

And Louisa felt herself excluded again from their life. She

sat in pain, with the tears of disappointment distilling in her heart. Was that all?

Alfred came upstairs. He was clean, and in his shirt-sleeves. He looked a workman now. Louisa felt that she and he were foreigners, moving in different lives. It dulled her again. Oh, if she could only find some fixed relations, something sure and abiding.

'How do you feel?' he said to his mother.

'It's a bit better,' she replied wearily, impersonally. This strange putting herself aside, this abstracting herself and answering him only what she thought good for him to hear, made the relations between mother and son poignant and cramping to Miss Louisa. It made the man so ineffectual, so nothing. Louisa groped as if she had lost him. The mother was real and positive – he was not very actual. It puzzled and chilled the young woman.

'I'd better fetch Mrs Harrison?' he said, waiting for his mother to decide.

'I suppose we shall have to have somebody,' she replied.

Miss Louisa stood by, afraid to interfere in their business. They did not include her in their lives, they felt she had nothing to do with them, except as a help from outside. She was quite external to them. She felt hurt and powerless against this unconscious difference. But something patient and unyielding in her made her say:

'I will stay and do the nursing: you can't be left.'

The other two were shy, and at a loss for an answer.

'We s'll manage to get somebody,' said the old woman wearily. She did not care very much what happened, now.

'I will stay until tomorrow, in any case,' said Louisa. 'Then we can see.'

'I'm sure you've no right to trouble yourself,' moaned the old woman. But she must leave herself in my hands.

Miss Louisa felt glad that she was admitted, even in an official capacity. She wanted to share their lives. At home they would need her, now Mary had come. But they must manage without her.

'I must write a note to the vicarage,' she said.

Alfred Durant looked at her inquiringly, for her service. He had always that intelligent readiness to serve, since he had been in the Navy. But there was a simple independence in his willingness, which she loved. She felt nevertheless it was hard to get at him. He was so deferential, quick to take the slightest suggestion of an order from her, implicitly, that she could not get at the man in him.

He looked at her very keenly. She noticed his eyes were golden brown, with a very small pupil, the kind of eyes that can see a long way off. He stood alert, at military attention. His face was still rather weather-reddened.

'Do you want pen and paper?' he asked, with deferential suggestion to a superior, which was more difficult for her than reserve.

'Yes, please,' she said.

He turned and went downstairs. He seemed to her so self-contained, so utterly sure in his movement. How was she to approach him? For he would take not one step towards her. He would only put himself entirely and impersonally at her service, glad to serve her, but keeping himself quite removed from her. She could see he felt real joy in doing anything for her, but any recognition would confuse him and hurt him. Strange it was to her, to have a man going about the house in his shirt-sleeves, his waistcoat unbuttoned, his throat bare, waiting on her. He moved well, as if he had plenty of life to spare. She was attracted by his completeness. And yet, when all was ready, and there was nothing more for him to do, she quivered, meeting his questioning look.

As she sat writing, he placed another candle near her. The rather dense light fell in two places on the overfoldings of her hair till it glistened heavy and bright, like a dense golden plumage folded up. Then the nape of her neck was very white, with fine down and pointed wisps of gold. He watched it as if it were a vision, losing himself. She was all that was beyond him, of revelation and exquisiteness. All that was ideal and beyond him, she was that – and he was lost to himself in looking at her. She had no connection with him. He did not approach her. She was there like a wonderful distance. But it was a treat, having her in the house. Even with this anguish for his mother tightening about him, he was sensible of the wonder of living this evening. The candles glistened on her hair, and seemed to fascinate him. He felt a little awe of her, and a sense of uplifting, that he and she and his mother should be together for a time, in the strange, unknown atmosphere. And, when he got out of the house, he was afraid. He saw the stars above ringing with fine brightness, the snow beneath just visible, and a new night was gathering round him. He was afraid almost with obliteration. What was this new night ringing about him, and what was he? He could not recognize himself nor any of his surroundings. He was afraid to think of his mother. And yet his chest was conscious of her, and of what was happening to her. He could not escape from her, she carried him with her into an unformed, unknown chaos.

XI

He went up the road in an agony, not knowing what it was all about, but feeling as if a red-hot iron were gripped round his chest. Without thinking, he shook two or three tears on to the snow. Yet in his mind he did not believe his mother would die. He was in the grip of some greater consciousness. As he sat in the hall of the vicarage, waiting whilst Mary put things for Louisa into a bag, he wondered why he had been so upset. He felt abashed and humbled by the big house, he felt again as if he were one of the rank and file. When Miss Mary spoke to him, he almost saluted.

'An honest man,' thought Mary. And the patronage was applied as salve to her own sickness. She had station, so she could patronize: it was almost all that was left to her. But she could not have lived without having a certain position. She could never have trusted herself outside a definite place, nor respected herself except as a woman of superior class.

As Alfred came to the latch-gate, he felt the grief at his heart again, and saw the new heavens. He stood a moment looking northward to the Plough climbing up the night, and at the far glimmer of snow in distant fields. Then his grief came on like physical pain. He held tight to the gate, biting his mouth, whispering 'Mother!' It was a fierce, cutting, physical pain of grief, that came on in bouts, as his mother's pain came on in bouts, and was so acute he could scarcely keep erect. He did not know where it came from, the pain, or why. It had nothing to do with his thoughts. Almost it had nothing to do with him. Only it gripped him and he must submit. The whole tide of his soul, gathering in its unknown towards this expansion into death, carried him with it helplessly, all the fritter of his thought and consciousness caught up as nothing, the heave passing on towards its breaking, taking him farther than he had ever been. When the young man had regained himself, he went indoors, and there he was almost gay. It seemed to excite him. He felt in high spirits: he made whimsical fun of things. He sat on one side of his mother's bed, Louisa on the other, and a certain gaiety seized them all. But the night and the dread was coming on.

Alfred kissed his mother and went to bed. When he was half undressed the knowledge of his mother came upon him, and the suffering seized him in its grip like two hands, in agony. He lay on the bed screwed up tight. It lasted so long, and exhausted him so much, that he fell asleep, without having the energy to get up and finish undressing. He awoke after midnight to find himself stone cold. He undressed and got into bed, and was soon asleep again.

At a quarter to six he woke, and instantly remembered. Having pulled on his trousers and lighted a candle, he went into his mother's room. He put his hand before the candle flame so that no light fell on the bed.

'Mother!' he whispered.

'Yes,' was the reply.

There was a hesitation.

'Should I go to work?'

He waited, his heart was beating heavily.

'I think I'd go, my lad.'

His heart went down in a kind of despair.

'You want me to?'

He let his hand down from the candle flame. The light fell on the bed. There he saw Louisa lying looking up at him. Her eyes were upon him. She quickly shut her eyes and half buried her face in the pillow, her back turned to him. He saw the rough hair like bright vapour about her round head, and the two plaits flung coiled among the bedclothes. It gave him a shock. He stood almost himself, determined. Louisa cowered down. He looked, and met his mother's eyes. Then he gave way again, and ceased to be sure, ceased to be himself.

'Yes, go to work, my boy,' said the mother.

'All right,' replied he, kissing her. His heart was down at despair, and bitter. He went away.

'Alfred!' cried his mother faintly.

He came back with beating heart.

'What, mother?'

'You'll always do what's right, Alfred?' the mother asked, beside herself in terror now he was leaving her. He was too terrified and bewildered to know what she meant.

'Yes,' he said.

She turned her cheek to him. He kissed her, then went away in bitter despair. He went to work.

XII

By midday his mother was dead. The word met him at the pit-mouth. As he had known, inwardly, it was not a shock to him, and yet he trembled. He went home quite calmly, feeling only heavy in his breathing.

Miss Louisa was still at the house. She had seen to everything possible. Very succinctly, she informed him of what he needed to know. But there was one point of anxiety for her.

'You *did* half expect it – it's not come as a blow to you?' she asked, looking up at him. Her eyes were dark and calm and searching. She too felt lost. He was so dark and inchoate.

'I suppose – yes,' he said stupidly. He looked aside, unable to endure her eyes on him.

'I could not bear to think you might not have guessed,' she said.

He did not answer.

He felt it a great strain to have her near him at this time. He wanted to be alone. As soon as the relatives began to arrive, Louisa departed and came no more. While everything was arranging, and a crowd was in the house, whilst he had business to settle, he went well enough, with only those uncontrollable paroxysms of grief. For the rest, he was superficial. By himself, he endured the fierce, almost insane bursts of grief which passed again and left him calm, almost clear, just wondering. He had not known before that everything could break down, that he himself could break down, and all be a great chaos, very vast and wonderful. It seemed as if life in him had burst its bounds, and he was lost in a great, bewildering flood, immense and unpeopled. He himself was broken and spilled out amid it all. He could only breathe panting in silence. Then the anguish came on again.

When all the people had gone from the Quarry Cottage, leaving the young man alone with an elderly housekeeper, then the long trail began. The snow had thawed and frozen, a fresh fall had whitened the grey, this then began to thaw. The world was a place of loose grey slosh. Alfred had nothing to do in the evenings. He was a man whose life had been filled up with small activities. Without knowing it, he had been centralized, polarized in his mother. It was she who had kept him. Even now, when the old housekeeper had left him, he might still have gone on in his old way. But the force and balance of his life was lacking. He sat pretending to read, all the time holding his fists clenched, and holding himself in, enduring he did not know what. He walked the black and sodden miles of field-paths, till he was tired out: but all this was only running away from whence he must return. At work he was all right. If it had been summer he might have escaped by working in the garden till bedtime. But now, there was no escape, no relief, no help. He, perhaps, was made for action rather than for understanding: for doing than for being. He was shocked out of his activities, like a swimmer who forgets to swim.

For a week, he had the force to endure this suffocation and struggle, then he began to get exhausted, and knew it must come out. The instinct of self-preservation became strongest. But there was the question: Where was he to go? The public-house really meant nothing to him, it was no good going there. He began to think of emigration. In another country he would be all right. He wrote to the emigration offices.

On the Sunday after the funeral, when all the Durant people had attended church, Alfred had seen Miss Louisa, impassive and reserved, sitting with Miss Mary, who was proud and very distant, and with the other Lindleys, who were people removed. Alfred saw them as people remote. He did not think about it. They had nothing to do with his life. After service Louisa had come to him and shaken hands.

'My sister would like you to come to supper one evening, if you would be so good.'

He looked at Miss Mary, who bowed. Out of kindness, Mary had proposed this to Louisa, disapproving of her even as she did so. But she did not examine herself closely.

'Yes,' said Durant awkwardly, 'I'll come if you want me.' But he vaguely felt that it was misplaced.

'You'll come tomorrow evening, then, about half-past six.'

He went. Miss Louisa was very kind to him. There could be no music, because of the babies. He sat with his fists clenched on his thighs, very quiet and unmoved, lapsing, among all those people, into a kind of muse or daze. There was nothing between him and them. They knew it as well as he. But he remained very steady in himself, and the evening passed slowly. Mrs Lindley called him 'young man'.

'Will you sit here, young man?'

He sat there. One name was as good as another. What had they to do with him?

Mr Lindley kept a special tone for him, kind, indulgent, but patronizing. Durant took it all without criticism or offence, just submitting. But he did not want to eat – that troubled him, to have to eat in their presence. He knew he was out of place. But it was his duty to stay yet awhile. He answered precisely, in monosyllables.

When he left he winced with confusion. He was glad it was finished. He got away as quickly as possible. And he wanted still more intensely to go right away, to Canada.

Miss Louisa suffered in her soul, indignant with all of them, with him too, but quite unable to say why she was indignant.

XIII

Two evenings after, Louisa tapped at the door of the Quarry Cottage, at half-past six. He had finished dinner, the woman had washed up and gone away, but still he sat in his pit-dirt. He was going later to the New Inn. He had begun to go there because he must go somewhere. The mere contact with other men was necessary to him, the noise, the warmth, the forgetful flight of the hours. But still he did not move. He sat alone in the empty house till it began to grow on him like something unnatural.

He was in his pit-dirt when he opened the door.

'I have been wanting to call – I thought I would,' she said, and she went to the sofa. He wondered why she wouldn't use his mother's round arm-chair. Yet something stirred in him, like anger, when the housekeeper placed herself in it.

'I ought to have been washed by now,' he said, glancing at the clock, which was adorned with butterflies and cherries, and the name of 'T. Brooks, Mansfield'. He laid his black hands along his mottled dirty arms. Louisa looked at him. There was the reserve, and the simple neutrality towards her, which she dreaded in him. It made it impossible for her to approach him.

'I am afraid,' she said, 'that I wasn't kind in asking you to supper.'

'I'm not used to it,' he said, smiling with his mouth, showing the interspaced white teeth. His eyes, however, were steady and unseeing.

'It's not *that*,' she said hastily. Her repose was exquisite and her dark grey eyes rich with understanding. He felt afraid of her as she sat there, as he began to grow conscious of her.

'How do you get on alone?' she asked.

He glanced away to the fire.

'Oh—' he answered, shifting uneasily, not finishing his answer.

Her face settled heavily.

'How close it is in this room. You have such immense fires. I will take off my coat,' she said.

He watched her take off her hat and coat. She wore a cream cashmere blouse embroidered with gold silks. It seemed to him a very fine garment, fitting her throat and wrists close. It gave him a feeling of pleasure and cleanness and relief from himself.

'What were you thinking about, that you didn't get washed?' she asked, half intimately. He laughed, turning aside his head. The whites of his eyes showed very distinct in his black face.

'Oh,' he said, 'I couldn't tell you.'

There was a pause.

'Are you going to keep this house on?' she asked.

He stirred in his chair, under the question.

'I hardly know,' he said. 'I'm very likely going to Canada.'

Her spirit became very quiet and attentive.

'What for?' she asked.

Again he shifted restlessly on his seat.

'Well,' – he said slowly – 'to try the life.'

'But which life?'

'There's various things – farming or lumbering or mining. I don't mind much what it is.'

'And is that what you want?'

He did not think in these times, so he could not answer.

'I don't know,' he said, 'till I've tried.'

She saw him drawing away from her for ever.

'Aren't you sorry to leave this house and garden?' she asked.

'I don't know,' he answered reluctantly. 'I suppose our Fred would come in – that's what he's wanting.'

'You don't want to settle down?' she asked.

He was leaning forward on the arms of his chair. He turned to her. Her face was pale and set. It looked heavy and impassive, her hair shone richer as she grew white. She was to him something steady and immovable and eternal presented to him.

His heart was hot in the anguish of suspense. Sharp twitches of fear and pain were in his limbs. He turned his whole body away from her. The silence was unendurable. He could not bear her to sit there any more. It made his heart go hot and stifled in his breast.

'Were you going out tonight?' she asked.

'Only to the New Inn,' he said.

Again there was silence.

She reached for her hat. Nothing else was suggested to her. She *had* to go. He sat waiting for her to be gone, for relief. And she knew that if she went out of that house as she was, she went out a failure. Yet she continued to pin on her hat; in a moment she would have to go. Something was carrying her.

Then suddenly a sharp pang, like lightning, seared her from head to foot, and she was beyond herself.

'Do you want me to go?' she asked, controlled, yet speaking out of a fiery anguish, as if the words were spoken from her without her intervention.

He went white under his dirt.

'Why?' he asked, turning to her in fear, compelled.

'Do you want me to go?' she repeated.

'Why?' he asked again.

'Because I wanted to stay with you,' she said, suffocated, with her lungs full of fire.

His face worked, he hung forward a little, suspended, staring straight into her eyes, in torment, in an agony of chaos, unable to collect himself. And as if turned to stone, she looked back into his eyes. The souls were exposed bare for a few moments. It was agony. They could not bear it. He dropped his head, whilst his body jerked with little sharp twitchings.

She turned away for her coat. Her soul had gone dead in her. Her hands trembled, but she could not feel any more. She drew on her coat. There was a cruel suspense in the room. The moment had come for her to go. He lifted his head. His eyes were like agate, expressionless, save for the black points of torture. They held her, she had no will, no life any more. She felt broken.

'Don't you want me?' she said helplessly.

A spasm of torture crossed his eyes, which held her fixed.

'I – I—' he began, but he could not speak. Something drew him from his chair to her. She stood motionless, spellbound, like a creature given up as prey. He put his hand tentatively, uncertainly, on her arm. The expression of his face was strange and inhuman. She stood utterly motionless. Then clumsily he put his arms round her and took her, cruelly, blindly, straining her till she nearly lost consciousness, till he himself had almost fallen.

Then, gradually, as he held her gripped, and his brain reeled round, and he felt himself falling, falling from himself, and whilst she, yielded up, swooned to a kind of death of herself, a moment of utter darkness came over him, and they began to wake up again as if from a long sleep. He was himself.

After a while his arms slackened, she loosened herself a little, and put her arms round him, as he held her. So they held each other close, and hid each against the other for assurance, helpless in speech. And it was ever her hands that trembled more closely upon him, drawing him nearer into her, with love.

And at last she drew back her face and looked up at him, her eyes wet, and shining with light. His heart, which saw, was silent with fear. He was with her. She saw his face all sombre and inscrutable, and he seemed eternal to her. And all the echo of pain came back into the rarity of bliss, and all her tears came up.

'I love you,' she said, her lips drawn to sobbing. He put down his head against her, unable to hear her, unable to bear the sudden coming of the peace and passion that almost broke his heart. They stood together in silence whilst the thing moved away a little.

At last she wanted to see him. She looked up. His eyes were strange and glowing, with a tiny black pupil. Strange, they were, and powerful over her. And his mouth came to hers, and slowly her eyelids closed, as his mouth sought hers closer and closer, and took possession of her.

They were silent for a long time, too much mixed up with passion and grief and death to do anything but hold each other in pain and kiss with long, hurting kisses wherein fear was transfused into desire. At last she disengaged herself. He felt as if his heart were hurt, but glad, and he scarcely dared look at her.

'I'm glad,' she said also.

He held her hands in passionate gratitude and desire. He had not yet the presence of mind to say anything. He was dazed with relief.

'I ought to go,' she said.

He looked at her. He could not grasp the thought of her going, he knew he could never be separated from her any more. Yet he dared not assert himself. He held her hands tight.

'Your face is black,' she said.

He laughed.

'Yours is a bit smudged,' he said.

They were afraid of each other, afraid to talk. He could only keep her near to him. After a while she wanted to wash her face. He brought her some warm water, standing by and watching her. There was something he wanted to say, that he dared not. He watched her wiping her face, and making tidy her hair.

'They'll see your blouse is dirty,' he said.

She looked at her sleeves and laughed for joy.

He was sharp with pride.

'What shall you do?' he asked.

'How?' she said.

He was awkward at a reply.

'About me,' he said.

'What do you want me to do?' she laughed.

He put his hand out slowly to her. What did it matter!
'But make yourself clean,' she said.

XIV

As they went up the hill, the night seemed dense with the
unknown. They kept close together, feeling as if the darkness
were alive and full of knowledge, all around them. In silence
they walked up the hill. At first the street lamps went their
way. Several people passed them. He was more shy than she,
and would have let her go had she loosened in the least. But she
held firm.

Then they came into the true darkness, between the fields.
They did not want to speak, feeling close together in silence. So
they arrived at the vicarage gate. They stood under the naked
horse-chestnut tree.

'I wish you didn't have to go,' he said.

She laughed a quick little laugh.

'Come tomorrow,' she said, in a low tone, 'and ask father.'

She felt his hand close on hers.

She gave the same sorrowful little laugh of sympathy. Then
she kissed him, sending him home.

At home, the old grief came on in another paroxysm,
obliterating Louisa, obliterating even his mother for whom the
stress was raging like a burst of fever in a wound. But something was sound in his heart.

XV

The next evening he dressed to go to the vicarage, feeling it
was to be done, not imagining what it would be like. He would
not take this seriously. He was sure of Louisa, and this marriage

was like fate to him. It filled him also with a blessed feeling of fatality. He was not responsible, neither had her people anything really to do with it.

They ushered him into the little study, which was fireless. By and by the vicar came in. His voice was cold and hostile as he said:

'What can I do for you, young man?'

He knew already, without asking.

Durant looked up at him, again like a sailor before a superior. He had the subordinate manner. Yet his spirit was clear.

'I wanted, Mr Lindley—' he began respectfully, then all the colour suddenly left his face. It seemed now a violation to say what he had to say. What was he doing there? But he stood on, because it had to be done. He held firmly to his own independence and self-respect. He must not be indecisive. He must put himself aside: the matter was bigger than just his personal self. He must not feel. This was his highest duty.

'You wanted—' said the vicar.

Durant's mouth was dry, but he answered with steadiness:

'Miss Louisa – Louisa – promised to marry me—'

'You asked Miss Louisa if she would marry you – yes—' corrected the vicar. Durant reflected he had not asked her this:

'If she would marry me, sir. I hope you – don't mind.'

He smiled. He was a good-looking man, and the vicar could not help seeing it.

'And my daughter was willing to marry you?' said Mr Lindley.

'Yes,' said Durant seriously. It was plain to him, nevertheless. He felt the natural hostility between himself and the elder man.

'Will you come this way?' said the vicar. He led into the dining-room, where were Mary, Louisa, and Mrs Lindley. Mr Massy sat in a corner with a lamp.

'This young man has come on your account, Louisa?' said Mr Lindley.

'Yes,' said Louisa, her eyes on Durant, who stood erect, in discipline. He dared not look at her, but he was aware of her.

'You don't want to marry a collier, you little fool,' cried Mrs Lindley harshly. She lay obese and helpless upon the couch, swathed in a loose dove-grey gown.

'Oh, hush, mother,' cried Mary, with quiet intensity and pride.

'What means have you to support a wife?' demanded the vicar's wife roughly.

'I!' Durant replied, starting. 'I think I can earn enough.'

'Well, and how much?' came the rough voice.

'Seven and six a day,' replied the young man.

'And will it get to be any more?'

'I hope so.'

'And are you going to live in that poky little house?'

'I think so,' said Durant, 'if it's all right.'

He took small offence, only was upset, because they would not think him good enough. He knew that, in their sense, he was not.

'Then she's a fool, I tell you, if she marries you,' cried the mother roughly, casting her decision.

'After all, mama, it is Louisa's affair,' said Mary distinctly, 'and we must remember—'

'As she makes her bed, she must lie – but she'll repent it,' interrupted Mrs Lindley.

'And after all,' said Mr Lindley, 'Louisa cannot quite hold herself free to act entirely without consideration for her family.'

'What do you want, papa?' asked Louisa sharply.

'I mean that if you marry this man, it will make my position very difficult for me, particularly if you stay in this parish. If you were moving away, it would be simpler. But living here in a collier's cottage, under my nose, as it were – it would be almost unseemly. I have my position to maintain, and a position which may not be taken lightly.'

'Come over here, young man,' cried the mother, in her rough voice, 'and let us look at you.'

Durant, flushing, went over and stood – not quite at attention, so that he did not know what to do with his hands. Miss Louisa was angry to see him standing there, obedient and acquiescent. He ought to show himself a man.

'Can't you take her away and live out of sight?' said the mother. 'You'd both of you be better off.'

'Yes, we can go away,' he said.

'Do you want to?' asked Miss Mary clearly.

He faced round. Mary looked very stately and impressive. He flushed.

'I do if it's going to be a trouble to anybody,' he said.

'For yourself, you would rather stay?' said Mary.

'It's my home,' he said, 'and that's the house I was born in.'

'Then' – Mary turned clearly to her parents, 'I really don't see how you can make the conditions, papa. He has his own rights, and if Louisa wants to marry him—'

'Louisa, Louisa!' cried the father impatiently. 'I cannot understand why Louisa should not behave in the normal way. I cannot see why she should only think of herself, and leave her family out of count. The thing is enough in itself, and she ought to try to ameliorate it as much as possible. And if—'

'But I love the man, papa,' said Louisa.

'And I hope you love your parents, and I hope you want to spare them as much of the – the loss of prestige as possible.'

'We *can* go away to live,' said Louisa, her face breaking to tears. At last she was really hurt.

'Oh yes, easily,' Durant replied hastily, pale, distressed.

There was dead silence in the room.

'I think it would really be better,' murmured the vicar, mollified.

'Very likely it would,' said the rough-voiced invalid.

'Though I think we ought to apologize for asking such a thing,' said Mary haughtily.

'No,' said Durant. 'It will be best all round.' He was glad there was no more bother.

'And shall we put up the banns here or go to the registrar?' he asked clearly, like a challenge.

'We will go to the registrar,' replied Louisa decidedly.

Again there was dead silence in the room.

'Well, if you will have your own way, you must go your own way,' said the mother emphatically.

All the time Mr Massy had sat obscure and unnoticed in a corner of the room. At this juncture he got up, saying:

'There is baby, Mary.'

Mary rose and went out of the room, stately; her little husband padded after her. Durant watched the fragile, small man go, wondering.

'And where,' asked the vicar, almost genial, 'do you think you will go when you are married?'

Durant started.

'I was thinking of emigrating,' he said.

'To Canada? Or where?'

'I think to Canada.'

'Yes, that would be very good.'

Again there was a pause.

'We shan't see much of you then, as a son-in-law,' said the mother, roughly but amicably.

'Not much,' he said.

Then he took his leave. Louisa went with him to the gate. She stood before him in distress.

'You won't mind them, will you?' she said humbly.

'I don't mind them, if they don't mind me!' he said. Then he stooped and kissed her.

'Let us be married soon,' she murmured, in tears.

'All right,' he said. 'I'll go tomorrow to Barford.'

TITLES IN THE NEW WINDMILL SERIES

Chinua Achebe: *Things Fall Apart*
Louisa M. Alcott: *Little Women*
Elizabeth Allen: *Deitz and Denny*
Eric Allen: *The Latchkey Children*
Margery Allingham: *The Tiger in the Smoke*
Michael Anthony: *The Year in San Fernando*
Bernard Ashley: *A Kind of Wild Justice*
Enid Bagnold: *National Velvet*
Stan Barstow: *Joby*
H. Mortimer Batten: *The Singing Forest*
Nina Bawden: *On the Run; The Witch's Daughter; A Handful of Thieves; Carrie's War;
    Rebel on a Rock; The Robbers*
Rex Benedict: *Last Stand at Goodbye Gulch*
Phyllis Bentley: *The Adventures of Tom Leigh*
Paul Berna: *Flood Warning*
Judy Blume: *It's Not the End of the World*
Pierre Boulle: *The Bridge on the River Kwai*
E. R. Braithwaite: *To Sir, With Love*
D. K. Broster: *The Gleam in the North*
F. Hodgson Burnett: *The Secret Garden*
Helen Bush: *Mary Anning's Treasures*
Betsy Byars: *The Midnight Fox*
A. Calder-Marshall: *The Man from Devil's Island*
John Caldwell: *Desperate Voyage*
Ian Cameron: *The Island at the Top of the World*
Albert Camus: *The Outsider*
Victor Canning: *The Runaways; Flight of the Grey Goose*
Charles Chaplin: *My Early Years*
Erskine Childers: *The Riddle of the Sands*
John Christopher: *The Guardians; The Lotus Caves; Empty World*
Richard Church: *The Cave; Over the Bridge; The White Doe*
Colette: *My Mother's House*
Alexander Cordell: *The Traitor Within*
Margaret Craven: *I Heard the Owl Call my Name*
Roald Dahl: *Danny, Champion of the World; The Wonderful Story of Henry Sugar;
    George's Marvellous Medicine*
Andrew Davies: *Conrad's War*
Meindert deJong: *The Wheel on the School*
Peter Dickinson: *The Gift; Annerton Pit*
Eleanor Doorly: *The Radium Woman; The Microbe Man; The Insect Man*
Gerald Durrell: *Three Singles to Adventure; The Drunken Forest; Encounters with Animals*
Elizabeth Enright: *Thimble Summer; The Saturdays*
C. S. Forester: *The General*
Eve Garnett: *The Family from One End Street; Further Adventures of the Family from One End
    Street; Holiday at the Dew Drop Inn*
G. M. Glaskin: *A Waltz through the Hills*
Rumer Godden: *Black Narcissus*
Angus Graham: *The Golden Grindstone*
Graham Greene: *The Third Man* and *The Fallen Idol*
Grey Owl: *Sajo and her Beaver People*
John Griffin: *Skulker Wheat and Other Stories*
G. and W. Grossmith: *The Diary of a Nobody*
René Guillot: *Kpo the Leopard*
Jan De Hartog: *The Lost Sea*
Erik Haugaard: *The Little Fishes*

Esther Hautzig: *The Endless Steppe*
Bessie Head: *When Rain Clouds Gather*
Ernest Hemingway: *The Old Man and the Sea*
John Hersey: *A Single Pebble*
Nigel Hinton: *Getting Free*
Alfred Hitchcock: *Sinister Spies*
C. Walter Hodges: *The Overland Launch*
Geoffrey Household: *Rogue Male; A Rough Shoot; Prisoner of the Indies; Escape into Daylight*
Fred Hoyle: *The Black Cloud*
Irene Hunt: *Across Five Aprils*
Henry James: *Washington Square*
Josephine Kamm: *Young Mother; Out of Step; Where Do We Go From Here?; The Starting Point*
Erich Kästner: *Emil and the Detectives; Lottie and Lisa*
M. E. Kerr: *Dinky Hocker Shoots Smack!; Gentlehands*
Clive King: *Me and My Million*
John Knowles: *A Separate Peace*
Marghanita Laski: *Little Boy Lost*
D. H. Lawrence: *Sea and Sardinia; The Fox* and *The Virgin and the Gypsy; Selected Tales*
Harper Lee: *To Kill a Mockingbird*
Laurie Lee: *As I Walked Out One Mid-Summer Morning*
Ursula Le Guin: *A Wizard of Earthsea; The Tombs of Atuan; The Farthest Shore; A Very Long Way from Anywhere Else*
Doris Lessing: *The Grass is Singing*
C. Day Lewis: *The Otterbury Incident*
Lorna Lewis: *Leonardo the Inventor*
Martin Lindsay: *The Epic of Captain Scott*
David Line: *Run for Your Life; Mike and Me; Under Plum Lake*
Kathleen Lines: *The House of the Nightmare; The Haunted and the Haunters*
Joan Lingard: *Across the Barricades; Into Exile; The Clearance; The File on Fräuline Berg*
Penelope Lively: *The Ghost of Thomas Kempe*
Jack London: *The Call of the Wild; White Fang*
Carson McCullers: *The Member of the Wedding*
Lee McGiffen: *On the Trail to Sacramento*
Wolf Mankowitz: *A Kid for Two Farthings*
Olivia Manning: *The Play Room*
Jan Mark: *Thunder and Lightnings; Under the Autumn Garden*
James Vance Marshall: *A River Ran Out of Eden; Walkabout; My Boy John that Went to Sea; A Walk to the Hills of the Dreamtime*
David Martin: *The Cabby's Daughter*
J. P. Martin: *Uncle*
John Masefield: *The Bird of Dawning; The Midnight Folk; The Box of Delights*
W. Somerset Maugham: *The Kite and Other Stories*
Guy de Maupassant: *Prisoners of War and Other Stories*
Laurence Meynell: *Builder and Dreamer*
Yvonne Mitchell: *Cathy Away*
Honoré Morrow: *The Splendid Journey*
Bill Naughton: *The Goalkeeper's Revenge; A Dog Called Nelson; My Pal Spadger*
E. Nesbit: *The Railway Children; The Story of the Treasure Seekers*
E. Neville: *It's Like this, Cat*
Wilfrid Noyce: *South Col*
Robert C. O'Brien: *Mrs Frisby and the Rats of NIMH; Z for Zachariah*
Scott O'Dell: *Island of the Blue Dolphins*
George Orwell: *Animal Farm*
Philippa Pearce: *Tom's Midnight Garden*